DATE DUE   OCT 0 5

MAY 11 '06			
GAYLORD			PRINTED IN U.S.A.

Fairway to Heaven

Fairway to Heaven

Roberta Isleib

THORNDIKE
CHIVERS

JACKSON COUNTY LIBRARY SERVICES
MEDFORD OREGON 97501

This Large Print edition is published by Thorndike Press®,
Waterville, Maine USA and by BBC Audiobooks, Ltd,
Bath, England.

Published in 2005 in the U.S. by arrangement with The Berkley
Publishing Group, a division of Penguin Group (USA) Inc.

Published in 2005 in the U.K. by arrangement with The Berkley
Publishing Group, a division of Penguin Group (USA) Inc.

U.S. Hardcover   0-7862-7756-4 (Mystery)
U.K. Hardcover   1-4056-3492-8 (Chivers Large Print)
U.K. Softcover   1-4056-3493-6 (Camden Large Print)

The text of this Large Print edition is unabridged.
Other aspects of the book may vary from the original edition.

Set in 16 pt. Plantin by Al Chase.

Printed in the United States on permanent paper.

British Library Cataloguing-in-Publication Data available

Library of Congress Cataloging-in-Publication Data

Isleib, Roberta.
　　Fairway to heaven / by Roberta Isleib.
　　　　p. cm. — (Thorndike Press large print mystery)
　　　ISBN 0-7862-7756-4 (lg. print : hc : alk. paper)
　　　1. Burdette, Cassie (Fictitious character) — Fiction.
　2. Women golfers — Fiction.　3. North Carolina — Fiction.
　4. Missing persons — Fiction.　5. Large type books.　6. Golf
　stories.　I. Title.　II. Series.　III. Thorndike Press large
　print mystery series.
　PS3609.S57F35 2005
　　813'.6—dc22　　　　　　　　　　　　　　　　　　　2005008766

For my dear father
and his Mary Jane

Acknowledgments

My warmest thanks go to all who helped this book become a reality.

To Pinehurst residents Judy Fitzgerald, Ellen Pfann, and Mary Scott and John Arnold, who took me on insider tours, answered urgent questions, and helped Pinehurst come alive; LPGA player Donna Andrews, fabulous golfer and copyeditor, for her time and enthusiasm; Faye Dasen, Joan Scott, and the Friends of the Given Library for their support; Tina Sheppard, Pinehurst Police Department patrol officer for her tour of the police station; Amanda and Mike Mammele, Pari Taichert, and Julie Nothstine, good sports who offered up their names for the sake of charity; the Shoreline Writers Group — Chris Falcone, Angelo Pompano, Karen Olson, Liz Cipollina, and Cindy Warm — for their willingness to puzzle through any problem and read as many pages as I can write; Sue Repko, for her good-natured online support; John Millman, USMC, who had enough ideas about how a retired Marine could go bad to fill a dozen books; the Royston boys, always good for a legal tickler; Marcat Knowlton for the alligator hat; Women in the Golf Industry, including Pat Baldwin, who brought me to Pinehurst for the first time; writing and traveling buddies Libby Hellmann, Deborah Donnelly, and Susan Hubbard; Hallie Ephron for reading the manuscript with fresh eyes; denizens of the mystery world — Sisters in Crime, Mystery Writers of America, mystery bookstores, and mystery fans everywhere; Roxanne Coady and the staff at RJ Julia Booksellers — I am so lucky to have you; librarians across the country, especially Madison's own Sandy Long; independent editor Nora Cavin for making all the difference; Cindy Hwang, Susan McCarty, and the great staff at Berkley Prime Crime; my indefatigable agent, Paige Wheeler.

I'm so grateful to my family and friends for providing the foundation that makes everything possible. And my love always to John, who talked over the details of the plot each time I needed him, and that was often!

Roberta Isleib
October, 2004

My luv is like a tall, thin mashie.
— Brad Burg

Chapter 1

Dr. Baxter opened his office door and waved me in. Well, it was the shrink's rendition of a wave, a distant cousin to the queen's royal greeting — a small nod accompanied by the brief eye contact that lets you know you're "on." I laid the dog-eared waiting-room copy of *Sports Illustrated* on the table and eased past what used to be Dr. Bencher's office. I'd found him lying there two years ago, nearly dead. Sometimes his last rasping breaths still seemed to rattle from the room. A sex therapist with a big bust and a sharp chin had taken over his office space. I wondered how much this new doctor had heard about the former tenant. And whether her patients ever spotted the faint mark under the desk when they were casting about the room to avoid looking directly at her.

Baxter crossed his left leg over his right and adjusted the crease in the pant leg so it pointed precisely to the laces on his shoe. You could have carved a roast with the crease in those pants. Who ironed them anyway? Mrs. Baxter? Or was it off to the dry cleaners after each day's wear?

"What are you thinking?" he asked.

I blushed and pushed away every thought I'd had in the last five minutes.

"Just can't believe I'm in this wedding up to my neck." I slid a paper out from the back pocket of my jeans. "Jeanine faxed me the draft of her wedding announcement this morning." I pressed the wrinkled paper out on my thigh. "They're putting on one amazing show." I cleared my throat and read a paragraph out loud.

"The bride wore a white strapless gown of French silk. The bodice featured an overlay of antique lace and seed pearls. The Basque waistline flowed into a floor-length gown with a chapel-length train. Her antique lace veil was attached to a diamond and pearl tiara, belonging to her grandmother, Tallulah Emory Bates."

I looked up at Baxter. "A Basque waistline? A tiara-wearing grandmother named Tallulah? But wait, there's more."

I read on. "The bride chose Cassandra Burdette of Myrtle Beach, South Carolina, as her maid of honor. Pari Noskin Taichert of Atlanta, Georgia, was the bridesmaid. Attendants wore strapless gowns of aubergine silk and carried loose bouquets of white lilies and glass sconces with candles." I shook my head. "We'll never make it up the aisle with those dresses intact — do you suppose silk just smolders when it's lit on fire, or would it actually burst into flames?"

Baxter didn't offer an opinion.

"People are throwing Jeanine four parties before I even get there — a recipe shower, a lingerie shower, a Chinese dinner party, and a Pampered Chef shower. She says that's the way it's done in Pinehurst." I read from the paper again. "Camellia Toussaint, the bride's maternal aunt, along with bridal attendants, Cassandra Burdette and Pari Noskin Taichert, hosted a bridal shower at the Forest Brook Clubhouse on November first. The theme of the party was 'Autumn Steeplechase.' "

I sank down into the upholstered chair until my chin rested on my chest. "Autumn steeplechase, my ass."

"Shall we talk about why you agreed to be in the wedding?"

I sighed. "You know I introduced them. And Jeanine is, well . . . sweet. All this stuff seems really important to her, like she honestly believes it's setting her and Rick up for a happy life. I couldn't turn her down. I couldn't hurt her feelings."

Baxter raised his eyebrows to delicate points.

"I know, I know. Then quit yer bitching, right?" We both laughed a little.

"You haven't mentioned how you're feeling about the tournament," said Dr. Baxter, palpating the ridge of his chin.

At the end of my second miserable LPGA season, I'd returned to see Baxter, my former shrink, for what he kindly called a "tune-up." More like a total engine overhaul. We'd already spent more money and minutes than I cared to count on the question of why I'd agreed to participate in the Pine Straw Three Tour Tournament, with my boyfriend Mike Callahan and my own father, Chuck Burdette, on my team.

"I'm trying not to feel anything. If I focus hard enough on the silly wedding, maybe the tournament will just go away." I shrugged. "Haven't you figured it out by now? My defense mechanisms may be primitive, but they're quite effective. At least in the short run." I stuffed the paper back into my pocket and glanced at my watch. "I have to get home and finish packing. We'll continue on Monday?" I added, before he could say it first.

★ ★ ★

My mother stood in the doorway of my girlhood bedroom and watched me poke underwear into the corners of the suitcase. Then I reached for the bridesmaid gown, balled up a handful of purple silk, and pretended to jam it into the top of the travel golf bag resting against the bed. Mom yelped and lunged forward to grab the dress and slap my hand.

"Don't you dare pack that in there!"

"It'll cushion the club heads perfectly," I insisted. "The titanium inset on my new driver scratches if you just breathe near it."

"Jeanine paid a thousand dollars for this gown. It's disrespectful and downright ugly mean to treat it that way." She hung the dress on a padded hanger and tucked it into the garment bag stretched across my pillow. "I thought I raised you better than that."

"I was joking, Mother. It was a joke." My mother's sense of humor has never been her strong point, but this wedding had impaired it even further. An edge had materialized in her voice the minute she heard that Dad's second wife and my two half-brothers would also be in attendance at the society wedding of the year. She did not receive an invitation. The semi-gracious truce she'd established with my father had been

15

strained to almost-rupture by these circumstances.

She sighed. "This purple turns your skin sallow. Did you pack the makeup I bought? You would have looked better in the green."

"I packed the makeup." I frowned and tried to jerk the garment bag zipper past a small catch in the fabric. "This is not about me, Mom. It's her wedding." Instantly sorry I'd given her an opening, I tensed for her standard barrage of questions.

What's going on with you and Mike anyway? Are you ever going to get married?

"You'll ruin the silk," my mother said, mercifully too intent on the dress to nag. "Let me do that." She zipped the bag closed, then stomped out of the room. Gin-and-tonic time.

It was childish to pretend to jam the dress in with the clubs. I knew that. Joe Lancaster, my friend and sometimes golf psychologist, would have celebrated that insight as an example of how much I was improving in psychotherapy.

"Half the battle is recognizing the stupid things you do," he'd say, "even if you plow ahead stupidly and do them anyway."

Now I felt guilty about the wrinkles in the silk. But knowing Jeanine, she'd have a corps of tailors standing ready, just to press the wedding party's garb.

Long-distance chats with Jeanine about the gowns had begun just after she and Rick made the formal announcement of their engagement. Recently they'd mounted into a daily blitz.

Should she choose the purple, which she called "aubergine," (appropriate for a fall wedding and guaranteed to burnish the bridesmaids' complexions to glowing) or the forest green (best suited as a background for the golf-theme tableware and centerpieces)? The aubergine, Jeanine informed me, would open the door to the lily family: picture a large spray of loose flowers cradled in my left arm, my right arm looped through Mike's elbow. The green, on the other hand, might call for white or yellow roses. And the roses would lend themselves to an elegant but more formal arrangement.

She had been frozen. She obviously preferred the purple, but was unable to surrender the golf-theme tie-in. My best friend and sometimes caddie, Laura, hypothesized that brides frequently focused on this sort of detail in order to avoid confronting the enormity of the leap they were about to make. Easy for her to pontificate: all she had to come up with was a dress — any dress — to wear to the wedding. And she was not obligated to prance down the aisle on the arm of a boyfriend who seemed to have mixed feelings about that status. And vice versa, of course.

So I'd finally lost it.

"Jesus, Jeanine. Why not choose sand-trap brown? With the amount of time Rick spends in bunkers, he'll feel right at home. He'll see all those bridesmaids in 'russet,' think he's at St. Andrew's, and forget he's getting married altogether."

That comment provoked an onslaught of tears and a second flurry of calls in which I pledged my friendship and assured her that I did in fact want to be a bridal attendant and was not making fun.

In truth, I had tried every maneuver I could think of to extract myself from any position other than back-pew observer. I couldn't afford the outfit: it would be her pleasure to purchase it. She had older friends who deserved the honor: I had introduced the two of them and simply had to appear.

And my trump card, I would feel uncomfortable up there with Mike, our own relationship in such constant turmoil. Strike three: Jeanine loved the idea of Rick's best man, Mike, escorting me down the aisle. Besides, all the bridal magazines promised that the glow of a wedding party was very likely to spread good karma to a couple in distress. From my perspective, it was hard to see how watching some other couple get married up close and personal could do anything but send a major tremor through an already precarious house of cards.

After that last phone call, she promoted me to maid of honor.

Then the purple gown arrived, insured for a thousand dollars, delivery practically requiring a notarized signature. Notwithstanding the tantalizing rhetoric of the bridal shop, it became immediately clear that this hue was not on my color wheel. According to my mother, who *knows* these things, my skin was reduced to a shade that suggested hepatitis, or at the least, a recent bout with pneumonia. She begged me to spend time in a tanning bed before the big event. Jeanine offered to pay for a professional spray job. I'd put my foot down — I was a golfer. Anyone who noticed that V-neck of tan skin would understand and forgive my splotchy coloring.

I tucked a couple extra pairs of golf socks into the suitcase, zipped it closed, and went to find Mom. She was at the kitchen table, drink in hand, phone against her ear.

"Charlie," she mouthed, the lines around

her eyes already beginning to relax. My brother.

"Send my love," I mouthed back, then leaned over to kiss the top of her head. "Call you later in the week."

I hoisted my luggage into the backseat of the old station wagon and set off from Myrtle Beach up Highway 501. Barring unforeseen disaster, I should arrive in Pinehurst in time to check into the Magnolia Inn and stop in at the Peterses' house for a buffet supper and a glass of champagne with the bridal party. I'd already warned Jeanine that I had an early curfew, what with an eight a.m. tee time for my practice round the following morning.

Ouch. The thought I'd been trying to dodge surfaced hard and sharp, and now I had three good, solitary hours to chew it over.

What in the hell was I doing playing in this silly tournament?

Jeanine had scheduled the wedding so her fiancé could both play in the Pine Straw Challenge and participate in most of the wedding celebrations. Which meant the tournament was convenient for me as well. But in the end, I'd only agreed because my father had asked. I owed him after he bailed me out of a tight spot at Stony Creek

Country Club last summer. Besides, he seemed to be making an earnest effort to atone for clocking out on me in my early teens. And finally, both Baxter and Joe Lancaster seemed to feel that the head-to-head competition with the men in my life could provide a breakthrough in my own wobbly career. And I was just desperate enough to try.

The tires thumped on the hardpan of the highway, seeming to croon a warning song. *Cassie and Michael standing on the tee . . . K-I-S-S-I-N-G . . . who'll make bogie, who'll make par, who will put it in the jar . . .*

I turned up the radio full blast and wailed along with Patsy Cline.

Chapter 2

It took three rotations around the traffic circle before I spotted a small sign for Pinehurst Village. After soda-fountain millionaire James Tufts proclaimed the climate "health-improving," he'd had Frederick Law Omstead design a resort on the barren sand hills. Since then, the town planners had been busy disguising its charms from joy riders and intruders. I shot across two lanes of traffic and made the exit. The tall pines lining the roadway had carpeted the ground beneath with pine straw. No accident the place had been named Pinehurst, rather than Maplewood, Oaklawn, Birchmont . . . I rolled past the neat red-brick and green-shuttered buildings of Main Street and pulled into the back lot of the Magnolia Inn.

I'd argued with Jeanine about this, too. She wanted me to bunk down with her childhood buddy, the girl I'd eclipsed as maid of honor. No way in hell, I'd said, slightly more politely than that. I needed breathing room to survive this weekend. The Holly Inn was out because Mike was staying there. We were definitely in a need-some-space phase — seeing him for breakfast every morning did not meet that standard. And the Carolina Inn meant close quarters with my father and stepfamily — a setup for losing it.

"But the Magnolia is so, so . . . funky," Jeanine had protested, "and wild!"

"Suits me to a tee, funky and wild. It'll be fine."

Inside an office choked with cigar smoke, I located the manager, a cheerful middle-aged man who instructed me to call him Zowie. We hiked up a staircase covered with a faded runner pinned down by brass bars. Zowie shifted the weight of my bags to accommodate the leftward lean of the stairs. He swung open the door to room Number Two with a gentle kick.

"Breakfast from seven to ten," he said. "The bar opens whenever the first customer comes in for a drink." He winked and deposited my luggage on the end of the four-poster bed.

Large, faded cabbage roses decorated the walls. The sour tang of stale wood smoke drifted up from the fireplace and hung in the room. I washed my face and hands, extracted the purple dress from the pile of luggage, and set off for Jeanine's parents' home.

Several miles outside the village, the gatehouse at Forest Brook masqueraded as a log cabin, each squared log chinked perfectly with concrete — not the kind of rough-hewn homestead you'd find crumbling in the North Carolina backwoods. An enormous azalea zigzagged up the flat stone chimney. A stern man in a security uniform emerged from the cabin carrying a clipboard. He approached my car without speaking.

"Cassie Burdette," I said with a smile. "The Peters family is expecting me."

He ran his finger over the paper attached to the clipboard and squinted back down at me. "Not on the list. Can't let you in unless Mr. Peters gives me the go-ahead." He crossed his arms and fixed his gaze over the roof of my car on a point in the far distance.

I tried smiling again. "I'm the maid of honor in Jeanine's wedding party."

The guard scanned the dents and rust spots on my Volvo, pausing for a beat on the tailpipe, which vibrated from the heavy rumble of my almost-shot muffler. "Why don't you pull over to the side for a moment, and I'll call the Peters." He scribbled something on the clipboard and retreated into the cabin.

I parked in a cul-de-sac just in front of the gate and followed the guard to his gatehouse. He had his ear pressed to the phone. "They're not answering." His gaze jumped to a monitor hanging from the ceiling. A dark Mercedes was pulling into the entrance to Forest Brook. A gold Land Rover was stopping on the way out.

"Damn," he said softly. "Mind having a seat for a minute, Miss . . ."

"Burdette."

"Miss Burdette. I'll be right with you."

I watched the screen as two men emerged from the vehicles. The body language alone suggested this would not be a friendly chat. I moved out onto the porch and perched on a wooden rocking chair.

"What are you doing here, Mammele?" asked the beefy man who'd been driving the Land Rover. "Get the hell off the property."

"Since when do you own Forest Brook?" The other man, slight and balding, brushed the lapels of his blue blazer and then adjusted his polka-dotted bow tie.

"Get the hell out!" The large man took several steps toward the Mercedes and banged his open palm on the roof. The guard moved smoothly in between the men. His words weren't loud enough to catch, but his voice was pleasant and conciliatory. He clapped the big man on the back and turned, pointing to where I rocked nervously on the deck.

"There's a young lady here who says she's in your daughter's wedding party," he said. "She's not on my guest list. Want to check her out?"

"Listen, Mammele," said the man who I now figured for Jeanine's dad, "the zoning question is dead. Your board voted it through. You're wasting your time. We're starting to clear tomorrow."

"The hell you are. I'm going to the courthouse to get a cease-and-desist order. This stunt you pulled has a name. It's called fraud," Mammele said.

Mr. Peters laughed. "Why don't you put all that energy into something useful? Like the crime spree we've had in the gated communities around here. We've got robberies like diarrhea on a cruise ship."

"Don't you worry about that," sputtered the bald man. "I am this close to cracking that ring wide open." He leaned forward with a sly smile and held his thumb and forefinger up, just an inch apart. "Pinehurst

No. 7 has loaned me their flash cam."

The guard steered him back to his car and opened the front door. "Take care of yourself, Mr. Mammele. Have a nice evening."

I offered my hand to Jeanine's father as he approached the cabin, his face flushed and glistening and his reddish hair standing up in a rooster comb. "I'm Cassie Burdette." He ignored my handshake and pulled me into a powerful, sweaty, lime-scented hug.

"Cassie Burdette, I am so glad to meet you. You sweet little thing." He winked at the guard. "My daughter has talked so much about you. Isn't she sweet, Pierre?"

Pierre flashed a noncommittal smile.

"Listen, darlin', I have to go into town and take care of some business before the ladies tie me up in knots over this wedding. But you go on to the house and get settled. Please tell Jeanine I'll be right along." He hugged me again and then patted my butt.

"I'll call Miss Peters and let her know you're on the way," said Pierre. "Sorry about the mix-up."

The waist-high white gates swung slowly open.

I drove through several streets of large, handsome, well-landscaped homes. Jeanine had explained that there were two main draws to the neighborhood: the exclusive golf club and Pierre's gate. Pinehurst No. 2 might very well be the most fabulous golf course in the world, but some folks preferred a private course where they could avoid rubbing putters with the crowds of visiting hackers. And Jeanine's dad had had the vision to buy his property at Forest Brook before the opulent clubhouse was anything more than a blueprint in some architect's dreams. I turned left on Payne Stewart Way. The Peterses' driveway was already lined with cars, including Mike's navy-blue Beemer and my father's Winnebago. My gut rolled. Hail, hail, the gang was all here.

I sighed, sucked in my stomach, and rapped a large, bronze lion's head against the door. Jeanine appeared and flung her arms around me.

"Cassie! You're finally here. It's so good to see you! I'm so sorry about Pierre. I never thought to tell him there would be two carloads of Burdettes coming through."

"I met your daddy at the gatehouse," I said. "He was on his way to town — said he'd be home soon."

Jeanine made a face. "He works too hard." As she took a step back to allow me into the foyer, she noticed the gown slung over my shoulder. "Oh, my God! Miss *Lucy!*"

An elderly black woman emerged from a rear room and creaked down the hallway. Her legs were wrapped to the knees in Ace bandages, and she wore an industrial chef's apron and a faded blue baseball cap perched on her wiry gray hair. It was hard to figure her connection to "Citifinancial."

"What's the trouble, Miss Jeanine?"

"Look at what Cassie's done to her gown!" Jeanine snatched the dress from me and cradled it like an injured child.

Miss Lucy took the dress, shaking her head, her dark fingers pressing smooth the wrinkled silk. "Don't you worry. I'll take care of that. You young ladies go have something to eat." She waggled one arthritic digit in my direction. "I'm not handing this back to you until just before the wedding. Miss Cassie, you can't be trusted."

"Come and meet the others." Jeanine pushed me down the hallway and around the corner into the family room. She dropped her voice to a giggly whisper, "Well, some of them you already know. I invited everyone over tonight. They had to eat somewhere, right?"

I shrugged. "Right."

A crowd of fifteen or so had gathered around a large slate pool table. "This is

Cassie, everybody. My maid of honor!"

I groaned inwardly. The unseated Pari Taichert would not need, or want, that reminder.

Rick Justice, the bridegroom, approached with a sweating Corona in each hand. "Welcome to the nuthouse," he said, kissing me on the cheek.

He handed me a beer. I clinked my bottle against his and took a long swallow. "How you holding up?"

"Not bad, considering he's about to sign his life away," called Mike, banking a shot into the far side of the pool table and sinking two striped balls.

"Cut it out, he's fine." Jeanine laughed and tousled Rick's hair. "This was all his idea anyway."

"Not all of it," Rick muttered.

Mike balanced his cue stick against the table and strolled over to kiss me on the lips. "How's my favorite partner? How was your drive?" He pushed a curl off my forehead, tucked it behind my ear, and stepped back to clear the path for my father.

"Hey! You told me I was your favorite partner." Chuck — Dad — winked at Mike and leaned forward to brush my cheek with his. "How was your drive?"

"Fine. Where are the boys?"

"They wanted to swim in the pool, so Maureen stayed back at the hotel with them. You'll see them tomorrow."

I couldn't blame my half-brothers for postponing our reunion — I hadn't laid eyes on them in almost four years. They'd be barely recognizable — gawky young teens with voices that sawed across the full range, from kid to almost-grown. It would take some work to break through the distance produced by our separation. Not to mention whatever misinformation Maureen had fed them about the sister from a strange land and stranger mother.

"In fact, I should be heading back now," he said. "See you at the practice range at seven? Or shall I pick you up?"

"See you at the range." I smiled and patted his back to file the edge off my knee-jerk reply. As often as I'd blabbed about my father to Dr. Baxter, I was far from reaching a comfortable conclusion about the guy. When I was thirteen, he'd been a rat jumping the ship of his unhappy marriage to my mom. Sometimes he still had the look of a rat, circling my ship, half-drowned and scrambling for a foothold back on.

Jeanine reappeared, grasping the forearm of a tall, dark beauty with sea-green eyes. A well-filled, lacy black brassiere winked through the thin black fabric of her blouse. "Cassie, this is Pari."

I pumped her hand vigorously, trying not to stare. She was dressed for the pages of Victoria's Secret. "I've heard so much about you."

This was true. I'd heard plenty. Jeanine had informed me that she was a genuine Iranian princess. Well, twenty-five percent of her anyway. From her detailed descriptions, I inferred that Pari Noskin Taichert was everything I was not — elegant, classically beautiful, and stinking rich. Even though her mother's deposed royal parents had lost their station and their wealth, Pari had scored her own small fortune modeling for underwear catalogs. I could see how this worked — she'd make anything she wore look good. The cash registers would sing as women with less-fortunate shapes handed over their trust and their MasterCards. *A body like Pari's — priceless.* Only when they broke out the packages in the privacy of their boudoirs would they have to factor in their own lumpy thighs and lapping bellies.

With the princess demoted from maid of honor to bridesmaid, I fully expected to be the target of her antagonism and disappointment. She wouldn't be the kind of girl who was used to taking second place. But none of that showed. Yet. Jeanine spun me around the room, offering introductions to Rick's brother and parents.

"Remember I told you that years ago Rick's parents played on the professional bridge circuit with mine?"

I didn't remember that, but I nodded and smiled pleasantly. Otherwise, she'd trot out the date and time of our alleged conversation and recount it in excruciating detail until I swore it had all come back to me.

"And Edward is Rick's older brother," she gushed.

I churned out another smile and pumped Edward's hand.

"And this is my aunt, Camellia Touissant. She's directing the wedding." Jeanine squashed her aunt into a hug. "Her job is to keep us all from going insane."

"Especially you." Aunt Camellia hugged her back.

A middle-aged replica of Jeanine buzzed into the room, her curly blonde hair cut to a flattering bob. She bore a large platter of fried chicken. Depositing the chicken on the sideboard, she wiped her palms on the tea towel draped over her shoulder, and came over to shake my hand. "And I'm Jeanine's mother, Amanda. It's too late to help me with the insanity issue."

"It's a pleasure to meet you," I said.

"Miss Lucy, you can put that potato salad right here." She trotted back to the buffet line and patted an empty spot next to a stack of white china plates. "Let's see, you all have drinks. We have sweet tea, too, and I'll bring the broccoli casserole and seven-layer salad right out. We'll have a chance to visit later, Cassie, you go ahead and get a plate now. Don't forget those biscuits, Miss Lucy," she called back in the direction of the kitchen. "And the gravy." She peered over the top of her reading glasses. "Everyone loves that gravy, but y'all leave room for Miss Lucy's coconut layer cake." Her voice trailed behind her as she hurried down the hallway.

Balancing a full plate, I squeezed in between Pari and Rick's brother, Edward, on the cream-colored leather couch underneath the bay window. Jeanine was counting on me to cultivate Pari's good will, so I squelched my concern about fried chicken and gravy meeting leather. She would have no such trouble — she had taken only a hamster-size serving of salad, and set about scraping off a thick layer of Miracle Whip. Her green eyes flitted across my dish, loaded with chicken, vegetables slathered with cheese and mayonnaise, and two of Miss Lucy's buttermilk biscuits. She worried a lettuce leaf to the rim of her plate with her fork.

"The tailor's going to be so busy this weekend. I just couldn't bear it if I had to ask for an emergency alteration," she said.

Meow. Another Corona might cushion the agony of talking with her, but I accepted a glass of sweet tea from Aunt Camellia instead. Baxter and I had settled on this compromise: I wasn't ready to give up drinking, nor did I believe I needed to. But I did agree to experiment by alternating an alcoholic beverage with a non. I wondered if I had to drink the entire glass of tea in order for it to qualify.

"Now where did you meet Jeanine?" I asked Pari.

"We've known each other forever," she said. "But most lately, we were sorority sisters at Chapel Hill. Pi Phi."

"Uh-huh. Secret handshakes and frat parties." What else to say about that? I'd been too busy traveling with the golf team during my college years, and hitting the bars on University Avenue in my free time. Groups of girls giggling about boys and fashion and table decorations just wasn't my thing, which should make this painfully long weekend even longer.

"I was a Skull at Washington and Jefferson," Edward told us. "Best years of my life. So far." He grinned, revealing a small cache of lettuce stored in the gap between his front teeth.

"So you're a golfer, too?" Pari's nose wrinkled up in what looked more like honest disbelief than distaste. "Are you well known? Have I heard of you?"

If she had to ask, my guess was no.

"Hey, anyone up for a pool tournament?" Rick asked.

"I'm there," said Mike.

"I want to be on your team," said Pari, batting her thick eyelashes in his direction. "I've been watching you handle that stick." Mike grinned.

Aha, so the hostility wouldn't be confined to comments about the size of my dinner portions. She was planning a two-pronged attack, at a minimum. If she got too close to Mike, I'd show her *my* skill with the cue.

Not that I could blame her for targeting him. He was a hunk, especially if you kept your distance. Tall, dark, broad-shouldered, and brooding, he was the kind of guy Emily Brontë parlayed into an all-time bestseller. He had a down side though: a tendency to moodiness that closely paralleled his golf game. The relationship was rough going when his putting was off. Lately, that was most of the time. And we'd never made much headway talking about feelings, as my shrink acquaintances were quick to point out.

Pari set her plate of salad on the floor at my feet and got up to claim a pool cue — and Mike. Jeanine teamed up with her husband-to-be. After a quick practice session for the ladies, Mike broke the first rack of balls. The purple seven ball slid past the ten into a corner pocket. He smiled at Pari.

"You start us off, partner. We're the solid balls. Contact is better if you chalk your stick."

I got up to stretch and study the display racks of golf balls arranged against the burgundy-and-green-striped wallpaper. The collection included balls from thousands of expensive resort destinations ranging from Disneyland to Ballybunion. I grabbed a third biscuit and returned to chat with Edward. Mike was not flirting, I told myself, he was being polite. He leaned over Pari's shoulder to assist her in lining up a delicate double-bank shot. I'd seen her miss a sure-thing, straight-in two-footer just five minutes earlier. He was dreaming. Or something. I slugged down the last inch of tea.

The doorknocker banged against the front door.

"Will you get that, Cassie?" Jeanine trilled. "My partner wants me to watch this."

I selected a fresh Corona from the cooler on my way down the hallway and threw open the door. Mr. Mammele stood on the top step, with two uniformed officers behind him. Pinehurst police, from the looks of the outfits. Officers Brush and Sturchio, their nametags read. I shifted the beer behind my back.

Officer Brush removed his hat, revealing a shaved head, and stepped in front of Mammele. "We need to speak to Mr. Peters."

"I'm Michael Mammele," said the man in the blazer, pushing back around the cop. He held his hand out and smiled. "Call me Junior. Everyone else does."

Jeanine danced up beside me. "Who is it?" Then her expression turned serious. "Oh, please come in, officers. How are you, Mr. Mammele? Is there a problem?"

"We need to speak to Mr. Peters," said Officer Brush a second time.

"I don't think he made it home yet. He may have come in the back way — let me check." Jeanine turned and walked quickly down the hallway.

"It's a lovely evening," said Junior Mammele, maintaining the same friendly smile. Officer Brush positioned his rigid body at an angle away from the party in the family room and faced a mural depicting the grisly finale of a foxhunt and a hat rack containing a cowboy hat and a houndstooth-check golf hat. Sturchio hovered behind him on the front stoop. Patrolman in training?

I backed away several steps. "I guess you won't be needing me."

Officer Brush's eyes lighted on my face, then returned to the painting.

Mrs. Peters emerged from the kitchen, wiping her hands on a Battenburg lace apron. "Can I help you, officers? Oh, Junior, nice to see you. Can I get you something to drink? Is our party too loud?" Her laugh did not match the tension in her eyes. "You know our only daughter's getting married this weekend. We've never had so much excitement."

Officer Brush cleared his throat and blotted his forehead with the back of one hand.

"Are you Mrs. Peters?"

"Of course she's Mrs. Peters," Mr. Mammele snapped.

39

"Can I help you with something?" Her smile fell away.

Mr. Mammele gestured to a wrought-iron bench in the foyer. "Amanda, would you like to sit down?"

Beads of sweat collected on her upper lip. "Whatever it is, please just tell me."

Officer Brush squared his shoulders, looked back to his partner, and glanced at the foxhunt again. "I'm sorry, ma'am. A man's been found dead on your husband's property on Midland Road. We need to have a word with him. Is he at home?"

Chapter 3

Mrs. Peters' pink cheeks paled to ivory. She sank onto the bench Mr. Mammele had suggested. "A man killed? How? Where?" Her eyes blinked rapidly, finally unable to contain a few tears.

The other partygoers abandoned their pool sticks and clustered in the entrance to the hallway. Aunt Camellia squeezed onto the bench with her sister, clasping her into a comforting hug. Her face had gone white, too, but mottled with pink splotches. Rick stepped forward and crouched beside Jeanine's mother.

"Can I bring you a drink of water, Amanda?"

She shook her head, inhaling shallowly, each breath punctuated by a small shudder. "Go ahead, Officer. Tell me what happened."

"I'm sorry, ma'am, but we really need to speak to Mr. Peters."

"What the hell is going on here?" Mr.

Peters took the front steps two at a time and waded through the cops and into the hallway. He patted his wife's shoulder and then turned to confront the men.

Mr. Mammele pushed out his chin. "We found a man dead on your Midland Road property. Almost certainly foul play. You need to come down to the station and answer some questions. And by the way, the place is a crime scene now, Peters. You won't be doing any clear cutting tomorrow." What chin he had jutted out even further.

"This is police business. Why are *you* here? And why pull this stunt in front of my family? You've frightened my wife half to death."

Officer Brush sagged slightly, looking as though he'd like to join Mrs. Peters on her bench. "I'm sorry, sir," he said in a loud voice, and "goddammit it all, Mammele" under his breath.

Mr. Mammele straightened his shoulders and ran his fingers over his bald spot. "I heard about the incident on the scanner. I thought it would go better for Amanda if I came along."

"And how well did it go?" Mr. Peters' voice vibrated with anger. He turned to Officer Brush. "I have a house full of guests here, as you can see. Okay if I come down to the station in an hour?"

"That will be fine, sir."

Mr. Peters clapped the officer on the back and propelled him toward the door. The second patrolman had already escaped down the front steps. "Would you care to stay for a brandy and cigar? There are some very pretty single young ladies in this house who might just find that uniform attractive . . ."

"Daddy!" said Jeanine.

"No thank you, sir," said the officer. "I'm very sorry for the misunderstanding. We'll see you shortly." He nodded to Mrs. Peters. "I'm very sorry to upset you, ma'am."

"Get the hell out, Mammele," said Mr. Peters.

Mrs. Peters struggled up from the bench. "Wait. Who was the poor man who got killed?"

"Don't worry, darlin'," said Mr. Peters. "I'll straighten all that out later on."

"But Daddy . . ." Jeanine started.

"This is a party," Dan said, shutting the door behind the men. "Drinks are on the house! Good to have you here, Cassie." Mr. Peters took my hand and squeezed until I thought I might never putt again. Or be forced to change over to the claw grip. "Quite an introduction to the Peters home.

Come on, all of you, let's celebrate! More champagne, Miss Lucy. I'd like to make a toast to my only daughter."

The party swung abruptly into almost-manic giddiness. I'd had this feeling before myself, after barely escaping a car wreck — euphoria fueled by a rush of relief over a near miss. For a minute, I'd been certain the cops had come to tell us that Jeanine's father was dead.

Mr. Peters toasted the happy couple. Rick toasted his future mother-in-law. Jeanine toasted her parents. Rick's mother toasted Jeanine. Large slabs of coconut cake were distributed by Miss Lucy and Mrs. Peters.

"This cake is amazing!" I scraped my plate and crammed in the last fluffy mouthful.

Pari nibbled at one bite, replaced her fork on the plate, and leaned over to whisper. "She must have used the kitchen's entire supply of Crisco for the icing."

Rick's parents and brother said goodnight, waving off doggie bags full of cake and paper cups of champagne "for the road."

"Gentlemen," said Mr. Peters to Rick and Mike. "Shall we adjourn to my study for brandy and cigars? Let's leave the ladies to discuss matters that don't concern us. Female matters." He grinned.

"He makes it sound like menopause," said Aunt Camellia, "but he means the bridal shower. I've tried to explain the modern tradition of the coed shower, but the concept does not compute."

Mike smirked over his shoulder as he started up the stairs behind Mr. Peters. He knew damn well that I'd fork over my first tournament winnings if I could skip the shower chatter and follow the guys.

"I'm so sorry to be rude, but that officer's visit quite did me in," said Mrs. Peters. "I'm afraid I'm going to have to retire."

"Are you all right?" Jeanine asked, coming to her side.

"I'll be fine, dear. I'll see you all to-morrow. Camellia, will you talk to the girls about the tailgating? The list is on the refrigerator door."

Jeanine led us into the living room and collapsed on a blue velvet couch. "Oh, my gosh, I didn't want to upset Mother by talking about it, but just how weird was that police thing?"

"Do they think your father's involved in the murder?" asked Pari.

"Of course not," said Jeanine quickly. She frowned. "The police never called it a murder. Did they say it was a murder, Aunt Camellia?"

Camellia shook her head.

"At first, I thought something had happened to Daddy," said Jeanine. "Don't you always think the worst when the police come?"

"The thought crossed my mind, too." I pulled a gold lamé pillow off the couch and stretched out on the floor. "I wonder who died?"

"No idea," said Jeanine. "My folks have only lived here five years. I'm really just home for holidays, so I don't know enough people to even guess. Daddy will get it sorted out."

"Who's Mr. Mammele?" Pari asked.

Jeanine shrugged. "He's the chairman of the Village Council. Retired Army." She winked. "He and Daddy don't see eye-to-eye on a lot of things. Daddy calls him the zoning Nazi."

I glanced around the room. It stood in total contrast to the family room: lilacs on trellises climbing the wallpaper, shelves crammed with arrangements of painted china knickknacks, an enormous armoire crowded with what appeared to be antique teapots and silver spoons, and swags of ruffled lace on the windows. Nothing to do with golf.

"This is Mother's room," Jeanine said,

46

watching me take in the décor. "The deal was, Daddy got to say what he wanted in the family room and his study — otherwise he shut up and wrote the checks. They have absolutely no overlapping taste. You can't imagine two more different people . . ."

"And yet they're still together," I said. "That's a good sign for you and Rick. This room is exquisite." In truth, I felt more comfortable in Mr. Peters' space.

Miss Lucy poked her head in the doorway. Her faded blue cap had drifted sideways almost parallel to her right ear. "I'll be right along to bring you girls some champagne."

"None for me, thanks!" I said. "I'm holding steady." My temples were already beginning to throb with the beat of a distant headache.

"Never you mind, this is a wedding party," said Miss Lucy, shuffling off toward the kitchen. "Everyone drinks too much champagne at a wedding."

Which was exactly what I'd tried to explain to Baxter: even if you didn't feel like drinking, the pressure squeezed in all around you.

"Okay girls, let's clear our minds for the fun stuff. Tell them about the shower," said Jeanine to her aunt. "Wait until you hear this. This is so cool!"

Aunt Camellia beamed. "Our Jeanine loves the steeplechase weekend in Pinehurst more than anything. But Rick wouldn't agree to have the wedding in the spring — that's when the race happens."

"Well, spring *is* prime golf season for professional golfers," I said. "It costs big, big bucks if you lose your momentum. And it kills your confidence, too."

"Priorities," said Aunt Camellia, shaking her head. "You only get married once."

"Not in my family," I muttered.

"Anyway, I got the idea of having our own steeplechase — at the shower."

"Horses at the shower?" Pari wrinkled her nose. "What about the manure?"

"Is the party at a stable?" I asked. If this thing got any more bizarre . . .

"It's at the clubhouse and there won't be actual horses, silly," said Jeanine. "But everything else will simulate the steeplechase."

Miss Lucy tottered back into the room with a tray of champagne flutes and a bottle of the good stuff. She set the tray down, filled the glasses, and methodically delivered one to each of us. "To Miss Jeanine," she said, holding up an invisible flute. "The prettiest bride there ever will be."

She watched with a satisfied look as we sipped, keeping a special eye on me. Then she collected the tray and left the room.

"She's sweet," said Pari. "The senior citizen Energizer bunny."

"We've tried to get her to retire," said Jeanine. "She doesn't get around that well, and she can hardly hear. She wanted to cater the wedding herself. Can you imagine? It would have taken her a week just to serve everyone dinner."

"Let's give the bride our gifts," Pari suggested. "I can't wait one minute longer." She deposited a large package wrapped in shiny gold paper and an elaborate arrangement of gold netting, ribbons, and stars on the coffee table in front of Jeanine.

"Shouldn't Rick be here?" I asked. "I thought you'd open the presents at the shower."

Pari snorted. "As if a man would care. Besides, this is a pre-bridal shower gift. It's for her, not for him." She moved the elegant package to Jeanine's lap. "It's for your side of the bed."

"Designer condoms? Pastel colors? French tickler?" I was the only one laughing.

Jeanine tore open the wrapping. "Oh, it's gorgeous! It's absolutely stunning! Oh, my goodness — it's Waterford!" Setting the carved crystal water pitcher and matching glass on the coffee table, she got up to hug Pari. "You are so sweet. I'll think of you every night."

I wouldn't put those on a nightstand on a bet. One grope for the phone in the dark, and *then* I'd think of Pari every night — each time I extracted another tiny splinter of glass from my bare feet.

Aunt Camellia handed a slender box to Jeanine. "The shop said you could exchange it if you don't like it."

Jeanine unwrapped the box and held up a shimmery lilac camisole and tap pants, and then brushed the fabric against her cheek. "They're lovely! Just my color, too. Thank you so much." She hugged her aunt.

I fingered the delicate silk and made appropriate noises of appreciation. I'd splurged on a silver place setting for a wedding present and a copper-bottomed wok as a shower gift. But somewhere along the line, I'd missed the etiquette lesson on expensive pre–bridal shower bride-only offerings. I'd have to squeeze a shopping expedition into my already too full day tomorrow. This maid of honor business was turning out worse than I'd imagined. And I'd imagined bad.

"Now tell them about the steeplechase," said Jeanine, practically bouncing up and down on the couch.

"Well, at the real race," Aunt Camellia said, "everyone sets up a tailgate station that they decorate like crazy. There are prizes for the best-looking booth and picnic."

"People take it very seriously," said Jeanine.

"Obviously the shower guests won't be asked to provide their own hors d'oeuvres, but we've enlisted small groups of them to decorate sections of the clubhouse," said Aunt Camellia. "The canapés will be spread around at these stations."

"Don't forget the hats," said Jeanine.

"We were planning to give prizes for the best hats," Aunt Camellia continued. "Now we're adding costumes, too. Why go halfway? Junior Mammele has been asked to serve as judge, like at the real steeplechase."

"Just keep him miles away from Daddy," said Jeanine.

"Cool," I said. *Bizarre,* I thought.

"We need you all here by noon to work on our hats," said Aunt Camellia.

I cleared my throat. "I'm playing the practice round tomorrow." I forced a laugh. "Mike will kill me if I tell him I can't play because I'm decorating my steeplechase *chapeau*."

"Don't worry Cassie, we know you're busy. Pari and I will take care of you," said Jeanine.

"Now the question I've been dying to ask," said Aunt Camellia, tapping her fingers on the coffee table. "Jeanine Elizabeth, have you chosen a husband who is just like dear old dad? I'm serious, I want an answer — one hundred words or less."

"*That's* the question you've been dying to ask?" Pari almost snorted. "I'm a lot more interested in what he's like in bed!"

Aunt Camellia looked like she'd been slapped. Jeanine cackled, glassy-eyed and giddy with too much excitement and champagne. Clearly ready to tell more than anyone really needed to know.

"I think your aunt's question is a good one," I said. "Isn't that what the shrinks say? We girls marry our fathers and boys choose someone like their mothers."

Pari smirked. "That gives me the creeps. And it's boring, too. But if everyone else wants to hear it, go ahead and answer, Jeanine."

"Well, Daddy's my hero. Well, I guess Rick is, too. Daddy's been a Marine all his life — up until a couple years ago. I just always knew he'd be there for me, no matter what. Even when he was off on his missions — and lord only knows what he was doing — I came first."

"I can attest to that," said Pari, her lip curling slightly. "When our families were stationed at Quantico, Jeanine always got the first hug from Daddy."

Jeanine frowned and smoothed a strand of blonde hair behind one ear. "Rick and I only had one fight over the whole wedding." She pursed her lips into a pink pout.

"She wanted more attendants," Aunt Camellia explained. "Rick refused to drag more than two buddies into this — he called it a dog-and-pony show."

Smart move on his part. I wished he'd held out for a justice of the peace. In Maui maybe. A couple of leis, and then a round of golf, followed by lots of drinks with little umbrellas in them.

"What about you, Cassie? Your Michael is adorable," said Pari. "Is he just like *your* father?"

"You know, that's a tough one. I'll have to give that some thought. Right now, I need to get going." I glanced at my watch. "Practice round starts early."

"Chicken," said Pari.

"Don't forget we all have appointments at

the spa on Thursday," said Jeanine.

"I wouldn't forget that," I said. "Which way is the bathroom?"

"There's a powder room down the hall or just upstairs on the left," said Jeanine.

I rattled the powder room door — locked. I sprinted upstairs and found the bathroom. As I opened the door on my way out, I came face to face with Mr. Peters and stumbled into him in surprise.

He steadied me with both hands, and then he slid one down the curve of my buttock. He leaned in close enough that I could smell the lime again. "You are such a doll. You be sure and let me know if that boyfriend of yours isn't giving you enough sugar. Okay, darlin'?"

I broke away and jogged down to the landing without looking at him, aroused, and horrified to feel that way. Mike emerged from the study and followed Mr. Peters down the stairs into the entrance hallway.

"I'm headed out, too," he said. "Just let me say goodnight to the bride." He pecked Jeanine's cheek. "It was a great party. And Rick is one lucky guy. Goodnight ladies."

As the front door clicked shut behind us, Mike reached for my wrist and pulled me roughly into a long kiss. He tasted like coconut and Cuban cigars.

"Hmmm, I thought you were making a play for the Iranian princess," I said when we broke to breathe. Never mind that my head was still spinning from Mr. Peters.

"Not my type."

I brushed a dark hair off his shoulder. "What is your type?"

"You're looking pretty good tonight." He smiled slyly. "I have missed you, you know."

Now my heart was pounding hard. For weeks, I'd spent my fifty-minute hours mulling over whether our relationship had to go. Somewhere between "Crazy" and "I Fall to Pieces" on the drive over to Pinehurst, I'd definitely sworn off Mike. If we hadn't been able to get it right yet, what was the point in continuing to try? On the other hand, I never could resist a broad-shouldered man in a white Oxford shirt and jeans. The taste of coconut clinched it.

He pulled me back close, and I felt my pledge turn to jelly.

"I guess I'm too late for the party."

I jerked away from Mike and gaped at Joe Lancaster, standing at the foot of the front steps, eyes red-rimmed and hair in disarray. He looked tired. Embarrassed, too.

Mike took a step down and shook his

hand, still keeping a firm grip on my wrist. "Yep. You missed most of it, though there's still a bridesmaid inside. Luscious and single." He winked at Joe. "We're just on our way out."

Chapter 4

Mike was long gone when my travel alarm shrilled at six. I had a vague memory of him laying his cheek against my forehead in the darkness before he left. Sweet.

Then embarrassment flooded in as I remembered that Joe had caught us kissing. So the hell what? What was so awful about kissing my own boyfriend? We'd been fully dressed, with zippers zipped and most buttons buttoned. Besides, Joe was not my parent. Why was he there anyway? And where was his precious Dr. Rebecca Butterman? I hadn't thought to ask.

I forced myself to think further. Some of my discomfort lay buried in the chat I'd had with Joe last week. He'd called right after my therapy session with Baxter — he has that kind of timing. And I'd foolishly announced that after this tri-tour nonsense, I was really done with Mike. Done with him running hot and cold. Finished with walking the tightrope of his grouchy moods. Through with his fragile golf game and his very mixed feelings about mine. Done. Kaput. Finito. And then caught necking and groping like a teenager with the very same guy. I blushed again.

Joe wouldn't mention it, I knew that. So anything I said to explain or defend backsliding on my "firm" decision would only make things worse. In the end, there was one flimsy defense: a girl has the right to change her mind. And ring her chimes.

I rolled out of bed, showered, and headed downstairs for the restaurant's signature French toast. The bread was crispy hot, slathered in butter, and drizzled with real North Carolina mountain maple syrup. Might be the highlight of the day.

On the half-mile drive to the clubhouse, I noticed modern sculptures along the roadside every couple hundred yards. There was a tall, rusted maze of intertwined pipes, a rough-hewn battering ram poised to crash a suspended tarp, and nestled into a stand of pines, a squatting woman chipped out of white marble. Someone had propped a roll of toilet paper next to her. The effect was more household refuse pick-up day than art exhibit, but what did I know? In my experience, athletic talent and artistic temperament are a zero-sum game.

The entrance to the Pinehurst grounds was lined with what else, towering pines. Both the croquet field and the bowling green were dotted with players dressed in white. I turned my battered station wagon over to a valet who gazed yearningly at the new Mini Cooper pulling in behind me. I stuffed a five in his hand to make up for the disappointment and headed into the clubhouse. Racks of expensive golf duds and Pinehurst-logoed resort wear lined the path through the pro shop to the portico just outside.

The day was a heartbreaker — warm but no humidity, the deciduous leaves hovering in the early stages of their fall splendor. What a shame if it were spoiled by a practice round from hell. I paused by the statue of Payne Stewart overlooking his fairway to heaven — the eighteenth green of Pinehurst No. 2. Now this was art: Payne immortalized in bronze as he celebrated the putt that clinched his 1999 U.S. Open victory — fist pumped, mouth open in a delighted yell — a mind-boggling coup in what had become a midcareer dry spell.

Three months after winning this coveted prize, Payne died in a bizarre plane crash, leaving his wife, kids, unfinished golf career, and newfound maturity behind. Made my family and boyfriend issues recede into pinpricks of irritation.

My best friend and caddie-for-the-moment, Laura Snow, came over for a bone-crushing hug. What she lacked in height and traditional hourglass shape, she more than made up for in strength, unflagging good humor, and common sense. Crucial attributes for a caddie. Excellent for a friend, too. Laura had caddied for both Mike and me, him on the PGA circuit, me on the LPGA. This was the first time we'd run into a head-to-head conflict over her services. I'd won the honors with a conference-call coin toss.

"When'd you get in? I could have used you last night at Jeanine's. Two hours of bridal shower chitchat almost brought me to my knees."

She grimaced and held me at arm's length for a careful visual inspection. "You look a little tired. Are you ready for show time?"

I shrugged. "I guess." I glanced over to the practice range. Mike's familiar form brought a little rush of warmth to my midsection. "Who the hell's standing with Mike?"

Laura snickered. "That's his caddie."

"No way! A dollar says he's pitched out

on his ass by the fifth hole."

The man's sharp nose protruded from a moon face, which was shaded by a black felt cowboy hat. Baggy plaid shorts brushed his knees, his skinny legs jutting out like number-two pencils underneath. Fashion disaster aside, he was crouched in the bar-stool position that golf instructors demonstrate to beginners — and he seemed to be explaining something about the movement of his hips to Mike. I could imagine the bomb on the computer screen of Mike's mind: fatal error.

A newly hired caddie should show up and shut up, offering nothing other than "one-twenty-five to the green, back pin," "which club, sir?" or "nice shot," if the compliment is really warranted. With Mike, unsolicited tips were a death knell. Having worked for the guy for a year, I'd learned his code of silence the hard way. And got canned anyway.

This new man was toast.

"Mike's going to eat that guy alive," I said. "Then we'll have another fight about which of our bags you'll carry. Jesus. Why did I ever agree to any of this?"

She squeezed my waist. "We'll figure something out. Let's go warm up."

"Hello!" called my stepmother Maureen

from the practice green.

I veered over to greet her. If I didn't go, my father would be commissioned later to find out why I was ignoring her.

The green palm trees embroidered on her cream-colored sateen Capri pants were studded with rhinestone coconuts that glinted in the sunlight. A matching rhinestone fringe tapped her calves as she walked. Her lime-green crop-top bared an inch of tan belly and a large keyhole of skin on her back. My good friend Odell Washington had stocked this ensemble in his pro shop back home at Palm Lakes. He returned them unsold — his customers weren't prepared to spend two hundred fifty bucks on a pair of pants that lacked pockets and could only be spot-cleaned and a shirt that didn't allow for normal female undergarments. Maureen seemed oblivious to the fact that her nipples showed right through the fabric — it was too chilly for the outfit, but she didn't seem to care. What could her boys be thinking?

I gave Maureen the distant-relation hug-pat and turned to my half-brothers.

"You remember Zachary," said Maureen, pushing forward the taller and blonder of the two boys. "It's your sister, Cassie."

I transformed his awkward handshake

into a stiff hug and faced David, my youngest brother, a skinny boy with my shade of hazel eyes and the same unmanageable tangle of dark curls. I hugged him, too. "This is my caddie, Laura Snow," I said.

"I'm carrying Dad's bag," Zachary announced. David's expression slid into a pout.

"Your time will come," Laura said, stepping over to shake his hand briskly. "You can learn a lot just walking along with us. You can help rake the bunkers and stuff. We'll probably have to clean up a lot after Cassie."

"Thanks, pal," I said.

Laura hauled my bag over to the range and set it up at the station next to Mike. It felt awkward, moving from lover to partner in the space of an hour. I wondered if it bothered Mike, too? Probably never crossed his mind.

The cowboy caddie introduced himself as Johnny Evans.

"I'm real excited to be working with your group," he told me. "If we can keep our eggs in the fairway and make a few snaking twenty-footers, I see this team on the top of the leaderboard."

Mike swung at the ball on his practice tee, drilling it left through the thin line of pines that marked the boundary of the eighteenth hole. "Fore!" he yelled in a disgusted voice.

"Lots of room down the middle for you today," Johnny said to me with a laugh. "You and Annika. Watch you don't clear that hip too late," he reminded Mike.

Which wasn't bad advice, but it didn't matter. This guy might not make it past the perimeter of the range with Mike's bag.

Off in the distance, my father walked out of the clubhouse and across the portico waving a newspaper. Joe Lancaster and Maureen fell in behind him as he passed the putting green.

"There's some terrible news! Apparently there was a fatal accident on Dan Peters' property last night. It's right here." Chuck arrived breathless and pointed to a short article at the bottom right corner of the paper.

"The cops came to the house after you left." I explained what had happened at the party the night before, suppressing the memory of my encounter with Jeanine's father.

"Weird, weird, weird," said Johnny. Then he noticed that Mike had removed the putter from his bag and was striding briskly to the practice green. He hustled after him. "I'm glad to see you've got yourself one of those belly putters. A lot of fellows over thirty could use one. Just don't have the nerves of the young guys. Hands start shaking a little, and trouble follows. Listen, I want you to try this new gizmo I brought today. It's called the Cameron Cube . . ."

Catching up, he slung his arm around Mike's slumping shoulders. I looked at my father and laughed. "Hope your game is sharp, because we can pretty much write Michael off."

" 'Morning all," said Joe. He reached for the newspaper. "I didn't get the chance to meet Mr. Peters last night. Did he know the victim?"

I shrugged, not quite meeting his eyes. "I haven't talked to Jeanine. Her father was going to the station to answer some questions after we left. The policemen bolted out of there like a sculled three-iron, with the village council chair right on their tail."

"Why was the village council chair there?" Laura asked.

"There's controversy about the development Mr. Peters has planned for his property. Best I could tell, Mr. Mammele, the chair, wanted to tell Mr. Peters personally about the death. He seemed pleased that it would delay the start of construction."

Maureen grabbed the newspaper from Joe and read aloud. "The body of Abraham

Lewiston of Southern Pines was discovered on Midland Road, the victim of an apparent hit-and-run. Anyone with information should contact the Pinehurst Police Department." She looked up, her eyes narrow. "It doesn't say anything here about the construction. Are you saying they killed this man to delay the building?"

"Probably no connection," I answered, studying Mr. Lewiston's headshot. He had thin blond hair and a wispy mustache that he should have shaved off. His eyes were set a shade too close together. He had not smiled for the camera. "They found the body on his property, that's all. Just a coincidence," I said firmly, handing the newspaper back.

"I heard a story like this on Dr. Phil's show . . ." Maureen began.

I tried to tune her out, wishing I hadn't said anything about Jeanine's father. Maureen loves knowing other people's official business. She attended the Santa Monica citizens' police academy twice and took a weekend seminar on firearms sponsored by the NRA. Her Christmas present to me last year had been a framed photo of her wearing a bulletproof vest and protective earmuffs, taken while aiming a rifle at a cardboard cutout at the shooting range. Yet she'd never come within spitting distance of a real crime. The fact that I've been involved in solving more than one murder case over the last two years just about killed her.

Once we finished warming up, Joe guided us to the first hole like a captain docking a loaded ferry. Mike moved onto the back tee, his new caddie following in a flash of plaid. Mike's drive was long, left, and uncomfortably close to the pines marking the out-of-bounds line. He stared down the fairway.

"Now that time you took the club inside," Johnny Evans said. Mike glared at him.

The rest of us advanced to the senior tee markers. My father's tee shot hung out to the right, hit the edge of the fairway, and nestled into a patch of wire grass.

"Remember your game plan," Joe whispered as I walked forward to the LPGA markers. "Block the rest of us out."

My game plan involved accepting the conditions of this tournament as a challenge — there was no other way. And if I could play well here, I should be able to break through on the tour, no question. It worked for Annika back in 2003. She spent two days battering through the men-only barrier on the PGA Tour, with an audience bigger and louder than a rock concert, including more media representatives than she could talk to in a lifetime of interviews. The pressure of that event pretty much molded her into a steamroller once she returned to the LPGA. Sure she had a little post-excitement let-down. But after that, nothing was going to faze her — she'd seen and felt it all.

So I picked out my spot on the fairway, ran through my pre-shot routine, and hit a nice draw that rolled just two yards to the right of my target.

And so went the day. Mike left, Chuck right, left, right, left, right — army golf, the hackers call it. Maureen nattered with Johnny Evans about who was doing what on the Senior Champions Tour. Who'd switched to a long putter, who was using ladies' shafts, who was banging someone's wife? She appeared to know it all. Halfway through the round it occurred to me to wonder why she was sticking close enough that I could hear every word: she was keeping a hawk-eye on Chuck. If he complimented one of my shots or started any other conversation, she stepped up with a bit of gossip about the tour. Same deal with her boys — she cut in between me and her new family like a border collie.

I wondered if she'd had a word with Dr. Baxter lately, too. From his perspective, some of my relationship issues stemmed from feeling like my father had favored me over my mother.

"You're an oedipal victor," he told me.

"What the hell is that?"

"You felt like you won — your father preferred your company to hers. You carry a lot of guilt about it."

Hard for me to see it that way — my father had left home when I was thirteen.

"It was equal opportunity abandonment," I told Baxter. "Nobody won that one."

His shrug suggested that a shrink with less patience might have given up on me long ago.

"Maureen's jealous of you," said Laura, when we stopped to use the bathroom on the ninth hole.

"I noticed."

"And what's with you and Mike?"

I shrugged. "I think the new caddie's getting to him."

She narrowed her eyes, by way of saying she'd take this up with me later when she wasn't obligated to keep me focused on golf.

Something clicked on the back nine. My swing felt effortless and it showed — I hit nine fairways and eight greens. I tuned Maureen, Mike, and Johnny out and listened to Laura chat with my brother David.

"Cassie hits a nine-iron one hundred and twenty-five yards," she told him on the thirteenth fairway. "But this pin's in back and the green's uphill. You see the way it looks like an inverted saucer?"

David nodded.

"If her shot is just a little short, the ball rolls all the way back off onto that flat spot in the fairway."

"So she'll want the eight," he said.

"And if she asks my opinion, I say . . . ?"

"Good choice. Stick it close," said David.

"My man!" Laura clapped him on the back. "Why don't you carry the bag for a couple of holes?"

Mike reached for Johnny's hand as soon as he replaced the flag on the eighteenth green. "Thanks for your help. I won't be needing you tomorrow."

Johnny rambled off, looking disappointed but not very surprised.

Mike picked his bag up from the collar of the green. "Damn, that guy was a zero. Who do you suppose they'll come up with tomorrow, Bozo the Clown?"

"You take Laura," I said. "I think David here can handle my bag."

My half-brother couldn't quite hide a smile. Maureen frowned and looked like she wanted to object.

"See you all later, I'm overdue at Jeanine's shower."

I admired Annika Sorenstam a lot. Still, she didn't have her stepfamily accompanying her over those two days at the Colonial. And she hadn't slept with one of her playing partners the night before, either. Let her spend a day getting ready for a tournament with this crowd. Then she could say she was mentally tough.

Chapter 5

My cell phone rang as I pulled into Forest Brook. Jeanine's voice came through loud, borderline hysterical.

"Cassie! Are you on your way? Did you see the article in the *Pilot* this morning? Oh, my god, everyone at the shower is talking about it. Even worse, we can't find Daddy."

"Slow down," I told her, nodding and smiling as Pierre approached my car. "I'll be there in five. Don't worry. I'm sure he'll turn up, and if he doesn't, we'll find him. Hang on a minute." I rolled down my window and turned to the guard.

"Keep this on your driver's-side dashboard." He stripped a guest pass off his clipboard and handed it through the window. "Then the other guys will let you in without a hassle when I'm not on duty." He paused, shaking his head at the Volvo, then smiled. "They do have lease options on new cars, you know."

I grinned back. "Struggling golfers don't have a great cash flow."

He returned to the gatehouse and the gate swung open. I revved the engine a little on the way through, my muffler popping him a salute.

I parked outside the Forest Brook clubhouse, an expansive tri-winged affair, Scarlett's Tara with a touch of Frank Lloyd Wright. The club's concierge directed me down the hall and around the corner to the right wing.

"Just follow the music," she said with a laugh. "Hope you brought your clogging shoes."

Jeanine had mentioned decorations. I'd imagined crepe paper streamers, white and purple balloons, maybe one of those fold-up, tissue paper wedding bells you find in a party store. And hats, of course. Wrong.

Partygoers, mostly female, mobbed the room. A bluegrass band stationed in the center of the ballroom pumped out "Rollin' in My Sweet Baby's Arms." I'd spent some time plucking at the banjo the year my mother decided all young ladies should play a musical instrument — this guy's banjo licks were for real.

A woman clasped my arm. It took a minute to recognize Pari under the crown dangling with plastic sea creatures and shells. Her blue-green bustier was covered in large cellophane scales that fluttered when she moved her arms. Her skirt, also rippling with scales, tapered to a narrow opening at the knees and dropped off behind her into a mermaid's tail. She hobbled in a full circle.

"Isn't this a stitch?"

"Who are you? What the hell *is* all this?" I fingered the rubber squid that hung in front of her face by a thread of fishing wire.

"It's Poseidon's Adventure. Can't you tell I'm one of the mermaids? Jeanine believes we have a good shot at winning the prize for most elegant theme," she said, rolling her eyes.

Jeanine hurried up and threw her arms around me, the hug made difficult by the hoop inserted in the frothy bridal gown that protruded three feet in front of her actual person.

"Isn't it supposed to be bad luck to have people look at your wedding gown before the ceremony?"

"Don't be silly! This is a costume." She leaned over to whisper. "Grab your outfit and meet me in the locker room in ten minutes. We *have* to talk." She smiled at a group of women just arriving and floated off in their direction.

"This is a bridal shower?" I asked Pari. "This is bizarre."

Aunt Camellia moved in between us, laughing. "It's the closest we could get to a replica of the steeplechase tailgate," she explained. "It's making Jeanine happy and that's what counts."

Now I felt like a wet blanket and a heel. And I still didn't get it. But it was Jeanine's show, and if she was happy . . .

"Wait until you see your hat," said Aunt Camellia. "Pari had some great ideas — it's perfect! You're going to love it!"

She propelled us toward the next booth. Here a foursome of women dressed in green togas and wearing spiked Statue of Liberty caps leapt to their feet and broke into a barbershop rendition of "God Bless America." I clapped politely and followed Pari to her undersea adventure. An aquarium the size of a pickup truck filled most of the booth. Enormous goldfish floated through a forest of heart-shaped balloons with "Jeanine and Rick" written on them in flowery script.

"We're serving sushi, of course," said Pari, thrusting a plate of raw fish at me.

I held up my hand. "No thanks. Maybe later."

I'd eat raw fish when hell froze over. Besides, it seemed downright cruel to serve sushi right in front of those live goldfish. Several women in grass skirts and leis swished by the booth. Startled, the largest fish shot backward and slammed into the rear of the tank.

"I've never seen anything like this," I said, and decided to let it go at that.

"Finish showing Cassie around, will you, Pari? Rick's mother just came in, I need to say hello. I'll catch up in a minute."

Pari tightened her grip on my elbow and nudged me to the left. "Your friend Laura's going to be stationed here."

We stopped in front of a booth constructed of wide weathered boards. Fresh straw covered the canvas tarp laid out on the floor. A cheese tray balanced on a large western saddle that had been mounted on a sawhorse in the center of the space. The walls were hung with bridles, saddle blankets, whips, and other riding paraphernalia.

"Only thing missing is the manure," said a large woman dressed in jodhpurs, tall boots, and riding helmet. "I'm Kendra Newton, Amanda Peters' bridge partner."

I accepted a mint julep from Kendra and shook her hand.

"She's very modest," said a second horse-woman. "Kendra is the person solely responsible for raising the level of culture in Pinehurst."

"Oh?" I said, snagging a stuffed mushroom from a passing tray.

"She cochairs the Sculpture Mile exhibit. I'm sure you've seen it in the village?"

"Oh," I said again. "Yes, I did see a couple of statues. Unusual. And very large."

Jeanine flounced up and nodded toward the large horsewoman. "Kendra founded the Hollyhurst Foundation, and they arranged to bring in all those fabulous sculptures."

"So I've been hearing."

"Not everyone is as fond of them as you are, my dear," Kendra said. The lines around her mouth tightened slightly, though she managed a small smile.

"Don't pay any attention to Daddy," said Jeanine. "He can be such a stiff old coot. We'll see you a little later — Cassie has to get ready."

Jeanine led me to a quadrant labeled "Pinehurst, the home of golf; an homage to Donald Ross." An old-fashioned sand putting green had been replicated on the floor, with a mural of the village in its 1920s splendor painted on the back wall.

"You're to be Babe Didrikson Zaharias," said Jeanine. "Here's the outfit." She held out a flapper dress and bloomers pinned to a padded hanger. "Come on, I'll show you the locker room." She tugged on my wrist.

"Babe would no way wear something like that — it's not even the right time period."

"So we took a few liberties — we thought you would have fun with it," Jeanine said with a tiny pout.

Pari glided forward, stumbling slightly on her tail. "We took some liberties with the hat, too."

She handed me a pith helmet. It had been carpeted with fake turf, with a golf flag glued to the indentation at the crown. A succession of golf balls circled the perimeter of the helmet. One plastic ball, cut in two and glued to the front of the hat, resembled alligator eyes. On the underside of the brim, tees were pasted, point-down, every few inches.

"It's the whole history of golf balls, right on your hat," said Jeanine. "Isn't it cool?"

"You're kidding, right? I can't even get this on without putting an eye out." The history of golf balls, my ass. Someone whose name started with P intended to make a fool of me. And she'd done a damn good job of it.

"Cassie, please, do it for me. You only

have to wear it until the judges have come around."

I frowned. I was already going out of my way for her, in my opinion. And I knew the hat was Pari's mean streak at work. And there would be photos shown for years.

Who the hell is the flapper with the weird hat?

Oh, you mean "Jaws of the Jungle"? That's Cassie, she played on the LPGA tour for a couple of years.

What was she thinking?

I settled the hat at a rakish angle. "Anything for you."

Jeanine waved to her mother, who stood on the far side of the room with Mike, Rick, and Rick's father and brother. Rick rotated in a slow circle, capturing the party with a video camera. The men began to work their way in our direction. Laura brought up the rear, wearing the same jockey getup that Mrs. Peters' bridge partner wore.

"Where's Dan, Amanda?" A woman with a replica of the entire downtown of Pinehurst Village perched on her hat sailed by. She had to hold her head at a precise angle to keep the church from sliding off into the cut-glass punch bowl that sat on a table at my station.

"Oh, you know Dan," said Mrs. Peters quickly. "They called him for a consulting job this morning. Everything he's asked to do is *urgent*. It's not much better than when he was in the service. They phone him, he packs his bag and goes. And he never tells us a thing about it. We wouldn't dare ask."

Her laugh was cheery but to my ear, slightly forced. And Jeanine looked suddenly miserable.

"Don't worry, Jeanine," said Mike, "if your father doesn't show for the wedding, we'll be fighting for the honor to escort you. It's the fellow meeting you at the end of the aisle that you have to worry about." He thumped Rick's back. "I'm keeping a close watch on this guy."

"No man in his right mind would show up at this event anyway," Laura grumbled.

"I was threatened with my life, that's the only reason I'm here," said Rick's dad.

"Dan'll be back for your rehearsal dinner, he wouldn't miss that," said Mrs. Peters. She glanced at the men, clustered in an uncomfortable knot of masculine angst. "Don't you think they've stood enough? Let's let them go. Give the camera to Laura, Rick, and take these fellows out for a beer."

With a kiss for each one, Jeanine excused them from the remainder of the party. I would have given my new three-wood to follow. Maybe the driver, too.

"Cassie, run like a bunny and put the rest of your costume on," said my Pinehurst booth host. "The judges are scheduled to be here in fifteen minutes. There's a ladies' locker room upstairs and down the hall to the left."

Laura leaned over to whisper. "Fifteen minutes and we are out of here. Trust me, I'm with you on this one."

I took the bizarre outfit and retreated up the stairs. The dress and bloomers would only make me uncomfortable. The hat was ridiculous. Next time I talked with Dr. Baxter I was going to get his professional opinion on why the men in the world get away with murder.

I closed the louvered door of the stall behind me and began to strip down. The door to the bathroom banged open.

"I can't believe he'd go to work today. He knows how much this party means to me." It was Jeanine. "Everybody's talking about it." She lowered her voice. "People think he had something to do with that man's death. Kendra Newton says he's hiding out because the cops think he's mixed up in it."

I peeked through the slats, surprised anyone would have said that to the already fragile bride.

"Don't be absurd. That's not even logical. The dead man totally ruined your father's plans to start construction on the property today. Why in the name of heaven would anyone think he was involved?"

"Then where is he, Mother?"

"He doesn't tell me anything about his assignments. He can't. He had to catch a plane to D.C. That's all he said." Mrs. Peters' voice crossed over from irritation to pleading. "The men weren't even supposed to be invited to the shower."

"But he promised he'd help with the judging. He tried on the hat and everything! Where could he have gone? Didn't he tell them he wasn't available this week?"

If his hat was as weird as mine, quite possibly the guy was laying low until this whole shower business was over.

"I don't know what he told them. I have no idea. He said he'd be in Atlanta overnight."

"Atlanta? You said D.C. a minute ago. What's really going on here?" Jeanine wailed. "What did he tell you when he got home from the police station?"

"It was an accident. That's all. An unfortunate accident." Mrs. Peters reached to smooth her daughter's hair. Jeanine pushed her mother's hand away.

"But who was that man? Is he one of

Daddy's friends? What kind of accident?"

"Jeanine Elizabeth. Take hold of yourself. We have two hundred guests waiting for us. We have the chairman of the village council arriving in five minutes to award prizes. Your father will be home as soon as he is able. Unless you collect yourself and come downstairs, you will ruin the party and embarrass the family."

"I can't believe he's not here!" Jeanine snuffled. "Something's gone very wrong."

"You know his job, dear. He needs to be able to come and go. If he gets home tonight and finds out you've made a scene . . . he'll be furious. You have mascara on your cheek," Mrs. Peters said, patting her own face. "I'll see you downstairs." The door thumped behind her.

I looked again through the slats of my louvered door. Jeanine was slumped on an upholstered hassock, still crying. I waited. Should I go out and comfort her or stay out of the whole mess? Even though she'd asked me to meet her here, I felt awkward about eavesdropping. Before I could decide, she shuddered and stood to look in the mirror. She dabbed at the errant mascara, fluffed her hair around the bridal tiara, and drifted out of the bathroom.

Chapter 6

After Jeanine left the locker room, I hitched up the bloomers and exited the stall. I didn't feel too good about failing to offer consolation, but maybe Baxter would be proud. He seemed to believe that I'd practically swept the horizon for the past two years, looking for excuses to keep me from the top of my golf game. Nosing into someone's domestic squabbles was a perfect example. This time I'd resisted.

I put the hat back on and looked in the mirror. Absurd. Then I heard a faint shout from the direction of the practice putting green behind the clubhouse. Then a scream and more shouting. I dropped the hat on the counter, stuffed my clothes into a locker, and rushed downstairs.

The crowd had pushed forward to the French doors and spilled onto the back terrace. I worked my way through the vestibule toward the window as quickly as my voluminous bloomers would allow.

"What's wrong?" I asked when I caught up with Pari.

She startled and turned, her green eyes wide. "Someone said there's a man in the wading pool." She shifted her tail so I could peer out. Hard to see anything through the crowd. I dragged a chair over to the window and climbed up on it. The waters of the decorative fountain in the small pond to the right of the eighteenth green arched up out of the mouth of a rearing stallion and splashed onto a seated figure.

"Who is it?" called out one of the toga ladies.

"What's the matter with him? Is he drunk?"

"Stand back," commanded a man dressed in the burgundy jacket of the club staff. "We've phoned the police. They're on the way."

Calling the cops seemed a bit extreme if the man's only problem was inebriation.

The bluegrass band's rendition of "Orange Blossom Special" ground to a halt. I edged out of the door and worked my way through the costumed women, looking for Jeanine. I found her up front, staring at the man in the fountain. Swirls of pale pink eddied around him. Blood was leaking from his abdomen. A tweed golf cap slowly sank to the bottom of the pool. I put my hand on Jeanine's arm.

She screamed. "Cassie! You totally scared me to death."

"What happened?"

"It's Junior Mammele. You met him last night — he's the village council chair. He was supposed to judge the contest with Daddy." She started to cry. "I can't believe this is happening. What's the matter with him? Why is he in the water?"

It looked like he'd been stabbed or shot, but pointing that out would only escalate the hysteria. I just patted her shoulder. "We'll find out."

Screaming sirens heralded the arrival of two Pinehurst police cars and an ambulance. They pulled around the clubhouse and screeched to a stop next to the eighteenth green. A crew of policemen hopped out of the vehicles and began to press the crowd back away from the fountain. Three paramedics in khaki uniforms hustled forward along the pathway the cops had cleared. Two of them waded into the pond, checking for a pulse, lifting eyelids, feeling for a puff of breath. They fished the sodden form out of the fountain and rolled him onto a stretcher. The uniform of the man who had lifted Mr. Mammele's torso was now streaked with red, and his polka-dotted boxers showed through the wet fabric of his pants. The dry paramedic began to apply pressure to the man's abdomen, while instructing the others to insert an IV and hook him up to oxygen. I gulped a breath of air, suddenly queasy.

"Everyone please return to the ballroom," boomed a cop with his hands cupped like a megaphone. "Remain there until we can talk with you individually. No one is to leave the premises without our express permission."

I clasped Jeanine's waist and guided her into the clubhouse. The shower guests bobbed around us in a noisy mass: some crying, a few eating, more sipping champagne. You can tell a lot about someone by the way they cope with tragedy.

Jeanine paced up and down the aisles, past my history-of-golf booth, to Poseidon's Adventure, to the stable and back. Women reached out with hugs and words of comfort at every stop.

"Junior's in good hands. You know our new health center will give him the best treatment," said one of the Statue of Liberty singers. "They're very good with accidents. Can you try to eat something? You need to keep up your strength." She pressed a platter of tiny sandwiches on Jeanine. A layer each of tuna and egg salad were sandwiched between three layers of pink, white, and blue bread.

Jeanine waved away the food. "I can't eat. I'm just so worried about Mr. Mammele."

"I'm sure he'll be fine," announced Kendra Newton, though her lower lip quivered. "He has an excellent constitution."

Jeanine nodded, her eyes filling with tears.

I slid two of the patriotic sandwiches off the plate. Feeling anxious always made me hungry. Maybe I was being pessimistic, but what I'd seen — a wound in Mr. Mammele's stomach — did not look accidental. Nor did it look like Mammele would be fine. But some of the guests at this party seemed to be opting for denial.

"Here, Miss Peters, have a little glass of champagne. You look so pale." A woman with blonde hair, dark roots, and a burgundy jacket with the Forest Brook crest on the pocket held out a tray of bubbling flutes to Jeanine.

"Thank you." Jeanine took a glass and leaned close enough to read the woman's name tag. "Thank you, Helen."

A burly cop worked his way through the

tailgate booths, cutting each shower guest from the pack and escorting her to the private dining area for an interview. The women waiting to be interviewed drank the beverages available at their stations and buzzed about what could have happened to Junior Mammele. I overheard more than one reference to Jeanine's dad. When my turn came, should I tell the police about the disagreements I'd witnessed between him and Mammele? I nibbled at an enormous walnut-encrusted cheese roll and paced the floor, shadowing Jeanine.

The whole scene looked like a crime investigation nightmare. Two hundred distraught, gossiping witnesses, two-thirds of them tipsy, all wearing bizarre outfits. I assumed it was a crime scene — why keep us trapped here if something criminal hadn't happened?

Mrs. Peters, one of the first guests interviewed, emerged red-eyed from the dining room. Her sister came instantly to put a comforting arm around her shoulders.

"What's going on?" asked Aunt Camellia.

"Mr. Mammele was definitely shot," said Mrs. Peters in a low voice.

Jeanine moaned softly. "Oh, my God, that poor, poor man. Do they know who did it?"

Mrs. Peters shook her head. "I have an idea they think it was a sniper. They asked if I'd seen a tall, slender man with very white legs."

"Very wide legs?" asked Jeanine.

Mrs. Peters looked confused. "White, I think he said white. We're not supposed to talk to anyone about it until they finish the interviews."

"Is the man going to be okay?" Laura asked.

Mrs. Peters shrugged and bit her lip. "They wouldn't say. I'd like to go home. I feel absolutely ill. Will you be all right without me, Jeanine?"

Jeanine hugged her hard. "I'll be there soon. Don't worry, Mama, it'll all be just fine."

She began to cry again as soon as she'd returned from seeing her mother to the doorway. "I wish Daddy was here."

"Do the cops know that your father is MIA?" I asked in a low voice. "It sounded like your mother thinks he's gone away on business."

She stared.

I admitted that I'd inadvertently eavesdropped from the bathroom stall.

"It might sound silly. He's a grown man, and he does have a job that takes him away suddenly all the time." She grabbed my hand and clutched it to her chest. "I just have this terrible feeling that something's wrong. First Mother says he's in D.C., then he's in Atlanta — she's not telling me something." She blinked. "It looks bad for him, though. Kendra Newton says the man who died on our property was the only thing stopping Daddy's development. And now Mr. Mammele's been shot . . ."

"More champagne, Miss Peters?" Helen the waitress hovered near us with the tray of drinks. Jeanine plucked up another glass, nodding her thanks. "I feel terrible about all this. Is there anything I can do?"

"Could you rustle me up a Budweiser?" I asked.

"Not a problem." She headed back in the direction of the kitchen.

"It looks bad, him not being here. You can see that, can't you?" Jeanine whispered. "He had a horrible relationship with Mr. Mammele. They were always arguing." A surge of tears welled up and washed out onto her cheeks. "I hope my mother is right about this. But I'm certain he wouldn't take a job the week of my wedding. I was counting on him. He knew that. Please Cassie. Please help me find him."

I didn't have any experience with fathers

you could always rely on, having adapted to my own father's absence at an early age. Things were better between us now, but I still wouldn't bet on him showing up for anything other than a tee time. Or maybe a dinner reservation if it was the right restaurant. Dr. Baxter was big on pointing out the echoes of this mistrust in the rest of my life. He saw them everywhere. Two weeks ago, he'd been late for our weekly appointment. I left after five minutes, assuming he'd forgotten. No point in wasting my time. In college when a professor was late, in our minds, class was canceled.

Baxter saw it differently.

"You expect very little from the men in your life," he said, "starting with your father and continuing through Mike. Now we're beginning to see it in here. With me."

I squirmed. Baxter considered it pay dirt when he could draw a parallel between life and therapy, but this felt like a stretch to me. We sat through a long silence.

"Would you say any of the men in your life qualify as reliable?"

I mentioned Odell, my mentor at Palm Lakes golf course, and then Joe.

"What's going on with you and Joe?" Baxter inquired.

"You could ask Joe to help," Jeanine interrupted my ruminations. "You two made such a good team at the ShopRite Classic."

"Yeah, I was the brawn and he was the brains."

She smiled, but the pleading look remained.

"I just can't, Jeanine. I wish I could, but I just can't. I have to focus on the tournament."

Jeanine fiddled with her pearl necklace and then straightened her shoulders. She sniffed and pulled a Kleenex out of her sleeve. "That's okay. I understand."

Trying to be brave made her look so damn pitiful.

No reason why I couldn't ask a few simple questions. Kendra Newton, for example, seemed to have strong opinions. And it wouldn't hurt to have a word with Jeanine's mother. After my brief interaction with Mr. Peters in the hall last night, I was very curious about the guy. And I had some free time after the round tomorrow. If it got more complicated than a couple questions, I'd turn it over to Joe. Or the cops, better still.

"I'll try," I said. "Maid of honor, right?" I clinked her glass with the bottle of Bud that Helen had delivered.

Half an hour later, Detective Warren

from the Pinehurst Police Department called me in for an interview. He was a tall, thin man with a receding hairline and a thin mustache. I explained my connection to the Peters family and my lack of connection to Junior Mammele. I had not seen him arrive at the party — I'd laid eyes on the man only briefly last night when he'd come to the Peterses' home to tell them about the hit-and-run. And no, I hadn't seen anyone with very white legs. Other than Mike's temporary caddie, Johnny Evans, and he'd have no business here at this club.

"Unless he was the shooter," said Detective Warren.

"I guess." Hard to picture an inept caddie as a sharpshooter. I pocketed the business card the detective offered, with assurances that I would call if I thought of any further helpful information. Then I bombed upstairs to get out of the damn costume.

I left the locker room, punching in the code for my voicemail on the way. There was a message from Mike. He was heading to a bar in Aberdeen for a couple drinks with the guys. If I wanted to come out, he'd buy me a beer. A beer and Mike's company both sounded great — the tragedy at the party left me feeling wrung out and depressed.

I ran into Laura on the way downstairs.

94

Her face had turned a bilious shade of green. "Are you okay?"

She shook her head. "Must have eaten a bad clam. Going back to my room. See you in the morning."

I found Jeanine finishing another flute of champagne in the near-empty ballroom. Helen swooped in with a tray to accept her empty glass and replace it with a full one. I mustered a cheerful smile.

"I'm meeting Mike out at the Tarheel Bar and Grill. I'll ask a few questions tomorrow after the round. With any luck, your dad will be home safe and sound by then and no need to worry. Meanwhile, get some rest. You're getting married this weekend, girl. You don't want big bags under your eyes."

She smiled another pale smile and staggered just a hair. "Thanks," she said.

Chapter 7

The Tarheel Bar and Grill was a squat cement block building sporting a sign that flashed "Ice Cold Beer" in flowing neon script to passersby. Worked for me. Once my eyes had adjusted to the smoky dimness of the room, I spotted Mike and company clustered at the end of the bar. Randy Travis wailed in the background about how a night in prison caused him to miss Christmas dinner with Mama, and she died later that same evening without affording him the opportunity to express his deep regret and sincere intention to turn his life around. Rick's brother — Edward, I thought he said — slid off his stool and waved me over. My attention was immediately drawn to his nose. Rick had the same distinctive nostrils and square chin, but dialed down enough to remain in the handsome range. The oversized tortoiseshell frames on Edward's glasses contributed to a

Groucho Marx mask effect.

"Have a seat. What are you drinking? I'm buying."

"Budweiser," I said. "Thanks." I bugged my eyes at Mike, to let him know that this was how real men treated their women and that a classic Roman profile was grossly overrated. Which also had the makings of a country song.

"That stuff is rat piss," said Mike. "Come on, drink like you mean it." He tipped a brown glass bottle of Sam Adams Oktoberfest at the identical beers held by Rick and Edward.

I shook my head and knocked on his forehead with my knuckles. "You're an idiot, Callahan. They bottle up the dregs from the bottom of the barrel and raise the prices for suckers just like you."

"How was the rest of the shower?" Rick asked. He glanced at his watch. "It must have gone on forever. All those gifts we'll never use," he groaned. "All those thank-you notes. And Jeanine made me swear in blood that I'd write half of them."

"Yeah, right," said Mike.

"We never got to the presents." I explained how the chair of the village council had ended the party early by getting shot and dumped into the fountain.

"He was shot right there at the club?" Edward asked, his nostrils flaring. His voice was incredulous and too loud, even for the noisy bar.

"Yeah. I don't know for sure. I guess so. He was bleeding from the stomach when they dragged him out of the pond. The police wouldn't confirm anything, but there was some talk about a sniper." My stomach dropped down two floors remembering the scene. I sounded more cavalier than I felt, by a long shot.

"A sniper! Jesus," said Edward. "Was anyone else hurt? Do they have a suspect?"

I shook my head. "But I'll warn you," I told Rick, "Jeanine's pretty broken up over the whole mess. And rightly so — it was awful. And things may get worse. The guy was a town pillar. And he didn't get along at all with your future father-in-law." How much to say? "Jeanine's dad never did show up at the party. People were talking . . . what with the body found on Midland Road last night, too. She's going to need a lot of support."

Rick dropped his head into his hands. "I knew getting married and playing in a tournament the same weekend was a terrible idea. But this is worse than I'd ever imagined. Poor Jeanine."

As I leaned against the rail and took a long swig of my Bud, I spotted Pierre, the Forest Brook gatekeeper, sitting on a stool at the end of the bar. He had changed out of his uniform into blue jeans and a faded polo shirt — he looked much more relaxed off-duty. Maybe he'd have some insight into the problems between Jeanine's father and Mr. Mammele.

"Excuse me a minute," I said to the guys. "I need to say hello to someone." I ignored Mike's frown and wormed through the crowd toward Pierre. His blonde companion seemed vaguely familiar. And angry. She had a lamprey's grip on his arm and appeared to be winding down a tirade. Pierre waved me over, probably pleased to have some relief. Too late to turn back now.

"How are you, Miss Burdette?" said Pierre. "I'm sorry to hear you ladies had a rough afternoon."

"Cassie, please," I said. "It was bad."

"Have you met my girlfriend, Helen?"

"You work at the club," I said, suddenly recognizing her as the waitress who'd hovered over Jeanine. "Thanks for being so nice to my friend." They both looked different out of uniform, younger and friendlier, in Pierre's case. Helen looked tired, pale, and just a little greasy. And now I could see she'd been crying.

"I felt so awful for Jeanine," said Helen. "All that planning, and then some lunatic spoils the day . . . not to mention poor Mr. Mammele."

I closed my eyes and shook off the invasive memory of his ghostly complexion.

"Do you think they'll go on with the wedding?" she asked.

"I imagine they will. No one's said anything different. There's a lot gone into it, and people are traveling here from all over."

"Didn't she look gorgeous in that dress? Wish I could be there for the ceremony. I can tell how elegant it'll be, just from spending that little bit of time with her. You're the maid of honor, right?"

I nodded.

"Doesn't she have any sisters?"

"Only child," I said. "And spoiled rotten." I smiled. "So I landed the position."

Helen scowled at Pierre. I was beginning to get an idea about the subject of their fight — the classic "she's ready to nail him down, but he needs more time" lovers' quarrel.

I turned to Pierre. "Last night when I arrived at Forest Brook, Jeanine's dad and Mr. Mammele were arguing. You broke things up and saved the day, from what I could see."

Pierre laughed. "I'm pretty good at defusing situations — the angry ex-wives, the bill collectors . . . Part of the job description that isn't on paper. The association pays us well to keep things safe and smooth, and we take the mission seriously."

"Can you fill me in on the zoning problem they talked about?"

"Honestly, I don't know the details." Pierre signaled the bartender to bring more drinks. "You'll understand that even if I did, my job depends on me keeping my mouth shut." He shrugged an apology.

"I can understand that. Any idea where Mr. Peters was headed after Mammele left Forest Brook last night?"

Pierre scratched his head. "His gym bag was on the front seat of his Rover. He's pretty dedicated to his workouts. Once a Marine, always a Marine."

It seemed possible, but not that likely. Mr. Peters knew the party was starting. "The cops must have asked you if you'd seen anyone come in or out of the neighborhood during the shower who didn't belong?"

"I worked the seven to three shift today, so Samuels had taken over by the time the shit hit the fan."

Helen rested her head on his shoulder.

"Why are you so interested in all this?"

"Jeanine's a good friend," I said. "She's worried about her dad. I told her I'd ask some questions if I got the chance."

I wished them both a pleasant evening and returned to my buddies.

"What was that about?" Mike asked.

"Nothing," I said. "Just wanted to thank that woman for being nice to Jeanine this afternoon." Mike's eyes narrowed. He wasn't buying it.

"They must be having a heart attack about security over at your tournament," said Edward.

"Speaking of which, are you two all set for the big event?" Rick asked Mike and me.

We gave him tandem eye rolls.

"Cassie played real well today," said Mike.

"Thanks. That's sweet. No one could have done much with your caddie."

"That's right, blame it on the caddie," said Rick. "Forget that Callahan's got a weak mind and an even weaker golf game." They broke into a mini scuffle, punctuated by escalating insults about how Mike putted like Alice and must have gotten his putter caught in his culottes. If I hadn't been so tired I would have protested that their worst slams involved playing like a girl.

Instead, I sipped my beer and felt the stress of the day wash over me. It was all catching up now — the morning's round, my family's demands and neuroses, the elaborately goofy shower, and then the tragedy at the party. Add in a crazy meal plan, not enough sleep, and a total lack of exercise — it was a miracle I didn't feel worse.

Edward returned from a trip to the men's room with another round of beers — three Sam Adams and a Bud for me. I opened my mouth to explain my alternating drinks theory, then snapped it closed. Too much history: these men did not need a personal introduction to my inner demons. Easier just to shut up, take a few swallows of the second drink, and avoid a scene. I made a mental note to describe this situation to Baxter in my next session. Let him sit drinking Perrier in his air-conditioned office and hold forth on how I should handle my life. He had no idea what the pressures of the real world were like.

I sipped the beer and listened to the men talk about the World Series. Mike's team, the New York Mets, hadn't threatened a series appearance in a number of years — to his chagrin and the great amusement of the Georgia contingent.

"I need to get home," I announced, hoping Mike would get the message, too. Tomorrow would be bad enough — I didn't want to know I was carrying the weight of the team before we even got to the first tee. I staggered slightly as I slid off the stool, banging my hip into the bar's overhang.

Rick caught my elbow. "Are you okay to drive?"

"I'm fine. Just need a good night's sleep. Don't stay out too late." I waggled my finger in Mike's direction.

"Sure, Mom." He kissed me on the lips and patted my butt as I walked away.

I stumbled out to my car, feeling slightly nauseous and unsteady. It had been a very long day. As I pulled out onto Route 5, the high beams of an oncoming vehicle startled me. I yanked the wheel right, bumped onto the shoulder, and lurched back left onto the road. I eased my foot off the gas and hunched over the wheel. "Careful, Cassie," I muttered. "Don't be an idiot."

Several miles down the road I noticed flashing blue and red lights in my rearview mirror. I pulled over to let the police car by, but it rolled in behind me. Now I really felt sick.

A blonde policewoman with a stern face approached the driver's side door. "License and registration."

With my heart hammering, I shuffled through the glove box and produced the registration and insurance papers, then handed her my South Carolina license. "Is there a problem Officer Cutler?" I asked, using the nametag pinned above her badge. My tongue and lips felt stiff and heavy.

The officer studied my license with her flashlight. A white cotton undershirt was visible through the open collar of her uniform. I wondered if a bulletproof vest gave her the barrel shape. She must be hot as hell in that outfit.

She directed the beam of light back to my face. "Have you been drinking tonight, Miss Burdette?"

"I had a beer and a half at the Tarheel," I said, "that's it. Boy Scout's honor." I suppressed the inappropriate urge to snicker. I should have said "Girl Scout's." Baxter would have a field day with that one. Penis envy taking the form of the Scouts of America. I giggled out loud.

Officer Cutler frowned. "Step out of the vehicle."

Rat piss, as Mike would say. I opened the door and climbed out. I'd had my fair share of driving under the influence incidents. This was not one of them. Still, I hated the jolt of shame and fear that ran through me. And I hoped Mike and company wouldn't spot my car on their way home. I'd never live it down.

"You should understand that by driving in North Carolina, you have given your implied consent to be tested for sobriety. Do you have a problem with that?"

I shook my head. "Honest, I'm not drunk, Officer."

"Walk along this line heel to toe for nine steps." She watched me step carefully down the road. "Now I want you to balance on one foot."

I raised the left leg up slowly, but the right one buckled and I lurched towards my car. What was wrong with me?

"I'm afraid I'll have to take you in. Pull your vehicle off the road and lock it, then give me the keys."

She fastened plastic cuffs around my wrists and guided me into the backseat of the cruiser. Off to the clinker bound up with twist ties — how much lower could I go? I struggled to remain optimistic. I wasn't intoxicated. Once she saw my blood alcohol reading, I'd be in the clear. Maybe they'd even apologize for the massive inconvenience.

The skeletal shadows of the pine trees

lining the road whizzed by on the way to the station. Somewhere along the way, we passed Dan Peters' property where the mystery man had died. Officer Cutler steered the police car to the rear of a new-looking red brick building. She punched a code into the remote clipped to her visor. The door to a double garage swung open, then banged shut behind us. I shuffled into the basement of the station ahead of the officer, wincing in the glare of the fluorescent lights. She deposited her gun in a safe by the door and snipped off my plastic cuffs.

"This way, Miss Burdette." I followed her into a cubicle just off the main hallway. "Take a seat. We'll be running a breath test." She pointed to a large machine laid out on a table. "Any objections?"

What good would it possibly do to argue? I shook my head, sinking into the molded plastic chair she pointed to. My head felt so heavy I could barely hold it upright. The officer sat behind a neat desk, scribbled my basic statistics on the papers in front of her, then called me over to the breathalyzer machine.

"Blow into this mouthpiece."

I placed my lips on the mouthpiece and heard the whoosh of my breath running the length of the plastic tube. She studied the readout as it emerged from the attached computer.

"Stay here," she said brusquely. She pointed back to my chair and left the room.

Bossy bitch. I rested my chin on my arm and let my eyes drift shut.

I heard her conferring with someone, a supervisor I presumed, in the office next door. "Driving was erratic," "flunked the road test," "puff test below the limit." Then came the rumblings of her consultant, too low for me to make out the words.

Officer Cutler returned to my cubicle. "We're not going to charge you with anything tonight. But you'll need to call someone to pick you up. You can recover your vehicle at our Aberdeen compound in the morning." She handed me a card. "We also need a signature on this." She pushed a paper across the desk. "Gives us permission to search your vehicle."

"For what?"

"Drugs."

"Drugs? That's ridiculous!"

She tapped the paper in front of me.

"You won't find anything. There's nothing there to find." I felt confused and then got pissed. "Hey, while you're looking, if you run across a divot repair tool with the Plantation Golf and Country Club logo on it, I dropped it a couple months ago and it never turned up. I've had that ever since I made it through Q-school, and I hate to lose it."

She stared me down and then continued with a lecture about responsible alcohol consumption, designated drivers, and dire consequences. I had a strong urge to protest. If I wasn't intoxicated, they should allow me to drive myself home.

"What was my reading?"

"Don't even bother arguing with me. You aren't driving anywhere tonight." She folded her meaty forearms across that barrel chest.

I tried Laura's cell phone first.

"You've reached Laura Snow. You know what to do and when to do it!"

She must have turned it off and gone to bed. I left a message saying I'd had car trouble and would need a ride to the club in the morning. If she was feeling well enough, could she please swing by the Magnolia Inn around 6:30 a.m.?

Then I hung up. Who was next? Joe or Jeanine? Mike, of course, was out of the question. He'd be knee-jerk furious, mostly upset that I'd gotten myself into any trouble, and maybe a little bit mad that I'd asked him to get involved. Joe, on the other hand, would be mother-hen worried. He'd think I was slipping backwards, and worst of all, lying about it. Who in their right mind would believe the one-and-a-half-beer defense? Jeanine seemed the least likely to launch into amateur psychoanalysis. She had enough problems of her own; mine wouldn't faze her. I just hoped she hadn't passed out cold from the champagne at the ruined shower. Or that she didn't get collared for driving under the influence, too, and we'd both spend the night in the Pinehurst drunk tank. She answered after one ring.

"Jeanine, it's Cassie. I need you to pick me up at the police station as soon as humanly possible."

"What are you doing there? What's going on?"

"Please come now." I used my firmest tone. "I'll explain it all later."

Her voice dropped to a whisper. "A couple of the council members are here talking to Mother. I can't leave right now. Give me half an hour."

Rat piss.

"It'll be half an hour," I told Officer Cutler.

"You can wait here," she said, escorting me to a small office with a two-way mirror and a video camera mounted on the wall. I curled up on the single chair and laid my head on the table. I felt awful. Woozy, bewildered, and pissed off. A short time later, I was startled by the sound of someone retching violently and banging on metal bars. The stench of vomit and sweat drifted into the room.

"Excuse me!" I called out, looking directly into the video camera. "Someone down here sounds very sick."

A second uniformed officer hurried through the hall toward the noisy inmate, carrying a mop and bucket. It was the blocky, young cop who'd hovered on the Peterses' front stoop when Mammele and company had come to break the news about the hit-and-run.

"He's sick all right, but it's his own damn fault." He unlocked what appeared to be a small cell. "He doesn't have the damn sense to know when enough rotgut whiskey is enough. And you might take a lesson from this yourself, little missy. Unless you plan to become a regular here, too."

He went into the cell.

"Son of a bitch, Luther. Who do you suppose is going to clean this mess up? Use the goddamn toilet if you have to puke again, you moron."

I heard the click and slop of the mop, the officer swearing and grumbling as he worked. I sank back down to my seat. Ten minutes later, he emerged from the cell, beaded with sweat and stinking of vomit. He paused by the door to my room.

"Cutler was a little overeager tonight, huh?" The officer shook his head and smiled. "She takes her job very seriously. You visiting the area?"

"I'm playing in the stupid Three Tour Tournament," I said, waving in what I thought might have been the direction of the golf course. "I won't be much of a representative of the LPGA tomorrow, thanks to all this."

"Sorry about that. We're just lookin' out for your safety. And the other folks out there, too."

I recognized a one-up situation when I saw one. "You're Officer Brush, aren't you? We sort of met at the Peterses' house the other night. Any news on Junior Mammele? I was there today when they pulled him out of the pond. That bullet wound looked bad."

"It'll be the headline in the *Pilot* tomorrow." He sighed. "Dead before he ever arrived at the hospital."

"So it was a gunshot to the abdomen." I tried to sound casual, in the know. "A sniper, like the police were saying at the shower?" The cops hadn't said that at all, some of the ladies had. But he wouldn't know that.

He nodded. "Looks it anyway. One of those high-powered rifle jobs."

"Any suspects?"

Brush squinted his eyes and laughed. "Got a whole town full of 'em."

I pushed on further. "What about the man who died on Dan Peters' property?"

"Hit and run. The guy had a blood alcohol reading off the charts. Best we can make out, he wandered out into the road and took a bad hit. Don't worry. We'll find the yellow bastard who clipped him and didn't have the guts to stop."

The phone on the desk rang. Officer Brush set his mop and bucket down just outside the door and came in to answer the phone.

"Your friend is here." He smiled and placed the receiver back in the cradle. "You've been sprung."

Not funny, I thought.

"Come back and see us, pretty mama," hollered the sick inmate.

Really not funny.

Chapter 8

Jeanine was waiting at the reception desk upstairs. "Cassie, you look awful! What in the heck happened?" She hurried over to offer a consoling hug.

I felt a surge of relief and shame. She didn't look too good herself, one side of her hairdo flattened against her head, and blue eyeliner and black mascara smudged around both eyes. I caught a whiff of stale alcohol and hairspray. "I'll tell you later. Let's get out of here."

Officer Cutler tapped on the glass behind the dispatcher's glass window and motioned vigorously to Jeanine. Cutler leaned down to speak through the microphone.

"Miss Peters? May I have a word with you? I have a few questions about your father."

Jeanine's face blanched, and she grabbed for my hand. Officer Cutler strode out of the dispatcher's cubicle and into the hallway. I followed her and Jeanine into a small room containing a table and five chairs.

"Please wait outside," the policewoman said to me. "We'll just be a couple of minutes."

Cutler dropped onto the nearest chair and leaned back, balancing on two legs while tapping the table leg with her heavy black oxford. My mother would have slapped her thigh and insisted she sit like a decent human being. Probably not a great idea here. I retreated from the room, leaving the door cracked open.

"Miss Peters, I would like you to run through the last known whereabouts of your father over the past twenty-four hours," I heard Cutler say as I wandered down the hallway. Then she got up and closed the door firmly behind me.

I was starving. The snacks from the steeplechase shower seemed like days earlier. I inserted a quarter into a candy machine with a label announcing that purchases would benefit the American Red Cross Disaster Relief Fund. The orange, basketball-shaped gumballs shifted inside the plastic dome, but none dropped into the delivery slot. I banged on the dome until the dispatcher frowned and shook her head.

"Out of order," she mouthed through her bulletproof, Plexiglas shield.

A warning sign would have been nice. I inserted a second quarter into a machine containing loose, mixed nuts. A handful clattered down the shoot of the dispenser. I don't really like nuts, and these were stale and chewy. Still better than nothing.

Then I studied the most-wanted-fugitive posters plastered on the bulletin board. Bessie Emory Andrews was wanted by the FBI for unlawful flight to avoid prosecution for murder. She looked like trouble, too: scraggly hair, puffy eyes, and a mean scowl. A potpourri of metal studs protruded from her nose, lips, and eyebrows. I wondered if she'd been caught yet — maybe snagged by an airport metal detector. Would Mr. Peters' picture be posted here next? God, I hoped not, for everyone's sake.

Farther down the wall hung the village council chair's top ten crime targets of the year and an American flag that had been presented to the Pinehurst Police Department by the students of Pinehurst Elementary School on September 11, 2002. I was examining some dusty sports trophies in a glass case when Jeanine emerged with Officer Cutler.

"Ready to go?" she asked brightly, as if I'd

been the one to hold us up. We hustled out into the cool night. The smell of burning leaves wafted through the air.

"So what was that all about?" I asked, sliding into the front seat of her mother's Audi.

"These seats have a bun warmer if you're chilly," said Jeanine. "Just roll that dial. Some people say it's like sitting in warm pee, but I love that toasty leather when it's cold outside. It heats up faster than the engine ever could."

"What did Cutler want from you?" I pressed.

"When did I see my father last? Where was he this afternoon? When do we expect him back? — that sort of thing."

"Is he a suspect in Mammele's shooting?"

Jeanine ignored the question, though her eyes had filled with tears. "They asked about you, too. Had I ever known you to be involved with drugs?" She turned to stare at me. "Why were you brought here, Cassie?"

I couldn't believe it. Of course I hadn't done drugs.

"This is bullshit. These cops are crazy. They don't have anything better to do in Pinehurst than harass visitors?" I flopped my head back against the headrest, feeling the warmth of the heated leather spread through the back of my thighs. "I felt sick on the way home, and I must have swerved off the road a little."

Jeanine wiped the tears off her cheek and tried to smile. "You know what? You ought to get a mini-breathalyzer. I got an e-mail about them the other day. They come on a key chain with a flashlight. They sell in stores for a hundred bucks, but you can buy one online for thirty-nine, ninety-five. This way you'll always know where you stand, and you'll never run the risk of driving drunk."

I briefly considered leaning over and wringing her neck, but I was pretty sure this was not consistent with maid-of-honor etiquette, nor advisable just outside police headquarters.

"I was not drunk. I do not carry drugs in my car. Let's drop it, can we?" I glared at her. "Honestly Jeanine, I have no earthly idea what happened tonight. Laura felt queasy after your shower, too. Maybe it was food poisoning. I definitely wasn't drunk."

"You don't have to bite my head off. It's not that far out — you have gotten loaded a time or two in the past."

I knew her laugh was an attempt to lighten the mood between us, but I was furious. We rode several blocks in cold silence. Jeanine pulled the car to a sloppy stop in front of the Magnolia Inn.

"I'm sorry Cassie. I'm not thinking straight. I'm sorry I hurt your feelings. Will you forgive me?"

I crossed my arms over my chest. It was a stressful time: the cops seemed to be fingering her father as a murder suspect. A decent friend would cut her some slack. "You said some council members came to interrogate your mother?"

She sighed. "Kendra Newton and another guy. You met her at the shower."

"The horsy woman in charge of the sculptures."

Jeanine nodded. "Daddy hates those things. They had a huge fight about the one on the green near the war memorials."

"What was the fight about?"

"Daddy thought it disparaged the veterans. It was a group of skulls that the artist called 'Heads-Up.' Daddy wanted it taken down immediately." She laughed. "He can come on a little strong and piss people off." She broke down into sudden tears.

"What now?"

"Kendra thinks he's involved with the shooting, too. Daddy had this blowout with Junior last week — about the property Daddy bought on Route Five. Something

119

about the zoning. I don't know. I've been so busy with the wedding, I didn't pay much attention to him." The tears on her face glinted in the streetlight. "Mother and Aunt Camellia keep telling me not to worry, he'll be home in a day or two." She was sobbing uncontrollably now. "Please, Cassie. You just have to help me find him."

I felt bad for yelling at her earlier. The girl was a basket case.

"I didn't get the chance to tell you this earlier, but your father and Mammele were arguing over the construction project when I got to Forest Brook yesterday. The guard broke things up before it got ugly."

"Shitbucket," said Jeanine.

"I talked with your guard in the bar, but he said he didn't know any details and couldn't have told them to me even if he did. Security guard confidentiality code." I chuckled mirthlessly.

She nodded, dabbing a drop of mucus from her upper lip.

"I'll keep my eyes and ears open. I don't really know what to look for," I said, finally.

She leaned across the center console and hugged me. "If we could only figure out where he is . . . I know he didn't kill Junior Mammele, I'm sure of it."

I wasn't sure at all. And just based on the

few minutes I'd spent with him, I was certain that her father was more complicated than Jeanine thought he was. "I should have a word with your mother." Jeanine nodded.

"Supposing we poke around and you learn some things you'd rather not know. Did you consider that?"

"Cassie! They think my father's a killer! What could be worse than that?"

Chapter 9

Laura picked me up at 6:30, as requested.

"Feeling better?" I asked.

"Lots. I thought I was getting the stomach flu, but maybe it was just a touch of food poisoning. Lord knows, I ate enough canapés yesterday to feed a Third-World village. And I saw most of them a second time."

"Ugh."

"What's up with your car?" she asked.

I never lied to Laura, and I hadn't planned it this time. But overcome by a surge of embarrassment, words just tumbled out.

"I came out of the bar last night — well before curfew I might add — and the thing was dead. Not a whimper. Had it towed to a garage in Aberdeen. Jeanine's going to run me over to pick it up later."

"Why didn't they give you a jump-start right there?"

I shrugged. "They tried. I guess the battery wouldn't hold a charge."

"You're the boss," she said. "Let's have dinner tonight and catch up, okay? Get away from wedding, golf, family, all of it."

I agreed, certain that she doubted my story. Over supper, I'd spill everything. Escaping the wedding and my family for a whole evening would be well worth the humiliation. And I could use her reliably lucid perspective. But I couldn't afford to hash it all out now before we teed off. Concentration was going to come at premium today as it was. She would understand that — I hoped.

She dropped me off at the players' entrance and went to park her car.

Except for biannual transcontinental competitions, like the Ryder and Solheim Cups, professional golfers rarely play in teams. Hackers play in teams so their partners can bail them out when their fragile games break down. On the professional tours, it's *mano a mano,* every man for himself, all men are islands. So figuring out how to manage teamwork with Mike and my father definitely shed a weird and unfamiliar light on the day.

The gallery had a different feel, too. In my experience so far at LPGA events, crowds had been sparse, except for the rounds I'd played with a big-name golfer. Some fans tried for a paternal relationship with any girls who allow it — taking them home, buying them dinner, offering rides. During my caddie days, the PGA tournaments had an altogether different tone — more fans, more beer, and more boors.

Today's group fell in the middle. Most of the biggest stars couldn't be bothered with the Pine Straw Three Tour Challenge. But middle-tier players use the postseason events — the silly season, we call it — to gain dollars and exposure. Right away I noticed that the audience here was on the sophisticated side — upscale golf clothes instead of rumpled T-shirts and baggy cargo shorts. Plastic cups of white wine and mint juleps instead of beer. From the comments I heard on the driving range, they were just as interested in deciphering the psychology of the teams as they were in individual golf shots. Burdette, Burdette, and Callahan could keep them busy all weekend.

I tried to outwit my jangled nerves by studying the details of the plantings on the first tee — mostly beach grasses, with bright clumps of chrysanthemums added for fall color. When that failed, I studied the features of the first hole. Architect Donald Ross was big on greens shaped like upside-down saucers, which meant small landing areas. Shots that were almost good enough chased off the edges into expansive grass bowls called collection areas. Just looking at the first green made me edgy. Staring at the bunkers sprinkled down the length of the hole wasn't much better — they reduced depth perception to a guessing game.

So I closed my eyes and listened to the buzz of conversation around me. Rick Justice's father, killing the half-hour before his son's tee time, talked with two gray-haired gentlemen dressed in pastel pants and cashmere sweaters. With Donna Andrews representing the LPGA and Tom Watson, the Champions tour, Rick's team would probably draw the biggest crowd of the day. In the good news department, after we stumbled off the first tee, my team should have been in the clear. We'd have Joe Lancaster following us — his calm, encouraging demeanor was always a bonus. On the other hand, Maureen would give us pretty much all the gallery we could handle.

The weather had turned a bit cooler. So she'd exchanged yesterday's skin-baring, palm tree ensemble for a pair of white corduroy knickers and a green sweater studded with fuzzy white circles that could pass for golf balls.

"Are you sure Cassie's bag isn't too heavy for you, honey?" She reached over to fuss with my brother David's collar, turning it down from his neck.

"Mom, I can *handle* it." Stiff with teenage scorn, he pushed her hand away and re-adjusted his collar to its original upright position.

"I took out everything I won't need," I told her. "It's not that heavy."

"Cassie, I'd like you to meet a couple of fellows," said Mr. Justice, waving me over to the ropes. "This is Bob Salivetti and Lance Pendleton. Former Marine colleagues of Dan Peters."

"Ooh-rah," said Pendleton.

"That's Marine-speak for how-do-you-do," said Salivetti, clapping his larger buddy on the back and shaking his head.

"Pleased to meet both of you," I said.

"Justice has been telling us what a fine golfer you are," said Salivetti. "Poised to break through, isn't that how you put it?" he asked Mr. Justice.

I groaned and laughed. "Maybe poised to break down. Are you guys here visiting or on business?"

"We live up near Raleigh. Just came down

to see some real golf."

"And you work with Mr. Peters?"

They exchanged a look. "Not anymore. Not now," said Salivetti.

"Next on the tee," hollered the marshal, "please give a warm welcome to Cassandra Burdette for the LPGA, Michael Callahan for the PGA, and Charles Burdette representing the Champions Tour."

"Good luck," said Pendleton. "Hit 'em straight."

Dr. Baxter and I had gone over this three-tour scenario a thousand times, a thousand ways. We both agreed it might succeed. I was not competing *against* my father or Mike. Not at all. And there were no inflammatory sexual politics like in the events Annika Sorenstam and Suzy Whaley played back in 2003. Nope, in this case, the PGA players had one set of tee markers, the Champions had another, and us LPGA golfers, our own. The girls played the girls, the boys played the boys, the older gentlemen played each other. My team's plan: play our own games, put up decent scores, and post a winning amalgam.

Who were we fooling?

As soon as Mike hit his first tee shot, a towering drive to the left center of the fairway, I realized how much mental energy would be spent all morning trying not to compare performances within our team. Comparing myself to other players had killed me so far on the tour.

"Nice shot! Pin's in back-left," Laura murmured to Mike. "You're set up perfect for a short iron into the green." She clapped his back and lugged his bag forward to the Champion tees.

My father looked more nervous than I would have expected. He winked at both his sons and me, then approached the tee markers. He milked the handle of his driver with both hands and waggled the club forward and back, four, five, six times. His swing was short and quick — too quick. The ball curved right and bounded into the heavy rough. Zachary sucked in his breath.

"Damn." My father spat, then smiled glumly at Zachary. "One shot at a time, son, one at a time."

David and I goose-stepped forward to my tee. He held out my driver, but let it slip from his hands before I had a grip on it.

"What an idiot!" he said to himself, dropping down to snatch it up from the grass.

"Hey, easy does it," I said. "No biggie. Let's just get off the tee and on the road."

He grinned and pulled the bag back to stand near Laura. I set up over my ball, took a deep breath, and eyed the line of my target. The ball shot off the tee and rolled just feet past Mike's. Which meant nothing, really. I'd started out almost half a football field in front of him. But we all noticed it just the same. Mike and I carded pars and watched my father struggle to a double-bogey six.

"Shake it off, honey," said Maureen, trotting along the ropes beside us. "Zachary, be sure to wipe his grips off. Do you need me to wet down your towel?" My blond half-brother rolled his eyes and picked up his pace.

"Next pin's in the front-left," Laura told Mike. "You'll want to land it right of the traps so you have a good angle in." She held out his three-wood, but he shook her off.

"Driver'll work just fine."

Just fine, as long as you didn't push, pull, or hook it. You had to hit it straight, a concept Mike hadn't mastered this week. He stomped off the tee box in disgust without even watching his ball settle comfortably into the farthest bunker. We finished the hole with two bogeys and my par.

"This is a great par four," I told David on the third tee. "You're better off focusing on where you place your drive rather than how long you can hit it. Most guys hit long iron so you have one hundred and fifty or so into the pin. Of course, some guys would rather try to drive the green," I added, watching Mike pull his big dog from the bag.

Laura whispered something to him. He frowned and continued with his setup. His ball screamed into the backyard of one of the homes lining the left side of the fairway. The owner gained a cool souvenir, but Mike was out of bounds with a two-shot penalty.

We straggled to the ninth tee with Mike three over par, my father six, and me holding steady at even par. My partners both hit beautiful iron shots onto the par-three ninth. I aimed for the front left pin and fell short into the bunker.

"Darn it!" said David, his face stricken.

"It's okay. I need to play patient today and not get so down on myself." I handed him my seven-iron. "I'm too hard on myself if things don't go well right away. Say I'm even par — like today — I start thinking about how the other players must be making birdies and what score's going to win. I panic and start to press." We approached the bunker. "Like here, I could get too cute and think I had to get close."

David held out my sand wedge. "Maybe you should play smart and make sure your shot lands on the green."

"That sounds like excellent advice." I splashed my ball within ten feet of the pin and sank the putt for par. "I see what you mean." We both laughed.

"Great up and down," said Joe.

Laura's amazed expression suggested a space alien had landed on the putting green in my place.

"Joe seems a little gloomy," I said to her as we waited by the tenth tee. Better to distract my mind dissecting Joe than think about what might go wrong on the back nine. "He doesn't have his usual springy step."

She looked up from the clubhead she'd been polishing. "He and Rebecca split up. He didn't tell you that?"

"He broke up with Butterman? You're joking."

"Actually, I'm not for sure who broke up with whom."

"Is he upset?"

"Hasn't said much about it. But he does seem a little gloomy."

I shot her an elbow to the ribs.

"You seem a little tense yourself," she added.

"Interesting night last night," I said. I flashed on my hours inside the police department pokey — the smell of vomit wafting out from the cell near mine, the clank of the barred door slamming, the police officers' grim faces. I rubbed a tender patch of skin on the inside of one wrist. A rush of worried thoughts followed: why had I felt so thickheaded and nauseous? Was it just the cumulative stress of the weekend? Maybe a case of the food poisoning that had laid Laura out?

David approached, wrestling with an enormous hot dog smothered in mustard and sauerkraut. Made me feel hungry, not sick, the way I might have if I'd had a bug.

If I didn't push these worries away, the back nine was really doomed.

"My caddie's doing a great job," I said, loud enough for him to hear.

"Forensic experts couldn't find any evidence that you'd been in that last bunker," Laura agreed. "I better be extra careful, or I'll find myself out of a gig."

"I know my mom won't let me drop out of school," David said, with a wide smile, "or you'd be in big trouble."

"Let's ask Joe to go to dinner with us," I suggested to Laura. "I've heard good things about the Holly Inn." I grinned at David. "You have any plans tonight?"

Maureen bobbed up behind him. "Don't swallow such big bites, honey. You'll choke on that hot dog. I already made reservations at the Carolina for the four of us," she said to me. And to David: "Daddy will be disappointed if you don't eat with the family."

My little brother scowled. "Isn't Cassie family?"

Time to cut this off before it got ugly. "I think your Dad could use your company tonight," I said. "We'll pick another night later in the week, and you choose the restaurant. Sound fair?"

No way was I going to get into a struggle with Maureen over who was the real family in this crowd. Nor did I want to spend the night with the four of them — the boys vying for my attention, Maureen jockeying for theirs, and my father trying hard not to show just how disappointing this outing had been. Besides, I hadn't been invited.

Dad arrived at the tee, stuffing the butt of a dog smothered in cheese and onions into his mouth. The last glob of mustard dropped onto his shirt. Maureen frowned. Hot dogs were definitely not on the low-fat, low-carb, all-natural, high-fiber diet I'd heard her brag about yesterday.

"Let's find out what kind of fun Donald Ross planned for us on the back nine," my father said, almost sounding jolly.

It all depended on your definition of

"fun." Mike made eagle on the long par-five tenth hole. Fun. My father took a double bogey. Not fun. My father chipped in for birdie on eleven, Mike saved bogey with a thirty-foot putt. We all took bogeys on the thirteenth, with three identical short-approach shots falling back off onto the fairway from the inverted green. On fourteen, my two partners tried it the other way: hitting shots over the green with a difficult pitch back and practically no chance to save par. By the time we reached fifteen, no one had the nerves to hit the precise tee shot required to hit the green. Two more bogeys and a lucky par for me.

Walking down the eighteenth fairway, my legs felt like rubber bands and my brain, a scrambled mess. I doubted the temperature had reached seventy, but I was drenched in sweat. The two boys looked beat, too — they had to be feeling the stress radiating from our team, even without a complete grasp of the undercurrents. I was tempted to blame Baxter for leaving me unprepared for the day. A prescient shrink would have insisted I consider the possibility that my partners could sink into a morass of truly bad golf, while I played on.

A smattering of applause greeted us as we putted out on the eighteenth green. The kid carrying our mobile scoreboard adjusted the numbers and hoisted the placard high for all to see: I'd managed to hold steady at one over par. Mike finished at five over, and my father brought up the rear with a whopping nine over. No scores in the black.

"Could he hold that goddamn scoreboard up any higher?" Dad joked. He shook hands with Mike and gave me a brief and sticky hug. "Sorry all. I'll try to bring my *A* game tomorrow."

"Tough round," I offered. It wouldn't matter what game he brought tomorrow. We'd pretty much played ourselves out of the tournament.

"Cassie, you were wonderful," my father added. "I'm very proud."

"Awesome," Mike grunted. "I'm impressed. Hard to keep your concentration with your partners playing like forty-handicappers."

He pressed on a fake-looking smile. Time to clear out before I said something inadvertently stupid that crashed through that thin veneer. Damn, he was hard work.

"Never would have imagined I'd be skunked by my own daughter," said my father.

"I won't ever beat you, Dad," said Zachary.

"Me, either," David added.

"That's my boys," said Dad, clutching one of his sons in each arm.

My big brother Charlie had never taken to golf. Somehow he knew the competition with Dad would do one of them in. So Dad got me interested instead. The consolation prize. Damn, he was hard work.

Kendra Newton was among the small crowd gathered at the eighteenth green. She followed me along the ropes lining the path to the scorer's tent.

"Don't you love our course? How about those greens? Isn't that amazing how the ball just rolls off if you don't stick it just right?"

"It's gorgeous," I said. "And very challenging." I loved the pride of ownership in her voice. Maybe she had a job on the maintenance crew as a sideline. Speaking of sidelines . . .

"I'd like to hear more about your sculpture project. Could I come by the next day or so and talk with you?" I couldn't really give a rat's keister about the sculpture, but I was sure she'd have some interesting comments about Jeanine's father.

"Anytime," she said, waving both hands. "I'll give you a virtual tour — or a real one, if you have the time. Anytime except Saturday afternoon. That's Junior Mammele's funeral." I thought she was struggling to hold back tears.

"I'm so sorry about that." I wrung her hand and headed into the tent to check over my scorecard and turn it in. "See you guys tomorrow," I called to my team. "Rest up, and we'll knock 'em dead, okay?"

Just outside the door, I was ambushed by Julie Nothstine, an LPGA rookie whose first year was mostly marked by the media attention she'd drawn for her perky blonde looks, a tendency to very short shorts, and comparisons to tennis star Anna Kournikova.

"Oh, Cassie! Did you have a good day? Isn't this fun? I wish we could play these kinds of events all the time!"

"Fun, fun, fun," I muttered.

Julie's team consisted of a wisecracking Champions tour veteran who probably had his batteries charged at the sight of her ass in those shorts. And her PGA tour teammate was a hot young Australian rookie who didn't know enough yet about the vagaries of competition to get moody.

"Could I ask you a favor?" Julie said.

"What's that?"

"You dated Mike Callahan for a while, right?" She didn't wait for me to answer. "We went out a couple of weekends ago, and then he said he would call. Do you think it would be okay for me to call him, or should I wait?"

I stared at her, dumbfounded. It was all I could do to shrug. "Can't really help you there," I finally managed. "Never did figure that guy out."

Chapter 10

I got as far as the parking lot before I started to cry. It never occurred to me that Mike would date someone else so soon. Obviously, we weren't getting along that well. And yes, we'd discussed needing space to see where we wanted to take our relationship. But he sure didn't waste any time translating speculation into action.

Did he sleep with her or just grab a beer? This sudden question added another layer of worry, considering that two nights ago he'd slept with *me*. By the time I'd crisscrossed the parking lot searching for my car, I had moved from tears to rage. That bastard didn't even have the courtesy not to foul my LPGA nest. And then I remembered that I didn't have a car here — I'd come to the tournament this morning with Laura. I waved down one of the other players and cadged a ride to the police compound in Aberdeen.

"Rough morning?" she asked.

"I won't rush out to sign up for this event again. Even if we end up earning something, it's blood money." I laughed a harsh honk and tried not to look like the world was coming to an ugly end. "On top of all that, my car breaks down. When it rains . . ."

"It pours," she finished.

After paying the impound fee, I headed back to Forest Brook for the chat with Jeanine's mother. I tucked away my outrage and hurt to deal with after the tournament — our team was in enough trouble. Besides, I was exhausted by the morning's events — flattened by a conflicting mixture of reactions. Playing like a real pro felt fabulous. Playing that well in the company of two struggling teammates — not so good. And I wasn't looking forward to pressing Mrs. Peters on the whereabouts of her husband. If she had any real clues about his absence, why didn't she come forward and tell the cops? I doubted she would share them with me. The dinner plans with Laura and Joe flashed like a beacon, guiding me to the close of a gruesome twenty-four hours.

I parked on the street. The driveway was filled with trucks — McGlinchey Plumbing, Nature's Design Landscapes, Perfect Parties Catering. Miss Lucy answered my

140

tentative knock after a long wait. She seemed a little out of breath.

"Sorry to keep you waiting, Miss Cassie. We have a man here working on the plumbing. I still haven't got the time to straighten your dress out. But it'll be ready by the wedding, never you worry. Come in, come in, you look tuckered out. How about a glass of sweet tea? Are you looking for Miss Jeanine? I think she went over to the Carolina Inn. Something about the center-pieces. Her mama's all worn out, too. She went to lie down."

"I'm right here, Miss Lucy." Mrs. Peters came down the hallway and took my arm. "Won't you come in and have a little late lunch with me? Miss Lucy makes the best chicken salad in the Carolinas. And I saw how much you enjoyed that coconut cake. We have a piece saved with your name on it. Camellia will be with us shortly. She's talking with the caterer and the landscaper about Sunday's brunch out in the yard. Then she was going to take a quick shower."

I followed the women into the kitchen and sat at the gingham-covered table. Mrs. Peters chattered about the million small de-tails of the wedding that were yet to be com-pleted. She definitely looked the worse for wear, her blonde hair faded and a touch frizzy, gray roots just creeping out around her widow's peak and temples. And in the merciless fluorescent light of the kitchen, her neck sagged into faint concentric lines and her eyes looked puffy and swollen.

"It must be hard to have your husband away with all the unpleasant excitement at the shower," I said disingenuously.

She nodded. "Though truth be told, Dan's not one to get involved in girl talk. He prefers to just stand back out of the way and write the checks."

I didn't see how the village council chair getting picked off by a sniper would qualify as girl talk. Especially with Mr. Peters himself a possible suspect.

"How long have you all been married?" I asked.

"Twenty-nine years next May." She smiled. "I can hardly believe where the time has gone."

"And our baby grown and getting married herself," said Miss Lucy. "Here you go, ladies. You enjoy lunch now, hear?" She clattered two plates of tomatoes stuffed with chicken salad on the table. Then she delivered a basket of warm biscuits and small bowls of butter and honey. I watched her hobble out of the room. She unnerved me a little — a character lifted straight out of

Gone with the Wind. I ran my finger along the strand of raised porcelain ivy that circled the rim of my plate.

"What kind of work does your husband do? You said he's retired from the Marines?"

"Five years now. Couldn't come soon enough. A career in the military can be very hard on family life." She carved off several dainty bites of tomato and arranged them in a semicircle, and then spread honey on a small square biscuit. "He travels more than I'd hoped, though. He's a consultant."

"For the military?"

She laughed. "I assume that's the case. He always says if he tells me too much he'll have to kill me. So I just stopped asking years ago. New brides don't understand this about marriage — you needn't know everything about your husband. Nor he about you. Leave some mystery, Cassie."

I nodded and took another biscuit from the basket she held out. It was not going to be so easy to get the facts from her. Either she really didn't have them, or she was reluctant to give them away.

"I'm sorry, you had a big day! And I forgot to ask how it went," she said.

"Not so good." I scraped up the last of my chicken salad and licked the spoon. Mrs.

Peters had barely touched her food, except to slide it around the plate like the pieces of an unsolved jigsaw puzzle. "There's something crunchy in here."

"Almonds. But the secret is the way they're cut — don't buy the slivers, buy the ones in little chunks. The contrast in textures between the chicken and the grapes and the nuts are what makes it so special."

"I'm not much of a cook anyway, but I sure love to eat."

"So what happened with your little team today?"

I sighed. "My father had a horrible day. And Mike didn't play so well, either. I was just average. It looked like Rick's team was on top of the leaderboard when I left. Amazing, considering he's getting married this weekend, too."

"He's a nice young man," said Mrs. Peters. She dabbed her lips. "We're so pleased about Jeanine's choice. We just adore his parents, too." She got up to clear plates and returned with a slab of cake for me and a sliver for her.

"The wedding plans are going well," she said. She listed Jeanine's last-minute menu changes — "no one eats beef these days" — and described the napkins they'd finally settled on. The cocktail napkins were paper,

"Jeanine and Rick" imprinted in gold script, but the dinner napkins were a simple and elegant ivory linen.

I stifled a yawn and tried not to gobble my cake. Was she warmed up enough to answer my serious questions?

"I hate to bring this up, but Jeanine's really worried that the police think your husband's involved —"

"Nonsense." She cut me off before I could finish the question. "Dan will get home tonight or tomorrow, and he'll straighten this all out. I'll talk to Jeanine, explain it to her."

Suddenly she was wound so tight it seemed that if I just touched her, she would shatter into a million pieces.

She smiled brightly. "You better run on now, you'll be late for the spa. It's brand new, you know, and they do a wonderful job over there — you'll come out feeling like a piece of cooked spaghetti."

Two glasses of sweet tea pressed on my bladder. "May I use the bathroom on the way out?"

"Go on upstairs — you're family. The plumbers have the whole toilet pulled out of the powder room. Lord knows what someone dropped in there."

I followed the wrought-iron railing up to

the second floor and turned left toward the bathroom I'd used two nights ago. Behind the locked door, I heard the shower running. I hesitated, then turned into the master suite and crossed the sitting area to the master bath.

While washing my hands, I noticed that the door to the medicine cabinet hung ajar. I hesitated again, then opened it all the way and glanced through the stash of medications. Along with supplies of Advil, aspirin, Pepcid AC, and Sudafed, Mrs. Peters had a renewable prescription for Xanax. Quite useful under the current circumstances. Mr. Peters had an old prescription for lithium carbonate, generic brand. Twenty-something years old, a very long time to keep a bottle of pills. Three refills had been unclaimed when the prescription expired. I propped the door open at its original angle and left the room. On the way out, I poked my head into Mr. Peters' study.

The walls were lined with leather-bound books and pictures of his family from across the years. His computer screensaver featured Marines in desert camouflage. Iraq maybe? The landscape's bleak features looked TV-news familiar. The desk was clear, except for a large calendar blotter. I walked around to take a peek. "Jeanine's wedding — do not double-book!!!" had been penciled in a feminine scrawl, with an arrow stretching across the entire week. I turned to look at the photographs. A rifle leaned against the window behind the desk.

"Can I help you find something?" asked a voice from the hallway.

Startled, I shot from behind the desk. Aunt Camellia stood in the doorway in a blue chenille robe and slippers, her hair wrapped in a towel turban.

"No, not, no . . . I didn't get the chance to have the tour of this floor the other night. And the powder room downstairs is out of order. It's such a beautiful home." I sounded like an idiot.

"Aren't you due over at the spa?" Aunt Camellia asked in a cheery voice that didn't match her frown.

"I'm just on my way."

She looked for a moment as though she would say something else. "Enjoy your massage, then," said Aunt Camellia. "It's been a bit stressful around here, hasn't it?"

"Weddings have that rap." I swished out past her and headed for the stairway. "On my way."

She laid a cool, white hand on my arm.

"Cassie. Remember that not every day in the life of a marriage is a fairy tale. You'll find dirt in any corner if you look hard enough. Presbyopia can be a blessing."

I nodded. Presbyopia? "Probably so. Well, have a good day."

What was all that about? I wondered on the short drive to the spa. One thing for certain, Aunt Camellia was delivering her warning about storybook marriages to the wrong gal.

Chapter 11

A tall Hispanic woman in a white uniform outfitted me with clear rubber flip-flops and a locker key attached to an expandable slip-on bracelet.

"I'll show you around," she said in a squeaky voice.

I followed her into an alcove papered with green and white stripes and lined with banks of polished wood lockers. She opened number 214 and presented me with a white terry robe: thick, soft, and perfumed with the scent of pine. The Pinehurst pinecone logo was embroidered on a chest pocket.

"Get changed here, and your esthetician will meet you in the waiting area. Showers are down the hall on the left, ladies' room on the right. Most customers like to visit both before their treatment. Enjoy your day."

I sat on the bench in front of the locker to remove my sneakers and stared at the brown pinecones woven into the carpet. Was I supposed to take everything off? Athletic training rubdowns in college had not prepared me for top-drawer spa protocol. I wasn't about to broadcast my ignorance by calling after the attendant. What the heck. I stripped down, stuffed my sweaty clothes into the locker, and traipsed off to the shower. I emerged into the waiting area, damp, a little nervous, and now enveloped in a mixed bouquet of pine and roses.

"Cassie!" Jeanine called. "Over here!" She reclined on a chaise longue, with Pari relaxing beside her. They wore white robes identical to mine. "I thought you'd forgotten."

I perched on the end of her lounge chair. "Not a chance."

"I am so looking forward to this," said Jeanine. "I love massage. It brings out all my deep and hidden feelings. Last time I cried all the way through it — and it feels a lot better than therapy, too."

Wouldn't be hard to vault over that low bar.

"Have you ever had a facial?" Jeanine asked me. I shook my head. "You're going to love it! I can't wait to hear what you think."

A woman wearing a white coat and a lot of

makeup approached our group. "Miss Peters? May I have a word?"

Jeanine struggled out of the chaise longue and padded over to confer with her a short distance away. As the woman talked, Jeanine looked first angry, then gloomy. The staff person was talking faster now, gesturing and smiling. She began to stroke Jeanine's back as though she were a large cat. Jeanine shook her off. She turned and poured a glass of spring water from a pitcher on the table along the wall and crossed the room to us.

"I have some bad news." She sipped the water.

"What's wrong?" The picture of her father arrested and taken away in cuffs came to mind. But how would the spa staff know that?

"I'm so pissed about this. I called months ago to book massages and facials for all of us, back to back." She was near tears. "Now they say the massage is no problem, but they only have space for one facial. Someone messed up and overbooked, and the other clients are already in the middle of their treatments." She tried to laugh. "We can't very well drag them out of the rooms with enzyme peel all over their faces. So I'll skip mine, but I'm so sorry, one of you is going to miss out, too." Her lip quivered.

"Don't be silly," I said briskly, patting her leg. "You're the bride. You absolutely have to have the facial." If this was terrible news, we could definitely field it.

Pari surprised me. "She's right. I can do this at home anytime."

After a few minutes of half-hearted protests, Jeanine agreed.

"You could get a manicure instead," she said hopefully.

"I don't want to have to worry about chipping my polish over a crucial putt," I said, laughing. "We'll be fine, right Pari?"

"At least let me get you a cup of herbal tea," said Jeanine. "They don't serve beer here." She giggled.

Considering the way I'd spent the night before, that comment felt a little mean. "I'm good," I said.

"You girls feel free to relax and enjoy the sauna, the hot tub, all of it, when you're done," said Jeanine. "You go right through that door. And the lap pool is just outside. Stay as long as you like. In fact you can use the facilities all weekend — one of the bridesmaid perks!" She dropped her voice to a whisper. "Did you talk to my mother?"

I nodded.

"I'll call you later."

A pudgy brunette in a white uniform stepped out from the steamy hot-tub chamber and into the waiting room. "Cassandra?" She peered around through fogged eyeglasses.

"That's me." I clutched my robe closed to my throat and clopped across the tiles to join her.

"I'm Violet. I'll be giving your massage today."

She placed one hand on my back and guided me past the hot tub, across the deck of the lap pool, and down a dim hallway. She held contact until we rounded a corner and entered a dark, sweet-smelling womb of a room.

"I'll wait outside while you get comfortable," she said.

That could be a long wait. I removed my robe and slipped into an envelope of sheets on her padded table.

"You be sure and let me know if you want me to work deeper," Violet said, running her hands along my spine. Then she folded the sheet down to my waist and began to rub my back with peppermint-scented oil. "My, you have very large stress knots," she whispered when she reached my shoulders.

"I'm a little tense right now."

A running commentary on the state of my

musculature would not do much to reduce the tension, either. So far, I wasn't having the experience that Jeanine had described — the sudden rush of emotions and ensuing relief. Instead, I felt my muscles compact into throbbing and painful lumps as questions about the events of the last two days swirled through my mind.

What the hell was up with Mike and me?

Violet dug into my neck. I winced and tried to ease away from her kneading fingers and that unpleasant and unanswerable question. I diverted my thoughts back to Jeanine. Why was Mrs. Peters oblivious to her husband's whereabouts? Or maybe more accurately, why did she choose to appear oblivious? Where was the guy? Had he been involved in Mammele's shooting?

Violet abandoned the knots and switched to rhythmic strokes extending from neck to buttocks. Another thought surfaced: I was not drunk leaving the Tarheel Bar and Grill. So what was wrong with me? I'd felt over-tired, off-balance, nauseous, and giddy — more than the reasonable aftereffects of less than two beers. My hands felt abruptly cold and then sweaty. Could someone have dropped something into my drink while I stood at the bar? But who and why? This new theory sounded ridiculous and paranoid. It must have been food poisoning.

Violet finished her work and instructed me to get dressed when I felt ready. "You'll want to drink a lot of water the next couple of days, wash out all the toxins I loosened up. And definitely take a hot tub and a sauna. Have you considered yoga?" she asked. "It might help with those knots."

"I'm a golfer," I said, as if that explained everything.

I crossed back through the pool area and into the ladies' lounge. Pari bobbed naked in the hot tub.

"How did it go?" she asked. "Come on in. The water is just wonderful."

I hesitated, again struggling with the clothing dilemma. Clearly Pari had no issues being nude. But who would, with boobs that stood straight out like the front half of torpedoes and a waist measurement smaller than the circumference of my thigh? I slipped out of my robe, slunk into the froth, and studied the signs on the wall above the tub, trying not to stare at those rubber-ball boobs.

Pregnant women, elderly persons, and persons suffering from heart disease, diabetes, and low or high blood pressure should not enter the hot tub without prior medical consultation and permission from their doctor.

"So you've known Jeanine's family a long time?" I asked, once we'd exhausted chit-chat about the benefits and pleasures of massage.

"On and off since we were kids. Our fathers were both stationed in Camp Lejeune. And they went to Okinawa together. Times have changed, though," she said. "The Peters have definitely moved up in the world in the last five years."

"They didn't come from money?"

She laughed. "Not that I know of. And believe me, not all retired military guys have achieved the standard of living that Dan Peters has managed. He's a gorgeous man, though, don't you think? And being filthy rich brings it out even more."

A gorgeous man? I hadn't thought of him that way exactly. Magnetic energy, maybe. His hand brushing my butt and the question he'd whispered flashed to mind. *Is your boyfriend giving you enough sugar . . .* or something to that effect.

" 'Do not use the hot tub,' " I read aloud, " 'while under the influence of alcohol, tranquilizers, or other drugs that cause drowsiness or that raise or lower blood pressure.' " I glanced at Pari. "I never knew hot-tubbing could be so dangerous."

Pari winked. "I'll tell you a secret. Dan

and I had a little fling maybe eight years ago. *He's* hot. And dangerous."

"You went out with Jeanine's father?"

"He took me to lunch. And something else ended up on the menu."

"How old were you?"

"Nineteen. Old enough to say, 'Yes sir, Lieutenant Colonel,' and enjoy the hell out of it." She grinned.

Was she telling the truth or trying to shock me? The jets of the tub bubbled up to fill the silence. Pari stretched, her boobs popping up to the water's surface. Were they real?

Do not use alone. Unsupervised use by children prohibited. Enter and exit slowly. Observe reasonable time limits, then leave the water and cool down before returning for another brief stay. Long exposure may result in nausea, dizziness, or fainting.

In the end, it wouldn't surprise me at all if she'd seduced Jeanine's father. I had a hunch — though my database was low — that he would have made an easy mark.

"Does Jeanine know?"

"Of course not. It didn't mean anything important, and she wouldn't understand. It was just a fuck."

"I think I'll try the steam room," I said. "Violet recommended it to me. I have stress knots." I grabbed the towel crumpled beside the tub and scuttled over to the sauna. Pari followed. I settled into the farthest corner, still wrapped in the towel.

Pari arranged herself naked on the first step. "I have a question."

"Yes?" I asked, leery of more conversation with her and claustrophobic in the thickening steam.

"Are you and that adorable Mike still an item, or is he available?"

"As far as I know, he's all yours. Be my guest."

I could barely make out her expression of astonishment. Probably she expected more of a fight.

"Oh, there's a little blonde twit who's interested in him, but he's one gentleman who doesn't prefer blondes," I added. "And he'll never go for another golfer. One was enough, thank you very much."

I surprised even myself by babbling on about just how available Mike was. I mean seriously surprised. And it wasn't just hearing about his date with the rookie golfer. Though that blow did land with a sickening thud. I loved Mike, I really did. But after today's outing, I could see what would happen if we both continued to play professional golf. It could only work if one of us played and failed — me in particular. Then he could act the consoling boyfriend — husband, even — and support my brave decision to move on to something else. Like a comfortable stool behind the desk in some pro shop. *Not.*

Hard as he tried to cover it up, my father's disappointment had mushroomed over the last two days. He'd postponed his dream for twenty years, then gotten into the game too late. I seemed to be turning a corner — I was not going to make the same mistake. Especially for a guy.

"I'm surprised you bothered to ask me," I told Pari. "Did you ask Mrs. Peters before you shagged her husband?"

Pari's throaty laugh bellowed through the steam. "I didn't have to ask. It was obvious he was available."

Now what was I supposed to tell Jeanine that I'd discovered so far? That her oldest friend screwed around with her own father? Or maybe she didn't, but she's telling people she did? And that in fact, it was believable because he'd practically made a pass at me right in front of Mike. And that Jeanine's mother was pretending to know nothing, but the truth lay somewhere else?

This is probably just what Baxter meant. Mind my own damn business and play golf.

Chapter 12

I walked the short distance from the Magnolia to the Holly Inn, still a little dizzy from too much time in the hot tub and sauna. And way too much time with Pari. Just a fuck. Who did she think she was? Diego Rivera?

There was no sign of Laura or Joe in the cool dimness of the Holly Inn lobby. I sprawled in an upholstered wing chair by the fire. The flames crackled higher, warming the dark paneling from molasses to honey and illuminating the quotation inscribed over the fireplace: *Time goes you say? Ah no! Time stays, we go.* Harry Austin Dobson.

"Sorry I'm late." Joe strode by the reception desk and across the purple flowered carpet. He leaned over to kiss me on the top of the head at the same time I turned my head to greet him. He caught half of my lips with his and pulled back like a scalded cat.

"How are you feeling?" he asked, blushing furiously.

"Limp noodle territory," I said, blushing, too. "Spent the afternoon with the gals in the spa." I hoisted my eyebrows full sail. "Thank God I have obligations besides the wedding festivities this week or I'd be going bonkers."

"Laura will be late — she's still out with Mike on the range." We both rolled our eyes. I wouldn't wish extra time with Mike after a lousy round on anyone. "Let's get a beer."

I followed him into the bar and settled onto a green leather barstool.

"I'm tempted to order a martini or a cosmopolitan." I pointed to the triangular glassware hanging from the ceiling. "I love the look." The bartender laid a napkin in front of me. "I'll try a Carolina lager."

"Ditto for me," said Joe. "You played really well under brutal conditions today." He squeezed my shoulder. "I've never seen you so calm. I'm proud."

"Thanks. It was every bit the bitch I expected. And more. But it helped to have David there. He was so nervous, I had to stay cool for his sake."

"He seems like a good kid. Zachary, too."

"Yeah, if Maureen doesn't hover the life

161

out of them." I shrugged. I knew from hovering mothers. "I feel sorry for my father. I'm afraid he doesn't have what it takes for the Champions Tour. And he sees it."

Joe massaged his head, leaving a standing wake of gray-tinged curls behind his kneading fingers. "Hard to say. He missed the years of professional competition that most of these other guys got playing on the PGA tour. Remember your first two years out there, all you could think about was missing the cut?"

"That's still all I think about!"

Joe laughed and waved dismissively. "Things are going to be different for you now. You have your eye on a different ball — winning, not just surviving."

"Maybe."

"I looked for you after the round to grab lunch, but you'd disappeared."

"I promised Jeanine I'd go talk with her mom. She's really worried about her father. Did you hear she was interrogated at the police station last night?"

Joe frowned, the skin crinkling around the corners of his green eyes. "No, I hadn't heard. Are you getting mixed up in their problems?"

I shook my head. "Jeanine just asked me to speak with her mother. She's really worried. Neither Mrs. Peters nor her sister seem very concerned, though."

"But this is how —"

"Sorry!" said Laura, rushing into the bar and plopping down next to me. "I needed to straighten a couple things out with your Mike. What's up with you guys?"

"Cassie's meddling again," said Joe, still frowning.

" 'Too late I stayed,' " I read aloud from the wall beside the entrance, " 'Forgive the crime. Unheeded flew the hours. How noiseless falls the foot of time, that only treads on flowers.' William Robert Spencer. This place is big on quotations and instructions. You should have seen the warnings in the spa."

"Don't change the subject, Cassie."

The officious tone annoyed me. But I needed help. And I knew Joe was afraid I'd sink up to my eyeballs into Jeanine's problems. If history was any kind of predictor, I probably would.

"This is the whole deal. Jeanine asked me to see if I could find anything out about her father. My plan was to ask a few people a few questions and tell her I did all I could. But then, something really weird happened."

I told them about my visit to the police

department the night before.

Laura's eyes widened. "So that's why you needed a ride to the course this morning."

"Your table is ready," said a square blonde woman wearing heavy rings of eyeliner. She seated us in a back booth. "May I tell you tonight's specials?" She rattled off a list, then gestured to her brass nameplate. "My name is Rudy. We have a new system here. Have you heard of our star points?"

I shook my head, just wanting her to clear out.

She explained that all guests were asked to fill out forms about the service they received. The staff could earn bonuses and extra days off depending on their point tally. She slid three papers onto the table and grinned. "Please keep me in mind."

"Guerilla marketing," said Laura. "Doesn't pay to be shy with this system."

"So get back to what happened in the bar." Joe hadn't taken his eyes off my face since I confessed to the police station incident.

"At first, I figured I had the stomach flu or food poisoning — like you did." I nodded at Laura. "I felt kind of giddy and thickheaded at the same time." I took a sip of the lager and studied my hands. "But then — I know this sounds crazy and paranoid and like I'm trying to weasel out of trouble — I had the thought that someone put something into my second beer."

Rudy returned to our booth, her pencil poised over her pad. "Are you ready to order?"

"I'll take the crab cakes with remoulade sauce and black-eyed peas. And another lager." I tapped my glass. "Wait, make that an O'Doul's." The others ordered, and Rudy bustled off to earn her points.

Joe pursed his lips and reached out to touch my hand. "To be honest, it sounds like you had too much to drink."

I pulled my arm away. "I was *not* drunk. Have you ever seen me drunk on less than two beers?"

"Not in my lifetime," said Laura.

I could tell Joe was alarmed. I could be lying about how much I had to drink in the bar last night — bad news — or someone could have tampered with the beer — even worse.

"Besides that, the feeling wore off quickly. I had a little nap waiting for Jeanine, and I felt much better by the time she arrived at the station."

"Supposing someone did drug your drink. Who and why?" asked Joe.

"It's hard to imagine," I said slowly.

"There's the tournament. Maybe someone wants me out. That doesn't make any sense, because we're liable to be slamming our collective trunks tomorrow even without any outside interference. Second possibility, someone doesn't want me to complete my duties as maid of honor."

"That's the most ridiculous motive I've ever heard," said Laura.

"I did bump Pari from the plum position."

"So she had you followed to this bar and had whoever followed you slip you a Mickey Finn? Like I said, it's absurd."

I shrugged. "Or someone knows Jeanine asked me to ask around about her father."

"Someone doesn't want him found?" asked Laura. "Let's start there. What do you know so far?"

Joe crossed his arms over his chest and said nothing.

"I have mostly questions, beginning with the pre-shower dinner that you two missed." I blushed suddenly, recalling that Joe had shown up at the end just in time to witness my make-out session with Mike. "Why did he go back into town instead of coming right to the party? Why didn't he react more strongly to the cops' news about the man killed on his property? Who is that man, and are they connected? Why did Mr. Peters have a rifle leaning up against the window in his study? Why was he taking lithium? How did he earn all the money he throws around? Did he kill Junior Mammele? If so, why? Has he had other affairs besides the one with Pari?"

"Whoa, whoa, whoa!" said Joe.

"He had an affair with Pari?" Laura asked. "That's sick."

Rudy slid my dinner onto the placemat in front of me. "Be careful. That plate is very hot."

"Thanks." I leaned back against the wooden ribs of the booth and faced Laura. "She's not currently seeing him, but she claims they had a fling a number of years ago. Which certainly raises the question of whether he's been involved with other women. Or has a girlfriend now."

"Is Pari a reliable source?" Joe asked.

"I wondered that myself. I'm certain she's pissed about her demotion from maid of honor. You can tell by the little digs. Would she lie in order to cause trouble between me and Jeanine?"

I spread a layer of cocktail sauce across one of the crab cakes and then squeezed a triangle of lemon over the top. Should I spill the beans about my own interaction with

Mr. Peters? I had a feeling they'd both make more of it, or something different out of it, than I would. To me, it had begun to feel as though he really noticed me as an attractive woman and cared that my boyfriend saw that, too. I sighed. "Mr. Peters did kind of make a pass at me the other night."

"He made a *pass* at you?" Joe asked.

"You don't have to make it sound that unbelievable," I snapped. "He just offered to help out if Mike wasn't giving me, you know, what I needed."

"What a jerk!" said Laura. "That's disgusting."

Joe was silent, his cheeks flooded with color again. This wasn't going well, and I wasn't sure I could fix it.

"Here's another thing that bothers me: even though she's wound tight as a drum, Mrs. Peters insists she's not concerned that her husband is missing. She says he's consulting for someone. Jeanine says he wouldn't have taken a job right before her wedding. And Aunt Camellia warned me that if I scratched the surface of any marriage hard enough, I'd find dirt. What did she mean by that?"

"If they suspect he's off visiting a girlfriend," said Joe, "they wouldn't want Jeanine to learn the truth. Besides Jeanine feeling hurt, it would be a terrible loss of face for Mrs. Peters."

"Back up," Laura demanded. "You're throwing an awful lot at us at once. And my brain doesn't work as fast as Joe's. Tell us about the rifle and the lithium."

Relieved that they both sounded interested, I described my lunch with Mrs. Peters and my spontaneous excursion into the master bathroom.

"Aunt Camellia caught me snooping in his study. She took that opportunity to warn me that not all marriages are fairy tales." My eyes widened. "Do you think *she's* involved with him?"

"You don't know enough yet to make a reasonable guess about the guy," Joe said.

"Anyone want to try the barbequed pork?" Laura asked. "It's delicious." I nodded and she sawed off a section of her tenderloin and put it on my plate. "Why would someone be taking lithium?" she asked Joe.

"Most often, it's prescribed as a mood regulator. A patient diagnosed with bipolar illness may respond well to lithium. It evens off the highs and lows. The problem is that while people don't like their lows, they do like the highs. So when they start feeling stable — and bored — they often stop taking it against their doctor's advice."

"Which could explain the unused refills," I said.

"Right. It's also prescribed sometimes for psychotic disorders."

"Do we think he's crazy?" asked Laura.

"We're not going to diagnose him based on one very old prescription," said Joe.

"But if he's crazy or manic, he could have just taken off without any real reasons, right?" Laura asked Joe.

"I didn't get the feeling at all that he was crazy or manic," I said.

"Let's go back to the bar scene. Who was around you that night?" Joe asked.

"Mike, Rick, Rick's brother, a couple other golfers, and lots of people I didn't know. The place was packed. And smoky."

"Did you order your own drinks? Did you see the bartender pour them? You said two beers, right?"

"Yes, I said two." I glared at him. "No, I did not order them myself. Rick's brother, Edward, bought me the first one." I tried to remember exactly what had happened. "He stopped on the way back from the men's room and bought everyone a second round. Which I hadn't requested."

I made a face at Joe and took a conspicuous swig of my O'Doul's. It has the same relationship to Budweiser that rabbit has to chicken — people insist you can't tell them apart. But you know damn well they're different species.

"Do you think Rick's brother is involved in this?"

"I can't see how. I only met him two days ago. What's the connection?"

"There are a lot of questions we can ask," said Laura.

I liked the sound of the "we."

"Mr. Justice introduced me to a couple guys who worked with Jeanine's father in the Marines — they were visiting for the long weekend. They might be able to fill in some of the gaps about Mr. Peters' consulting business. They were very quick to assure me that they no longer work with him. And Kendra Newton. She's Amanda Peters' bridge partner, but she's had a feud with Mr. Peters over the sculpture exhibition around the village. She invited me over for a tour — I was planning to talk with her while I was there."

"If he's been fingered for murder, you have to ask about his relationship to the guy he supposedly shot. And why in the hell would he shoot the guy at his own daughter's shower? That does sound crazy," said

171

Joe. "I'll see what I can find out about Junior Mammele."

He appeared to have abandoned his "don't meddle" policy. And I was grateful.

"Maybe I can stop by the local paper and ask about the man who was found dead on Peters' property," said Laura.

"I don't think we're going to like what we find out about Mr. Peters." I sighed. "Jeanine adores him."

"That's not so unusual," said Joe. "Even kids who have been abused and neglected by their parents get very, very attached to them. Daughters love their fathers. It's in the blood."

I squinted my eyes closed; I didn't want to hear any more about fathers and daughters.

Rudy cleared our plates and brought coffee and cheesecake to Laura and Joe. My heart was set on a chocolate milkshake from the soda fountain I'd passed on the way over.

"I'm going to bed," I said. "We can touch base on this stuff tomorrow night. See where we stand."

I phoned Jeanine on the walk home, sucking the thick, sweet shake up through a straw. "Can you talk?"

"I'll go in the other room." I heard her excuse herself and then muffled footsteps.

"There. Did you love the spa? Did you have a good time with Pari? I so want the two of you to get along."

"We had an interesting afternoon. The spa is fabulous. I could get used to that."

"Mother said you two had a nice lunch together." She laughed. "She thinks you're just the cutest thing. Did she tell you anything about Daddy?"

"Not much," I said. "She wasn't even willing to talk about his absence. I think it's time for you and her to have a heart-to-heart. And find out why your father has a rifle in his study, while you're at it."

She sniffled into the receiver. "That was a BB gun, Cassie. He'd never leave a rifle lying around the house. He shoots at the squirrels if they get in the birdfeeder. That's all."

For her sake, I hoped it was that simple. I wouldn't know a rifle from a high-quality water pistol. Not that I liked the idea of him shooting at squirrels, either. "Have that talk with your mother," I suggested again. "I'll see you at the golf course tomorrow."

Thursday night was karaoke night at the Magnolia Inn bar, I learned later as I lay in bed trying to fall asleep. Relentless rhythms of rock 'n' roll oldies were punctuated by tuneless wailing and bursts of hysterical laughter that grew louder as the minutes ticked by. I got up to check the deadbolt on the door and stuffed my ears with wads of toilet paper. I still couldn't sleep.

What had happened between Joe and Rebecca Butterman? They seemed like such a good match from the outside: both headshrinkers, so they could talk without hiring a translator; both apparently stable and emotionally mature; they even looked good together. She tucked in just below his shoulder and steered him toward choosing outfits that matched, for a change.

With three advanced degrees, Joe's the kind that analyzes everything to death before making a move. That didn't seem to bother Butterman. I scraped by a state university through the grace of God and the dean of the college. I prefer the close-your-eyes-and-charge-full-steam-ahead method of decision making. Hard not to get impatient with Joe.

My mind wandered back to our conversation about Jeanine. In some ways, I had it all over my friend. Wrapped in her blind adoration of her father, she was poised for a disappointing fall. My illusions about my own father had crashed early and hard.

Chapter 13

A loud banging woke me the next morning. I rolled out of bed and staggered to the door.

"Who is it?"

"Open up, knucklehead. It's Laura."

I slid the chain across the slot and clicked open the deadbolt.

"You look like hell."

"Good morning to you, too." I stepped aside to let her in and tried to shake the sleep snarls out of my hair. "You wouldn't look so good either, if you'd listened to karaoke until two a.m. What time is it? Did I ask you to pick me up? Where are we going?"

"Nowhere. I have something I want to show you." She held up a small, silver video camera. "Recognize this?"

I shook my head. It was only 6:15 — hard to recognize anything without a large infusion of caffeine. Pieces of the previous day began to sift into my conscious brain. "I'm not even talking to you until you come back with coffee."

She groaned and headed out of my room and down the leaning staircase. The sound of her voice sweet-talking the breakfast cook wafted back up the stairs. Laura herself appeared a few minutes later and handed me a large white mug of steaming java.

"Mmmm," I said, inhaling its fragrance. "Heaven, thanks."

"I found the camera in my backpack this morning. Remember Mrs. Peters had Rick give it to me at the shower? So I looked over the footage he shot. You're not going to believe this." She flicked the camera on and held it out to me.

I watched a miniature version of the tailgate shower. "Gosh, you look ridiculous in that outfit," I chuckled.

"Shut up and keep looking."

The camera swept around the banquet hall at a dizzying speed. "This is making me sick to my stomach."

"Almost there," said Laura. "Stop!" She froze one frame on the viewer. "Take a close look, in the back."

"Nice hat." A bright green-and-white check, it looked like Payne Stewart meets Goodwill Industries. "Wait just a minute! Is that Jeanine's father?"

"That's exactly what I wondered. It's a little hard to tell from the back, but . . ."

"But if he was away on business, he couldn't have been at this party."

"Not unless he does time travel." She pressed the play button and the camera swept across the faces of Rick's parents, Kendra Newton, and Helen, the wait-staff person who'd plied Jeanine with champagne.

"This reminds me, we should have a word with Rick's parents. They used to play bridge with the Peters on the professional circuit and could give us a feel for what he was like in the old days."

"Though if their son is marrying into the family, I don't know how candid they'll be," I added. "Especially if Mr. Peters was a bad boy."

My cell phone sang "Somewhere Over the Rainbow." "Hello?"

"Cassie?" Jeanine's voice was muffled by the sound of her weeping.

"What's wrong?"

"I need you to come over to the house right away."

"What's wrong?" I asked again.

"I'll tell you when you get here." She hung up.

"Jeanine. She wants me to come over now. She sounded awful." I pulled my T-shirt off and quickly dressed in khaki pants and a yellow turtleneck sweater.

"I'll drive you," said Laura. "Maybe Miss Lucy will be serving something good for breakfast. Like biscuits and sausage gravy. Or omelets — bacon and cheese for me. Grits on the side . . ."

My stomach now rumbling, too, I followed her down the crooked stairs and out into the crisp and sunny morning. Minutes later, we approached Pierre standing sentinel inside the Forest Brook gatehouse. He waved us through with a small smile. I guessed he was at the end of his shift and too tired for chitchat, which was fine with me.

Jeanine threw the front door open and ran down the steps before Laura even had the car parked. "Act natural!" she hissed. "Hurry up! Come in."

"What the heck is going on?"

She glanced left and right at the neighboring homes. "Inside! Hurry! Mother and Aunt Camellia are waiting." She hesitated, looked at Laura, then waved her in, too.

Once we'd stepped into the vestibule, Jeanine slammed the door behind us and flung her arms around my neck. "I'm so glad you're here."

I patted her back and extricated myself from her grip. "What's the matter?"

Mrs. Peters emerged from her living room and led us back in. "Thank you for coming right over so early," she said, sitting down and tapping the blue velvet cushion beside her.

"I hope we didn't wake you," said Aunt Camellia from her seat across the room. They both looked exhausted, the skin under their eyes bruised with weariness and some kind of pain.

"Someone's kidnapped Daddy!" Jeanine burst out. "I told you something was terribly wrong, and it is." She shot a reproachful glance at her mother.

"What do you mean?" I asked, dropping down on the couch. Laura sank into an upholstered rocker next to Jeanine's aunt. "How can you be sure?"

"They sent a note," said Mrs. Peters. "It arrived this morning. Then Jeanine told us she'd asked you to look for Dan." Her lips quivered. "I must request that you discontinue your inquiry." One tear slipped out and slid down her cheek. "They say they'll kill him if anyone finds out about the note. We just can't risk having them think we've told you to ask questions."

"Did you call the police?" asked Laura,

her voice firm and strong.

"They said they'd kill him if we contacted anyone, especially the authorities," said Aunt Camellia. "Whatever Jeanine asked you to do, we must insist that you stop."

"I'm so sorry. This is terrible. This must be terrible for all of you. Where did you find the note?" I asked.

"I went to pick up the newspaper this morning at the end of the driveway. The envelope was rolled up inside."

"May we take a look?" I asked. "Did they ask for a ransom?"

Mrs. Peters glanced at her sister and cinched tight the belt of her silk peach bathrobe. "I don't see the harm, Camellia. They already know about it. They said they won't talk about it to anyone outside." Her eyes shifted back over to Laura and me. "Right, girls?"

We hadn't agreed, but I nodded anyway.

"Don't touch it," Aunt Camellia cautioned. "Fingerprints. In case we take it to the police later. Of course ours are all over it. We didn't realize right away what it was."

"We couldn't believe it," Jeanine said with a moan.

Aunt Camellia picked up a pair of yellow rubber household gloves from the coffee table and pulled them on. Then she slid a page of computer paper out of an envelope lying on the coffee table. She smoothed a tear in the corner of the paper and motioned us close.

The page was a sheet of plain white paper with black type — Any Computer, USA. The message was simple: "The colonel has landed. We will exchange him for one million dollars. Will contact you with further instructions within the next three days. Do not call the police unless you want him to die."

"I don't get it. What does this mean? How do you even know it's Mr. Peters?"

Mrs. Peters wiped her eyes and tried to smile. "It's our family code. Whenever he was sent on top-secret missions, he'd call and leave the message 'the eagle has landed.' It was a joke, but I'd know that he'd gotten there safely."

"When he got his promotion, and he was so proud of the new rank, we just started teasing him with 'the colonel has landed,' " said Aunt Camellia. "No one else would think to use that phrase. It's him. They must have asked him for a phrase we'd recognize."

"Who are these people? What do they want?"

"I guess kidnappers don't clip and paste

letters out of a newspaper anymore," said Laura.

Mrs. Peters started to cry, and Jeanine bawled along with her.

"I'm sorry," Laura said, rising from her rocker to distribute pats to each of them. "I was trying to lighten things up. It's not at all funny. How can we help? We've had some experience with this kind of thing."

I glared at her. In my opinion — and I had a well-deserved reputation for meddling in things that weren't my affair — this was police business, pure and simple.

"If it was my father, I'd call in the cops," I said. "Right away. They know just how to handle this kind of incident."

"No police," said Aunt Camellia sharply. "It says right here, they'll kill him." Jeanine and her mother keened in unison.

"They said don't call the cops, but they didn't mention private detectives or other professionals," I said slowly.

"We're not calling in anyone," Aunt Camellia insisted.

"Okay, okay," said Laura. "No phone calls. But let's just think this through a minute. Who could be behind this? How the hell do they expect you to come up with a million bucks?"

"Someone who knows Dan's business

would know Amanda could manage it, given time," said Aunt Camellia. Mrs. Peters nodded.

Miss Lucy shuffled into the room carrying a tray loaded with a silver coffee pot and five china cups. The china clattered with each shaky step.

"Can I help with that?" Laura asked. She wrested the tray from the old woman and deposited it on the coffee table. Jeanine's mother leaned forward to pour.

"How about some breakfast for y'all?" asked Miss Lucy. "I could cook up some home fries and flapjacks. It's no trouble to make the biscuits . . ."

Carbohydrate heaven. In spite of the unfolding nightmare, I suspected that Laura had the same celestial dreams. When the going gets tough, we get hungry.

"Just the coffee is fine," said Aunt Camellia. Laura shot me a mournful glance.

"Any guess about who sent the note?" I asked again, once Miss Lucy had left the room.

All three women shook their heads.

"He seemed very stressed about his work lately," said Aunt Camellia.

"The military consulting," I said. Mrs. Peters nodded.

"Then there's the matter of Junior

Mammele's shooting," said Laura. "But why kidnap Mr. Peters? And why would Mr. Peters shoot Mr. Mammele?"

Jeanine banged her cup down on the coffee table and the hot liquid sloshed over the edges onto the polished cherry wood. "He wouldn't shoot anybody!" She ran a fingertip through the spill. "Sorry, Mother," she said softly, standing. "I'll get a rag."

"What do you plan to do about the wedding?" Laura asked.

"We've talked about that." Aunt Camellia sat up tall and squared her shoulders. "We don't see any other option. We're going forward with everything, exactly as planned. Until we hear something different."

"You're going on with the wedding without the father of the bride?" I asked. "Won't people think that's odd? Maybe you should consider postponing — announce that someone's ill or something. An elderly aunt whose heart would be broken if she missed the event?"

"Absolutely not," said Mrs. Peters, with more backbone than I'd seen all week. "Once it got out that we were postponing for any reason, Lisa Justice wouldn't stop with the questions until she'd squeezed every secret out of us." I hadn't noticed that side of Rick's mother.

Jeanine returned, sopped up the spilled coffee, and slumped cross-legged on the floor at her mother's feet. "We're also afraid if we change the plans, the kidnappers will think we've contacted the cops . . . or, who the hell knows what they'll think? What kind of people would do this anyway?" Jeanine was crying full bore how. Mrs. Peters stroked her hair.

"Will you call us if they get in touch with you again?" I asked. "We already know you got the note. We could at least try to help you think through the next move."

Mrs. Peters looked at her sister. "We'll call you," she said.

Chapter 14

"This is horrible," said Laura when we reached her car.

"I still don't get why they don't cancel the wedding," I said.

"They're absolutely terrified," said Laura.

"And maybe in denial, too. Just hoping he'll walk back in the door and it will all blow over." I leaned against the headrest. I felt exhausted by my short night and wrung out by the Peters women. "What now?"

"I'm famished," said Laura. "We were so close to those biscuits."

"Let's make a deal. You go with me for a light workout, and then we get breakfast. I'll buy."

She groaned.

"You're the one who's always nagging me about staying in shape. This way we'll have a big breakfast and time to visit with Kendra Newton. When we get to the golf course, all those carbs will be in just the right state of digestion."

"So you're not going to quit nosing around about Mr. Peters?"

"I'm interested in the sculpture project: the juxtaposition between free speech, artistic license, and the right to choose one's cultural stimulation in Pinehurst."

Laura snorted.

"If the topic of a rocky relationship between Mr. Peters and Mr. Mammele happens to crop up as we chat . . ." I shrugged. "I think the Peterses are making a big mistake. They should call the cops right away."

"It's strange," Laura agreed. "They're scared to death and frozen in place. Joe might know what to do."

"They said don't tell —"

"They didn't mean Joe. He can be trusted. I'll fill him in later while you're warming up at the range. Off to the spa first?"

"Not the spa," I said. "I don't want to risk running into Pari. She gives me the creeps. There's a perfectly functional gym near the hospital. Jeanine told me we could get a day pass there if we wanted to use it."

We parked outside the health and fitness center and signed in with a friendly attendant who set us up with lockers and rough, white towels. His eyes brightened when he discovered our connection with the Pine Straw Three Tour Challenge.

"Maybe you gals could help me with my slice," he said hopefully. Then he planted himself in front of the floor-to-ceiling mirror next to a universal weight machine, picked up a broom, and began to demonstrate his swing.

"What do you think, Doctor?" Laura asked, covering a smile.

"The basics are sound," I lied. "Maybe you have a little excess lateral movement." My standard diagnosis and true for almost every duffer. In other words, he swayed like a reed in the wind.

"I knew it!" he exclaimed. "I sway! Any tips for a poor old man?"

"This always works with Cassie," said Laura. "If she starts to move around on the takeaway, I tell her to imagine she's standing in a doorway with her feet wedged against the jamb on either side. Try it and see if you don't feel more solid."

Handing Laura the broom, the man arranged himself in the door and pantomimed his swing.

"Oh, bless you," he said. "I feel the difference right away. I can't wait to get out and try this on the course. I have a tee time tomorrow morning on Number Seven, and I was just dreading spending the day in the woods hunting for my ball."

"Thirty minutes on the treadmill," I told Laura once we'd escaped from our new friend's enthusiasm. "That's really all I need."

She deposited her towel and water bottle at the Stairmaster next to my treadmill and began to climb. Within minutes her gray T-shirt was soaked with sweat.

She paused for a gulp of water. "What do you make of Aunt Camellia?"

"She's awfully bossy. And I bet she's keeping secrets. At least from Jeanine, and maybe her own sister, too. Everyone seems to think Mrs. Peters is so fragile. I'm not convinced it's really true. She understands that her husband makes a big splash wherever he dives in, and she chooses not to let it bother her."

"She might not like what she saw if she looked too closely," Laura agreed. "She must know that."

We showered, dressed, and left the locker room. The attendant grabbed Laura for a last-minute review of his swing tip. I waited, leaning against the counter near the front door and staring out the plate glass window. Suddenly I remembered my conversation with Pierre in the bar. He'd thought Mr. Peters might have been headed to the gym after his confrontation with Mr. Mammele outside Forest Brook on Tuesday evening.

"Say," I said to the friendly, slicing attendant. "Can you tell me whether Dan Peters made it in here on Tuesday night?"

"I can check for you." He picked up a clipboard from behind the counter and leafed through several pages. "He's generally an afternoon exerciser, but this week he signed in Wednesday morning." He tapped the clipboard with the pen that hung on a string around his neck. "Regulars. You can set your watch by 'em. Not everyone's that dedicated — you get your drop-ins and your dropouts. You can tell by the size of the belly how long they laid off." He patted his stomach and laughed. "Human nature is lazy, mostly."

"Speaking of big bellies, where's the best breakfast in town?" Laura asked.

"Besides my wife's kitchen?" The man chuckled. "The locals go over to the horse track to a little hole-in-the-wall. You might have to wait to get a seat, though."

"Let's just go back to the Holly," I said. "Maybe we can catch up with Joe."

"So Mr. Peters was definitely in town the morning of Jeanine's shower," I said, once we'd driven away in Laura's car. "And that attendant would tell anybody anything about who was on what schedule."

We parked in back of the Holly and threaded through the rear halls to the breakfast room. The walls were paneled in dark wood and the ceiling seemed low — a cavelike effect for guests who couldn't yet tackle the day. Right away I saw Joe at a table with Mike, whose back was to us. They were deep in conversation. I grabbed Laura's arm and started to backpedal. She barged ahead.

"Hey you guys! What's good this morning? We've been to the gym already, and I'm ravenous."

"Blueberry pancakes," said Mike. "Bacon on the side." He stood quickly, looking uncomfortable. "Take my place. I'm heading over to the course early." He didn't quite meet my eyes.

The image of the blonde rookie golfer panting for her second date with him snapped right to mind.

"See you over there." He squeezed my shoulder as he passed by. "How are you, partner?" He kept walking without waiting for the answer.

"What's up with him?" asked Laura.

"The yips again," said Joe.

I could have sworn the guy was lying. I'd seen Mike through a lot of putting problems, and this was something different.

"And he really feels bad that he isn't part of the PGA Tour Championship this week."

The PGA Tour Championship was the last official tournament of the year on the men's tour. Only the top thirty money winners for the entire season received an invitation.

"He wasn't anywhere near the top thirty," I said.

"So he should feel good that he didn't just miss the cut?" Laura asked. "Give the guy a break sometimes."

"He should make the best of it and give his damn best to the tournament he committed himself to," I said, feeling the irritation finally boil over.

"He is, he is," said Joe. "That's why he went over early to putt."

"You won't believe what happened this morning," Laura whispered, leaning across the table to spear half a sausage from Joe's plate. "Someone delivered a ransom note to Jeanine's family."

"Say what?"

"You can't say a word about this to anyone," I whispered to Joe. "We swore we wouldn't tell."

"I swear," he said, lifting his right arm and extending the left to an imaginary Bible.

Laura described the note and the reactions of Jeanine and her family. I was still pouting about Mike, temporarily too annoyed to get interested in talking about anything else — even the alleged kidnapping of Mr. Peters. I'd begun to wonder if the guy had just holed up somewhere.

Damn, I was crabby.

"They have to call the cops," said Joe. "More kidnapping victims are killed by far when their loved ones refuse to involve the authorities."

I winced. The man had a boundless supply of tips and facts. "We weighed in heavily with that same opinion. They won't consider it."

Laura shrugged. "We stopped at the gym this morning," Laura continued. "The attendant told us Mr. Peters signed in Wednesday morning. And we think we have him on videotape at the shower."

She stopped talking long enough to order the Hungry Golfer: three eggs over easy, home fries, biscuits, and sausage gravy. I went with the Hole-in-One: Mike's buckwheat, blueberry pancakes. No point in ignoring his good taste in food just because I wanted to scratch his eyes out.

Joe pushed a section of the newspaper across the table. He had it folded open to the editorial page, a column titled "Birdies and Bogeys."

Laura read it aloud. " 'Birdie: By Miss Kendra Newton, top dog at the Hollyhurst Arts Council, for having the vision to bring the Sculpture Mile to Pinehurst. We're already proud of Kendra for her leadership at the Given Library and the Women's Club. Pinehurst attracts residents because of its golf, its weather, its community, and now its cutting-edge visual arts. Thanks, Kendra.

" 'Bogey: By the vicious prankster who stole the airplane sculpture out of the tree on the green. The artwork is placed there for the enjoyment of all the residents. Your irresponsible theft deprives us of a unique opportunity, as well as a sense of safety and pride in Pinehurst.

" 'Double bogey: By Mr. Dan Peters, who refuses to consider the spirit in which the zoning laws were passed in our township. Regardless of the literal wording in the paragraphs he is so fond of citing, longtime residents understand the importance of retaining the beauty of Midland Road. Mr. Peters, maybe you should consider moving back to the big city.' "

"Boy, they lay it all on the line in this newspaper," I said.

"And this," said Joe, flipping to the obituary page.

"Mr. Abraham Lewiston," Laura read aloud. " 'Mr. Lewiston, fifty-three, of Pinehurst died on Wednesday, the victim of an automobile accident. A private memorial service will be conducted for the family by the Reverend Dwight Juliani. Calling hours will be held from five to seven p.m. on Friday at the Unger and Haskins Funeral Home in Aberdeen. Surviving are his wife, Vonda Lewiston, and two sisters, Cynthia Ray Vaughn and Mae Catherine Lewiston of Atlanta. Unger and Haskins Funeral Home is handling arrangements for the family.' "

"Isn't that the same preacher who's supposed to do Jeanine's wedding?" I asked. "I was surprised they had an Italian minister in Pinehurst."

"Someone should drop by the calling hours," said Laura. "If the Peterses won't call the cops, at least we should have our eyes and ears open."

"I should be able to stop in after the tournament," said Joe. "Right now, I better get over to the golf course. Your partner needs all the help anyone can give him."

"I better stick close to him, too," said Laura. "Do you mind going to see Kendra Newton alone?"

"Fine," I said.

"Don't spend too much time at it," said Joe, tousling my hair. "You need to get mentally set for your round."

Breakfast finished, I moved to a wooden chair outside the building and rocked gently in the sun with the last of my coffee. I glanced down. A scum of oil floated on the surface. Somehow, the morning had gotten away from me. It felt sour, like milk kept just a day too long. I left the mug sitting on the porch and walked back into the center of town.

Chapter 15

Kendra Newton's Hollyhurst Foundation occupied a small office in the heart of the village, nestled in between The Gentlemen's Corner and Christina's Southern Comforts. From the looks of the Christmas decorations, town planners had mandated tasteful green wreaths, with traditional red bows, to be installed early in the season. Kendra's tall, rectangular form materialized in the window as she twisted open the blinds. She motioned me in.

The space inside was far from traditional. A rusted metal gyroscope-like object dominated the center of the room. Photographs of other sculptures hung on the walls, two of which had been painted purple and two tangerine. The largest photo, featuring a white metal airplane hanging from a pine tree, was draped in black crepe paper. *In memoriam,* read the hand-lettered sign beneath the poster. A memorial for a fake airplane?

"Someone stole that piece right out of the tree on the town square. Can you imagine the gall that takes?" Kendra asked. "How are you, Cassie? Shouldn't you be over at the golf course?"

"I'm going soon. But I saw you opening up and wanted to hear more about your sculpture project. And hey, congratulations on your birdie in the paper this morning."

"Oh, that." Her neck flushed red. She picked up a pamphlet, waved it back and forth across her face, and then handed it to me. "You can take yourself on a little tour around town using this guide. Or let me know, and I'll set you up with one of our docents. I just adore this whole project — the exhibit brings a depth to the village that has been lacking. We've always had sports here, of course, and history, but now we have the arts in a big way, too."

I pointed to the gyroscope. To my mind, some sandblasting and a coat of varnish would have done it a world of good. "I saw several of these rusted pieces in town. Is this a trend?"

"A lot of our artists like the look — it's organic, it ties their art to nature."

"And easy to keep up, too." I laughed. "You said that Dan Peters opposed the Sculpture Mile?"

Her face darkened. "It's one thing to hold a dissenting opinion on a topic. But that man is a thought warden. If he doesn't like something, he takes it down. I mean he goes at it with all his energy until it's obliterated." Her gaze shifted to the photograph rimmed in black.

"You think he stole your airplane?"

"Who else?" Kendra demanded. "It wasn't just a prank. It was too big a job for that — the piece weighed close to a thousand pounds, and it had been installed thirty feet above ground. It had to be someone with resources and equipment."

"Why would he object to the airplane?" I asked. "It seems lighthearted, just something fun."

She scowled again. "Dan Peters sees things the way Dan Peters sees things. He's not a team player."

"Were there other sculptures he didn't like?"

"The group of skulls on the green — you may have seen them on the open space in front of the church. The artist calls it "Heads Up: The 57th Infantry." He designed the piece to honor the American soldiers who have served in Iraq. Peters went completely crazy over that one and demanded we move it by Veterans' Day."

"Why?"

"Because he claims it's a slap in the face to the military. He thinks the artist was linking death to war and not in a positive way. And his opinion is always correct." She was really scowling now, and her voice harsh. "Especially in this case, because he's the big Marine colonel, and therefore he's the only one capable of determining what makes a proper veterans' memorial."

I just nodded, determined not to say anything that would shut off the stream of information.

"Here's another one he hated." She grabbed my elbow and pulled me along until we stood in front of a photograph in the back of the room. It was a mask of a man's face, but covered with crawling insects.

I stifled a yelp and tripped backwards. "That's disgusting!"

"Look more carefully," she said, her hand gripping my arm and propelling me forward. "It's only shells and seaweed."

"It looks like bugs to me."

She shrugged and then grinned. "The librarians reported that it's scaring some of the children, too. So maybe he was correct on this one. But you know what he considers art? Fiberglass Labrador retrievers decorated by the town schoolchildren."

"Sounds a little silly," I said.

"You know the Peters have only been in town five years, right?"

I nodded.

"He didn't have the common courtesy to get a feel for the village and what we're all about before trampling all over us. This is the South. We move slowly. And this is Pinehurst. We're very concerned about preserving our history."

"It's important," I said inanely. Anything to keep her talking.

"He owns some property over on Midland Road — you probably drove right past it. Everybody understands the importance of keeping that area beautiful — it leads right into our town. Some people call it the Fifth Avenue of Golf because it runs from Pine Needles, host to the U.S. Women's Open, to Pinehurst Number Two, host to the U.S. Open. Others have compared our road to the seventeen-mile drive through Pebble Beach."

I stifled a giggle. The seventeen-mile drive was a spectacular winding trip along the Monterey coastline — comparing the two was definitely apples to oysters. Kendra frowned.

"Everyone knows Midland Road sets the tone for the whole town. The value of neighboring properties depends on it being preserved intact. Not Dan Peters — he has no respect for zoning guidelines other than what suits him. He wants a shopping center there. Nothing can stop him from putting it up. Sure, he's technically correct. But he's got a lot of people angry."

It sounded like Kendra had had a hand in bestowing Mr. Peters the newspaper's double bogey this morning. "What actually happened with the zoning issue?"

"He pushed it through the commission by agreeing to dedicate half of the property to open space. The zoning board assumed that the open space would be along the highway, with the retail establishments set back out of sight. It seemed a reasonable compromise, though Junior never liked it."

Sudden tears filled her eyes. She pulled a crisp white handkerchief out of the pocket of her slacks and wiped them away. "I'm sorry. I miss him terribly already."

"And I'm so sorry about . . . all that." I waited a minute, then asked: "But there was a loophole?"

"Yes." She grimaced. "The zoning amendment didn't specify where the construction had to be." She sniffed. "Junior was prepared to fight Peters to the death on that roadside stripmall/Wal-Mart would spoil Pinehurst over his dead body."

She took a deep breath and stalked over to a file cabinet behind the desk. She extracted a fat folder from the second drawer. "Letters to the editor," she said, holding it up. "Every one of them against his stupid, ugly shopping center." She motioned me around the desk and pressed on my shoulder until I dropped into her chair. "Just take a look."

I opened the file and leafed through the top pages.

"Not a single letter in his favor, not one. Are you seeing the picture?"

I skimmed through four or five letters exhorting residents to preserve history, prevent deforestation, and defend Pinehurst from destructive intruders.

One letter, buried at the bottom, complained about people who'd appointed themselves "the pine tree police." What I was beginning to see most clearly was how much Kendra disliked Jeanine's father.

"How does Mrs. Peters fit into the equation?" I asked. "Are her politics controversial, too?"

Kendra sighed. "That's the very hard part. We all adore Amanda. She's my duplicate partner at our Monday game. She's the sweetest thing. Her bidding gets a little fuzzy when she's got a big hand. But I frankly don't understand what she sees in that man."

"Have the police made any inroads with Mr. Mammele's murder?"

"Nothing." She shook her head sadly. "That's my heartbreaking task for the day. His family asked me to say a few words at the funeral."

"And what about the man found on Peters' property on Tuesday? Any news on all that?"

"You probably heard his blood alcohol level was off the charts . . . but I shouldn't waste your time with gossip. You have a golf tournament to play. I wish you all the best today."

"Thanks." I held up the sculpture brochure. "And thanks for your time. I'll look forward to seeing the rest of the exhibit."

Rats. She'd cut me off just when things were starting to get interesting. I turned on my cell phone and checked for messages. The first was from my big brother, Charlie. We don't stay in touch the way I'd like. He's the only person in the world who can totally appreciate the craziness of my family. With our mutual stepfamily in town, there was a lot of drama to report. I'd call him later when I had the time to elaborate on the gory details. The second message was a hysterical plea to call Jeanine. Oh, my God, what now? I punched in her number.

"Is there news?" I asked when Jeanine picked up the phone.

"No. No. Aunt Camellia asked me to call and make sure you understood you can't go to the police." She started to cry again.

"I wouldn't do that, Jeanine. I'd never hurt your family." I felt immediately guilty about grilling Kendra.

She blew her nose. "Aunt Camellia would kill me if she knew I said this, but please keep your eyes and ears open. I can't stand waiting around and doing nothing . . ."

"Will do. I'll keep you posted. Have you told Rick what's going on?"

"I can't." Her voice sounded different now, firm. "He'd go nuts. He was so worried about playing in the tournament and having the wedding the same weekend. I promised him it would run like melted butter."

"But Jeanine, if your father's in trouble, Rick would want to support you."

"I know what's best for us," she snuffled. "I also wanted to remind you that there's dinner at the clubhouse tonight. We've invited all the people who came in from out of town for the wedding. I don't know how I'm ever going to get through this, but Aunt Camellia says the best way we can help Daddy is to carry on."

"I'll do whatever I can. I promise. Maid of honor. I'll be there."

Chapter 16

Against all odds — not enough sleep, pissed at Mike, and way too many outside distractions — it was going to be a good round. I felt that promise the minute I hit the range. The pancake carbo loading helped and so did Laura's advice to the gym attendant. With my feet braced inside that imaginary door, my golf shots started out straight and went long. I glanced over at my father. Weird to see him take the same setup I did, the same baseball grip on the club, the same pause, glance, pause, waggle, pre-shot routine. Not so weird when you figured he taught me all of it when I was a kid. Besides, I had fifty percent of his genes.

But my father's swing today looked fast and jerky. After he'd struggled through a dozen balls without settling down, I tried joking with him about a tip he'd given me when I was twelve.

"Imagine you've had a metronome implanted in your brain," I said. "It's set to your own personal rhythm. Tick-tock, tick-tock."

He smiled and nodded, but his eyes were the eyes of a condemned man.

"Where's Maureen?" I asked, when we both stopped for a breather ten minutes later.

"Migraine. She's going to try to get here at some point, maybe catch the back nine. Right now she can't even lift her head off the pillow." He hesitated and tucked his shirt into his Sansabelt slacks. "This is hard for her." He tipped his head in the direction of my half-brothers, slouching next to Laura on the outer edges of a group of caddies. They already wore their white caddie bibs over their polo shirts, with "Burdette" written in green across both their narrow backs.

By "this" I didn't imagine he meant his boys' interest in the golf world. He meant me.

"It's not a competition, you know," I said. "She's their mother. And your wife."

"But I'm your father. And you came first."

"You never would have known that," I muttered.

"I'm sorry, Cassie. I tried." He sighed, a

heavy gust of peppermint. "I really screwed up a lot of things." He flung one arm out to encompass the clubhouse, the range, Payne Stewart's statue, the first hole. "I'm not going to make it out here."

"You don't know —"

"Don't," he cut me off. "I know you see it. Who can say if it would have turned out different if I started younger?"

Used your energy to play golf instead of chasing women, I wanted to say, but didn't.

"I'm not in the same league with these other guys," he continued. "I can't hit it as far, and I don't have the nerves. My putting stinks, to frost the cake."

"You could try another putter . . ."

He lifted the long-shafted putter from his golf bag and let it drop hard to the bottom. "Don't you think I've fooled with everything manufactured within legal limits? It's not the arrow, Cassie, it's the Indian. I could spend a couple of years in the minor leagues, maybe travel the feeder tour in Florida again. But that wouldn't be right for my family." He winced. "I already screwed one family up good. Your brother Charlie won't even take my calls."

"I'm sure he's just busy." I crossed my arms and gazed off into the distance. This is how things always ended up with him. By the end of the conversation, you felt so sorry about some crisis in his life, it was hard to hold on to the mad.

"What I'd really like to do — and I hope you'll consider it — is to take the money I'd have used on the satellite tour and put it toward your expenses. You don't have to answer me now . . ." *Wow.* That was a shocker. Both him quitting and him handing over a chunk of dough.

"Let me think about it," I said. "Thanks for the offer. We'd better get over to that putting green. We're on the tee in twenty minutes."

"About Mike." He spat on the bottom of his driver and rubbed at a white slash with a corner of his golf towel. "I know I haven't earned the right to give you fatherly advice, but here goes anyway: I'm not sure he's the best guy for you." He laughed, threw one arm across my shoulder, and squeezed. "Not that I'm an expert on the subject of successful relationships, either. But I do want you to have the best."

I bristled and pulled away. He wasn't so far off — I was starting to think the same way. But I wasn't ready to accept it from him.

Pari was talking with Mike near the first tee. She stood closer to him than social norms would dictate. If I were feeling generous, I would have attributed this to a cultural difference — Iranian princesses weren't taught the niceties of American body language. But she'd been a U.S. citizen her whole life, and besides, I wasn't feeling generous. She reminded me of a vulture, her beak diving into the carcass of my relationship with Mike while it was still warm.

The starter called our names after we'd spent fifteen worthless minutes on the putting green — me, obsessed with ending things with Mike; my father, jabbing helplessly at a pile of balls; and Mike, missing short putt after short putt, who knows what on his mind. Joe hovered nearby like a worried mom. And Maureen surfaced, chalky white and painted with makeup to hide the rings under her eyes.

The cheery promise of the day was gone.

"Next on the tee, from the PGA Tour, Mike Callahan; from the Champions Tour, Mr. Chuck Burdette; and from the LPGA Tour, Cassandra Burdette." Even the enthusiasm in the starter's voice had paled compared to yesterday.

We all three hit our drives in the right-hand rough and trudged down the first fairway without speaking.

The caddying got off to a poor start, too. Slung over David's shoulder, my clubs rattled like a chorus of beginning percussionists. Laura noticed me scowling and wound a golf towel in between the shafts. Zachary realized halfway down the first fairway that he'd left Dad's driver back on the tee. So Laura carried two bags while he sprinted back to recover the club.

Once we had straggled to the green, I heard Laura reminding the boys not to stand in the line of a player's putt. Next she took up the importance of not walking near the cup.

"Even a lightweight like you guys can make a footprint that could cause someone's putt to go off-line." She leaned over and added in a loud stage whisper: "Or so they think. They're all prima donnas, remember."

Everyone tried — but as the boys shuttled away from Mike's or Dad's putting line, they seemed to move into mine.

Or maybe I noticed every small error more clearly today. In the throes of a bad round, every noise, every movement, becomes magnified. If they hadn't been relatives and young enough to have their sensitive psyches scarred by an abrupt dismissal, they would have been gone. If not axed by me, certainly by proxy alone, Mike.

The magic had gone from the boys' eyes, too. It was one thing to carry the bag of a professional golfer in top form. It was quite another to be snapped at by three cranky players performing well below any professional standard.

The golf course took us to our knees. We found patches of wire grass I never even noticed the day before and bunkers that had remained pristine over the previous rounds. And the greens proved elusive.

As we putted out on Donald Ross's final magnificent hole, I noticed that Maureen looked furious. I shook hands with the boys, my father, Mike, and Laura, and headed off to the flimsy shelter of the scoring tent. Maureen followed.

"If you didn't want David to caddie for you, you should have said so," she said.

"I did want him. I never would have asked him otherwise."

"You bitched at him all the way around."

"He has to learn the etiquette," I said. "This isn't a casual country club round." Although we played as if it had been.

"You expect to be treated like royalty," said Maureen. "Chuck would never behave that way. He would never blame the caddie for his own disappointing play."

I bit my tongue. Didn't matter if he'd made three nasty remarks to his boys for every one of mine. She would believe the version she saw in her own mind. And I was way too miserable to be gracious. I walked past her in silence and stomped into the tent to sign my card. I murmured words of encouragement about the next time that would never come. We'd all roast on a spit in hell before we played together again, and we all three knew it.

"I've got to dash for a shower. I'll see you over at Forest Brook," I said. "Jeanine needs me a little early."

"We're going out for a family dinner," said Dad, apologetically. "I'm afraid I have some fences to mend here." He ducked his head in the direction of Maureen, who had a son wedged firmly under each arm. The ranks had closed.

Chapter 17

Back in my room at the Magnolia, I stepped into the antique bathtub. The water sluiced down my back, the thin curtain clung to my legs, and I cried. I hate crying, especially without a firm grasp of the reason. It couldn't just be one lousy round. I pushed myself to flesh out the sadness.

If I looked closely enough, I could see I was drowning in blown opportunities. The chance for our threesome to jell into a team. The chance for me and Mike to grow together instead of splinter apart. The long-gone chance for me to have a real family. A *Father Knows Best* kind of family, with pot roast and mashed potatoes on the kitchen table and two emotionally stable parents asking their kids about the math quiz or the senior prom. Maureen might show signs of being Mommy Dearest, but at least my half-brothers had two, count them, two parents who cared about their lives.

Get a grip, Cassie. Jeanine has problems a lot worse than yours.

I toweled off and dressed in black Capri pants, sandals, and a V-neck, rose-colored sweater. I ran my fingers through my wet curls and flicked on a layer of brown mascara. Talk about going out of my way for a friend . . .

With half an hour to spare before I was due at the dinner, I stretched out on the bed and called Charlie. Only the fresh coat of mascara kept me from starting to cry again when he answered.

"Cassie, how are you? I miss you!"

"Same here," I said. "Could have really used you today — we had the Nightmare on Pine Street." I filled him in on the scene with Maureen, the struggle with the teenage caddies, and my team's floundering games.

"How is old Chuck doing?" asked Charlie. His voice was light, but I knew his issues with the old man lurked just below the surface. He preferred to work them out at a sensible and comfortable cross-continental distance. In a word, denial.

"He thinks you're avoiding him," I said.

"Clever man."

"He dropped a bombshell today," I said. "He claims he's giving up his tour aspirations. He wants to donate the funds to my cause."

"Just say yes," said Charlie, laughing. "Take the money and run."

"Besides that, Maureen's really bent out of shape about me playing with Dad. My hiring David pushed her right over the edge. I think the kid felt the pressure, too. Everything he remembered and did just fine yesterday, he screwed up today."

"Poor kid. He's got some crazy genes. Maureen alone could keep your psychologist buddy Joe in change for years if he got her on his couch."

"Dad claims she's obsessed with which of his little families is more important."

"She can have him. We don't need him anymore," said Charlie. "How's the other curmudgeon in your life?"

"I'm about to throw him out on his ass, if he doesn't get to me first. But never mind that. I need your advice for Jeanine." I hesitated a minute over spilling the beans about the kidnapping — a second time — when the Peters women had begged us not to tell anyone — twice. But Charlie had years of legal training in keeping people's confidences, and he had his head screwed on right besides. "Her father disappeared two days ago after a man was shot at Jeanine's bridal shower. This morning, the family received a ransom note."

"You're not serious?" His voice was suddenly worried. "He's been kidnapped?"

"They told Mrs. Peters to get together a million dollars, and if she calls the cops, they'll kill him."

"How are the police handling it?"

I cleared my throat. "Like I said, the Peters haven't called — they're afraid to."

"Cassie . . ."

"Don't lay the big-brother tone on me. I'm not involved, except to hold Jeanine's hand."

"Tell her I said, and this is my legal opinion, that she should let the professionals deal with this. They could lose both the money and her father."

"I'll tell her. But they're panicked about making a mistake. And you're a corporate bankruptcy lawyer, for whatever that's worth."

"You said a man was shot at the shower? What happened? This is some nightmare wedding."

I explained the tragic chain of events at the steeplechase, taking a small detour to describe the outlandish costumes, and the hors d'oeuvres. Charlie got the same gene combination as me when it came to enjoying food. "So maybe the police think Mr. Peters killed this man — they were at loggerheads over town politics. To me it doesn't hold together. Why would he kill a guy at his own party?"

"Who does Jeanine think nabbed her father?" he asked.

"She doesn't know. But the kidnapper was clever enough to include an inside joke in the note, so the family would believe they really had him."

"Like, put the ball in the hole, you egg-sucking bed wetter?"

I laughed out loud. Charlie and my father never did get along well on the golf course, but that had been the low point. Even when the day comes that we can't remember which hole on what course they'd been playing, my father will never, ever live that line down. And if a kidnapper uses it, we'll certainly believe he's got Dad. I'm not so sure we'll come up with a ransom.

I said good-bye, scooped up the pink cashmere shawl that Jeanine had insisted I borrow, and left the room.

The guard at the Forest Brook gatehouse, a blond man with broad shoulders that I hadn't seen before, glanced at the guest pass on my dash and waved me on. The lights in the clubhouse sparkled in the gathering dusk — a fairy tale, made "Grimm" by the underlying catastrophe. I prayed that Jeanine's father had made a miraculous appearance. Maybe he'd greet me at the door. I'd even overlook a tweak on the rump.

Then I noticed a police car parked in the shadows of the lot. A uniformed officer leaned against the vehicle, the end of his cigarette glowing red in the dying light. I hustled past him, pulling the shawl tight around my shoulders, and muttered "good evening" without making eye contact.

Aunt Camellia greeted the arriving guests just inside the clubhouse door. From the pinched expression around her eyes and the cop in the lot, I was pretty sure Mr. Peters had not returned.

She flashed a brittle smile. "How are you, dear? You look lovely."

A waiter serpentined through the crowd carrying a tray of champagne glasses.

"Bring Miss Burdette a beer, will you please, Randall?" Aunt Camellia asked.

He nodded and headed in the direction of the bar. The room was decorated with bursts of silver and gold stars. A string quartet played softly in one corner, no competition for the lively conversation of the party guests.

"How's Jeanine?" I asked in a low voice. "Any news?"

She shook her head and turned to greet Rick's parents.

"Derek and Lisa, you've met Cassie, haven't you? She's Jeanine's maid of honor. Will you please excuse me, I have to check on the dinner." She placed my hand on Mr. Justice's arm and swished off toward the buffet table.

The waiter returned with my beer in a frosted mug.

"That looks good," said Mr. Justice. "Could I get one of those, young man?"

"How was your day?" Mrs. Justice asked me.

"Rough going," I said. "We didn't even scare the cut. And Rick?"

"Second place, so far," Mr. Justice said with a proud smile. He leaned closer. "Actually, I think the tournament is keeping his mind off the wedding. And that's for the best all the way around." He chuckled. "I remember how nervous I was getting married. Even though I had the pick of the litter." He winked at his wife, who smiled and excused herself to offer assistance to Mrs. Peters.

The pick of the litter? *Sheesh.* Did he whistle for her when it was time to leave a party? "You've known the Peters a long time," I said.

"We ran into them from time to time on the bridge circuit. We never met Jeanine though — just saw her in their wallet photos. She was just a little thing then — so cute and blonde. A butterball, but don't tell her I said so! She's a real beauty now. My Rick's a lucky man." He practically licked his lips.

"What kind of players were Mr. and Mrs. Peters?" I asked, nudging him off the topic of Jeanine's charms.

"Amazing how your personality comes through in the bidding. Do you play?"

I shook my head. "I was practicing chip shots when the rest of the dorm was learning. Maybe should have put more time into bridge, the way things are going with golf."

"Dan was a wild card in those days — still is, I hear. Where is that cagey bastard anyway?"

"I — I understand he got called away on business."

Mr. Justice frowned slightly.

"You started to tell me about their bridge games," I prompted, before he could formulate any doubts about his former opponent.

"The amazing thing about the Peters was how Amanda handled anything he threw at her. If he jumped to seven-no-trump — that's the highest bid in the game — she didn't even blink. She could read him perfectly, and she played a wonderful supporting hand. Of course, it didn't go quite as smoothly if she took the lead."

"Sounds a lot like finding the right caddie," I said. "One of the pair had better be the natural leader. In the case of golf, it damn well better be the player."

He nodded and laughed. "Some couples, as aggressive as Dan played, would never have survived one evening as partners. Lisa and I had our share of spats." He glanced across the room at his wife and grimaced.

"So the Peters dropped out because of his bidding?"

"Not at all." He looked puzzled. "Or that's not what they said in public, anyway. His job got too demanding, so they had to quit."

He flagged down a passing waitress and grabbed a boiled shrimp with one hand and a phyllo triangle with the other. He popped the shrimp into his mouth.

"In the end, though, Dan wouldn't have made it to the highest level because he was incapable of holding back. He'd bid to the max, even if the cards weren't there."

Rick's brother, Edward, joined us, carrying a beer for his father. "Are you boring poor Cassie with the golden days of bridge? I remember a lot of arguments when they got home," he said to me. "Rick and I would lie in bed and listen, scared to death our family was headed for divorce."

Mr. Justice laughed again. "We weren't fighting, we were just rehashing the tournament rounds. That's how we improved, not to mention how we blew off steam. It's pretty tense at that level of play. You can't really call it 'play' at all. Well, Cassie, you would understand all about that."

Across the room, Mrs. Peters tapped on a glass with a fork. The buzz of conversation quieted quickly and the string quartet tailed off to silence.

"I wanted to thank you all for coming tonight and to make a toast to my new in-laws, Derek and Lisa Justice. My husband and I wish to thank them for their wonderful son, Rick. Dan and I are so grateful to have three wonderful additions to our family."

"Here, here!" cried a voice from the back of the room.

"Don't forget Edward," Jeanine added, smiling brightly. "We're gaining Edward, too."

"And Edward," Mrs. Peters said. "Sweet Edward. And ladies, intelligence reports tell me he's single." Several women in the crowd tittered. "Dinner is served. Please help yourselves to the buffet. Thanks again for sharing this special time with us."

No mention of Mr. Peters, except as part of the happy bridal parental unit. I wondered if anyone else had noticed the strain in her voice. Possibly not — she was a Southern lady, bred and trained to cover internal turmoil with a gracious and pleasant exterior.

Joe cut in behind me and nudged me toward the buffet line. "Heard you had a lousy day. How are you?"

"Good," I lied.

He looked skeptical.

"Okay, lousy, then. Is that what you wanted?"

We loaded our plates with smoked turkey, cornbread spoon pudding, green bean and almond casserole, and Caesar salad. He steered me toward an empty table in the corner of the room. Two plastic golfing figurines were posed as the centerpiece — a woman in midswing, with red short-shorts and her bust bursting out of her shirt, and a man lining up a putt on a felt putting green. It was shaped like the one on the eighteenth hole of Pinehurst No. 2. I knew it was replicated accurately, as I'd taken three putting strokes to finish the hole earlier this afternoon.

"Is that the proposed dress code for the LPGA Tour?" Joe asked.

"Cabernet or Pinot Grigio?" asked a passing waitress.

"None for me, thanks," I said. "But could I trouble you for a glass of water? Oh, Helen, hi. I didn't recognize you for a minute. This is my friend, Joe Lancaster. Helen took good care of Jeanine at the tailgate shower."

"Nice to meet you," said Joe. "I'll try the Cabernet, please."

Helen smiled and filled Joe's glass to the brim with red wine. "Enjoy the party," she said as she moved to the next table.

"I think she likes you."

He waved at me with his fork. "Women and dogs find me irresistible."

"She doesn't know you're a shrink with an annoying habit of constantly asking your friends how they feel about things," I continued.

Joe chewed and grinned.

"How was your day?" I asked.

"Interesting. I think I may have landed a couple of new clients. It pays to hang out at the eighteenth hole and watch which golfers post scores in the red."

"Did you stop in for Lewiston's calling hours?" I asked.

He leaned in close. "I decided we shouldn't get involved in this without contacting the police. Mr. Peters' life is at stake here, and we don't have the skills or the training to be of any use. We'll blunder around, piss someone off, and —"

"Can we join you?" Jeanine, Rick, Laura, and Edward approached our table and took the four open seats. Pari and Mike trailed behind.

Joe stood up quickly. "I'll get a couple of chairs."

"Don't bother," said Pari. "We'll find another table." She smiled and prodded Mike away from our group.

Bitch.

"Watch out for her, Cassie. She has her sights on him." Jeanine appeared glazed and slightly disheveled, a lacy bra strap exposed and a hank of hair loosened from its elegant upsweep. All signs pointed to her having doused her problems in champagne.

"You guys look so serious," said Rick.

"Cassie had a rough day," said Joe.

I wasn't interested in arguing about the kidnapping in public any more than he was, but I certainly didn't want to hash through my miserable golf round for the table.

"I'll get over it."

"Red or white wine?" Helen was back, without my water. She topped off Joe's glass and moved over to fill Jeanine and Rick's. "How's our bride tonight?" she asked.

"Very well, thank you! Cassie had a rough time the other night, too," said Jeanine to our tablemates, slurring the *s* in *Cassie*.

"Can I get anything else for you all?" Helen asked, looking mostly at Joe.

He covered his glass with his hand. "All set, thanks."

"Edward," said Jeanine slumping forward to rest both elbows on the table. "Maybe you could help figure this out. You were there at the Tarheel Bar, right?"

"Well, yes. Did something happen at the bar?" His nostrils flared wide.

"It's okay, Jeanine. No need to worry Edward . . ." I started.

"She thinks someone put something in her drink!" Jeanine's voice echoed loud in the sudden silence at our table.

Where in the hell had she heard that? There were only two possibilities. I glared at Laura and then Joe.

"I can't believe it," said Edward. "Why? Who?"

I shifted my glare to Jeanine. "There's no need to discuss this."

"It's just Edward," she said sternly. "He's family now."

"Do you remember seeing anyone near those drinks when you picked them up at the end of the bar?" Laura chimed in. She shrugged at me, as if to say the cat was already out of the bag.

"Lots of people," said Edward. "It was very crowded that night. Why? What happened? Did you get sick? Now I feel terrible."

"It's not your fault," I said, patting his hand. "And I'm fine."

"Here's a thought," said Laura. "If we go over to the bar for a nightcap, Edward might remember something — have his memory jogged just by being back in the same environment."

"And we could get drunk on champagne." Jeanine giggled.

"You're already drunk on champagne, sweetie," said Rick. Poor man looked almost as glazed as she did, though I didn't think the culprit was alcohol.

"So what's the point?" asked Joe. "Let's just enjoy the party."

"Maybe the guy who spiked your drink hangs out there on a regular basis," said Laura.

"Count me in," said Jeanine.

"I'm going, too," said Edward. "I feel just awful about this."

"Me, too," said Jeanine. Then she leaned over and threw up, spackling Rick's shoes and ankles with bits of green bean casserole and shrimp.

"Oh, gross," he groaned. "I begged you to elope." He swabbed at his feet with a napkin and helped Jeanine out of her chair. "Sorry all. Come on, honey. I'm taking you home."

"Sure I can't drop you back at the Magnolia?" Joe smiled at me.

"You're bailing out?"

"I'm turning in." He raised his shoulders just slightly.

"Turning into Mike," I muttered, and then with a fake grin, "See you tomorrow, then."

As we left the clubhouse, Aunt Camellia pulled me aside. "Are you available tomorrow morning at nine? We've decided to hold the rehearsal then, with or without Dan. I know Rick's busy on the golf course, but they scheduled Junior Mammele's funeral in the afternoon. It would be just too gruesome to overlap. You saw how Jeanine's holding up, and my sister's not much better."

"I'll be there."

In the parking lot, Kendra Newton was unlocking the car next to mine. Which reminded me that she hadn't finished telling me about the man who'd been found dead on Mr. Peters' land.

"Thanks again for the chat today," I said. "I'm going to take myself on that sculpture tour tomorrow. I've got some free time since we washed out of the tournament."

"Sorry to hear about that, dear." She slid into her driver's seat.

I draped my arms over her open door. "I was thinking about that man, Abraham Lewiston, you know, the one killed on the Midland Road property? You were starting to tell me his blood alcohol level was high."

Kendra's eyes narrowed as a swath of headlights brushed by. "All I know is what was in the police report. It looked like the man was drunk, and who knows, stumbled into the road? And the driver who hit him didn't stop. A terrible accident." She shook her head, making a clicking noise with her tongue. "Well, good-night."

As Kendra pulled away, I heard raised voices from a dark corner of the lot.

"I'm not even sure you want to get married!" This from Jeanine, shrill and hysterical.

"I told you my time would be limited if I

was playing in the tournament. What is it that you want from me, Jeanine?"

Rick's voice was as harsh as I'd ever heard. I slid into my Volvo and started the engine. Maid of honor or not, no way was I going to mediate a drunken lovers' spat.

Chapter 18

By all appearances, Friday was a big night at the Tarheel Bar and Grill. We wormed through the crowd single file toward the bar, ducking beneath a darts game on the way. A smiling but faded Bill Clinton, his arm draped around Monica Lewinsky's waist, had been pinned onto the bull's eye. A heavy haze of cigarette smoke hung at shoulder height, and Randy Travis pounded out a raspy love song in the background.

"I don't see anyone here I know," said Edward, his face red and beaded with sweat. His nostrils had taken on a life of their own. "I don't recognize a soul."

"Take your time," Laura told him. "Relax and look around. Maybe you'll notice someone familiar."

She ordered three Carolina lagers and leaned back against an oak rail, oiled dark by previous patrons' hands. "Same bartender as the other night?" she asked, voice soothing as a lullaby.

"I think so," said Edward, looking even more worried. "Maybe. Seems like he was bald or wore glasses or something. I don't know. I just couldn't swear to it."

Edward was shaping up as a poor eyewitness, too anxious to commit himself to any one memory. And I'd been too distracted, first by Mike, then by feeling sick, to notice much about the bartender at the far end of the room. I couldn't even be sure I'd ever seen this man pour drinks before.

"I'll check it out," said Laura. "What should I ask? Did anyone spike your patron's drink the other night?" She laughed and turned back to the bartender, who was busy adding celery salt and liquid hot pepper to a Bloody Mary. I wished Joe were here — he'd have a lighter touch. Besides that, I didn't like fighting with him. Sparring with Mike was bad enough. Where was Mike anyway? Had he gone home with Pari? That thought made me positively ill. I wished I didn't care.

"Say, a couple of friends of mine were here the other night." Laura gestured at me and Edward. "This lady felt sick after she drank her beer. I wondered if you might have noticed someone dropping something into her drink."

The man stopped mixing the cocktail, stone-faced. Then he frowned and stirred. "Nope. Nothin' like that happened here." He moved away to take a twenty from a patron down the bar, still frowning.

"That went well," said Laura with a rueful grin. "Next plan?"

"Let's forget about it." I took a long swig of my beer and scanned the room, wishing again that Joe had come along.

"I feel bad for Jeanine," said Laura. "Puking in the middle of her own party. This business with her father must be really getting to her."

"What business with her father?" asked Edward.

"Shit," I said, meeting Laura's horrified gaze.

"Never mind," said Laura. "It's nothing."

"You have to tell me," Edward said sternly. "You can't just leave me hanging . . ."

I shrugged. "Swear him in, that's all. It's too late now."

Laura whispered a short and whitewashed version of the kidnap note delivered by rolled-up newspaper. Edward's eyes widened with each word.

"Did you talk with Kendra Newton this morning?" Laura asked me.

I nodded. "I went by her office. Mr. Peters has made enemies in this town, and she's one of them. He hates her pet project — the Sculpture Mile. She even suspects he vandalized one of the pieces. And Junior Mammele had a longstanding fight with him about a development project Mr. Peters plans to put in on Midland Road. She showed me an entire file folder filled with letters to the editor protesting the project. She was practically frothing at the mouth."

"This whole thing is so bizarre," said Laura. "It would make more sense if someone shot Mr. Peters, not Mammele. Instead, he gets kidnapped. Who's got the guy and why? It gets more complicated everywhere we turn." She deposited her empty beer bottle on the bar and pointed to the bartender to bring another. "Tell me about that first night at Jeanine's dinner party. You were the only eyewitness, Cassie."

"No, I was there," said Edward.

"Good." Laura smiled and straightened his collar. "A second pair of eyes. What happened when Mammele came to the door with the cops?"

"Mammele definitely took the lead," I said. "One of the officers never came inside. The other cop tried to take over, but Mammele stayed in the mix."

"He seemed eager to be there," Edward offered. "We were playing pool but we could hear the voices. When we all came out to the hall to see what the problem was, he was acting very solicitous to Mrs. Peters, like he wanted to help her handle the bad news."

"After she got over the first shock, she wanted to know who the victim was," I said.

"But Mr. Peters shooed them all out fast and said he'd take care of it later," said Edward. "He was furious with Mammele, it was obvious they disliked each other."

"Why would Peters rush them out — wasn't he concerned about the dead man?" Laura asked.

"That's a very good question," said a familiar voice behind me. "Perhaps he had something going on that he didn't want hashed out in front of the dinner guests. Or the cops."

It was Joe. I grinned. "Nice to see you."

"I was worried you three could get into big trouble on your own." He smiled back. "But I haven't changed my mind about staying out of this."

"We're just talking," said Laura. "Here's another question. Mr. and Mrs. Peters are hosting a bridal shower party for their only daughter. Why is he at the gym?"

"He seems to come and go as he pleases at odd times, and the girls don't ask many questions," I said. "Anyway, it wasn't the shower. Though he ended up missing that, too. And he wasn't at the gym, remember? He went there the next morning. We don't know where he went that night."

"What about Aunt Camellia? How did she take the news when the cops came to the door?" Laura asked.

"She mostly seemed worried about her sister." I looked over at Edward and shrugged. "What would you say?"

"That's pretty much what I remember."

"There's something about Camellia . . ." Laura mused.

"You don't think she kidnapped her brother-in-law?" Edward asked.

"No way," said Joe and Laura at the same time.

"She knows something that could hurt her sister, maybe," I said.

I smiled, a little smug. Joe raised his eyebrows — I thought he looked impressed.

"But her sister behaves the same way," said Joe, flattening my theory.

"At the party, you mentioned that you and Rick used to listen to your parents argue when they got home from nights playing bridge with the Peters. Say more about that," I suggested to Edward.

"You heard Dad," said Edward. "His story is quite different from my memory." Joe nodded encouragement. "We'd be in a hotel room somewhere with a baby-sitter while my folks played cards. When they got back, they'd go into the bathroom and yell. It wasn't just the cards they fought about." He pursed his lips and whistled softly. "Rick was too young to realize this, but I'm pretty sure they argued about Peters."

"About Dan Peters?" the three of us chorused.

"Dad insisted he was flirting with my mother. And worse still, she flirted back. He was furious. She denied it, of course. But it went on for quite some time. Until the Peters stopped playing."

"Flirting during a professional bridge tournament sounds very distracting," said Joe.

"There were parties associated with the tournaments. They'd stay late after the games and get trashed." Edward took his glasses off and rubbed one eye, then the other, with the back of his hand. "I worried we'd turn out like the Miller family down the road. Their father left home and started another family, and those kids were never the same. They had a kind of haunted look. We all kept our distance after that."

I wondered if that's how people had described Charlie and me.

"Do you suppose they had an affair?" Joe asked gently.

Edward looked sad. "I suppose I wouldn't be surprised. It would explain why I had such a strong fear that our family was about to split into pieces."

Joe nodded. "Even if the arguments didn't spell it out, you recognized the intensity of their feelings."

"I'm sorry," said Laura, touching his arm. "You'd never know it from looking at your parents now. They seem so happy together."

"Those guys look a little familiar," Edward said, suddenly. "I wonder if they were here the other night." He pointed across the smoky room to the two men I'd met on the first tee a day earlier.

"Your father introduced them to me the other day," I said. "They're Marines, I think. But I don't remember seeing them in this bar. I'm going over and have a chat."

"I'll come with you," said Laura. Maybe

she wanted a break from Edward's abrupt and painful sadness as much as I did.

"Fancy meeting you here," I said as we approached the men. They'd clearly been drinking a while. Anything less hackneyed would have been wasted on them. It took a minute for them to recognize me.

"You're the golfer!" said the small thin man, extending his hand. "Bob Salivetti."

"Ooh-rah!" grunted his buddy.

"This bozo is Lance Pendleton. How'd it go today?" His words bordered on slurred. I moved out of butt-pinching range.

"Got our keisters kicked," said Laura, reaching across me to shake their hands. "I'm Laura Snow, Cassie's sometimes-caddie and all-the-time friend."

"I'm also in Jeanine Peters' wedding," I announced. "Maid of honor. You guys worked with her dad, right?"

Both men nodded. "Loosely speaking." The small man nudged the other, who staggered and then laughed. "The Marine Corps is a big operation, ma'am," he said.

"Could I be honest with you? We're worried about him. The wedding's on Sunday, and the guy's disappeared. Mrs. Peters says he's been called away on business. Is there any reason he might be in danger?" Subtle, Cassie. Laura gave me a pained look. Good thing the witnesses were too smashed to know they were being led.

Salivetti's expression shifted from jovial to serious. "We terminated our business with him on Tuesday."

"Tuesday night?" I asked, flashing a look at Laura. "Was your work completed?"

"In our minds," said Pendleton.

"Sounds like you guys called a halt," said Laura. "Mind if I ask why?"

"Plenty of reasons. The guy's gone with some dumb options," said Salivetti, widening his eyes.

"In our humble opinion," Pendleton added.

"Dumb options?" Laura asked.

"Let's put it this way, ma'am." Pendleton straightened his shoulders and saluted. "As you serve the nation, you see opportunities to earn money that span a range of ethical choices."

"If that asshole had the chance to go out on a limb for the sake of the bottom line, he went," said Salivetti. "And he wanted us to go out with him."

"Morals of a moron," said Pendleton, draining the last of his cocktail.

Laura waved down a passing barmaid. "Bring another round for these gentlemen?"

"Johnny Walker Black, rocks," said

Salivetti. "Make it a double."

"Seven-and-Seven," said Pendleton. "With a twist."

"I'm holding steady," I said. "What exactly is Peters doing now?"

"He's a military contractor — advises countries in conflict how to rebuild their military infrastructure. You've seen the news — our troops can't handle the staggering amount of work that needs to be accomplished in those hellholes. So defense contractor companies hire retired military guys — they know the territory, they know the equipment. It's an easy transition." He took a long swallow of the fresh drink. "Peters recommends new equipment purchases."

"Which puts him in position *A* when it comes to influencing decisions. And why not choose the company that's willing to throw a little extra in Dan Peters' Swiss bank account?" asked Salivetti with a sneer. Laura was tolerating the arm he'd slung around her shoulder pretty well.

"And why not pad the budget, too, while he's at it," said Pendleton. "Slide a couple thou' over to that same account each time a major transaction is made. Call it overhead."

"Wouldn't the military stop this?" I asked.

The men laughed. "You think someone's running a tight show on the budget in Iraq?"

"No one wants to know too much about it," Pendleton explained. "If something happens to Dan while he's working, it's not nearly the PR problem it would be if he was in the Marines. He's paid well for taking the risks, and he's doing it voluntarily. No one's going to blow the whistle. And no one cares if he makes a couple of extra bucks while he gets the job done."

"Except," I said, "if he's cheated someone and pissed them off."

"With Dan Peters involved," said Salivetti, pointing his finger in my face, "that is a very good bet."

We wandered back to the bar and reported the conversation to Joe and Edward. I felt lousy about the way things were going. Jeanine and her family had sworn us to secrecy and we were telling just about anyone within earshot that he'd disappeared. I hoped to God it wouldn't backfire. I glanced down the bar and noticed a couple with their heads bent close together, deep in conversation.

"I just remembered something else," I said. "Pierre, the security guy, and his girlfriend were here the other night. I had a conversation with them about Mr. Peters and Mr. Mammele because Pierre saw them arguing. He actually broke up the fight."

"So what?" said Laura. "You think one of them drugged your beer?"

"I don't even know them." I shook my head. "Just wondering if they might have noticed someone, something, I don't know." I stared at Joe. "I'm beginning to really wish the Peters women had called the cops."

Chapter 19

Thin slats of sunlight poured through the narrow, leaded glass windows of the church. Jeanine reclined face-up on the red cushion of the first pew, her skin pale to the point of translucence. Pari perched next to her, stroking Jeanine's blonde hair away from her forehead.

"Don't say a word," Jeanine moaned. "I know I made an awful fool of myself."

"I doubt anyone noticed a thing," I said. Hard to miss the bride barfing on her fiancé's shoes and shrieking at him in the parking lot, but my job was to reassure and support. "Anyway, brides are supposed to be high-strung. People expect drama, and they'd be disappointed if you didn't come through."

Pari stood and stretched as I squatted down next to Jeanine. "No news?" I asked softly.

"Not a word," she whispered back. "I begged Mother to cancel the rehearsal this morning, but she insists we have to carry on. She's obsessed with what Lisa Justice will think."

My knees cracked as I straightened up. "We'll just get through it the best we can." I squeezed her hand.

Aunt Camellia strode down the center aisle carrying a stack of parchment paper and a can of soda. "Before the others arrive, could you girls get started with the ribbons on these programs? Just roll the program loosely and tie a bow. Try to keep the bows about two inches and the ends the same length," she added. "We'll snip the ends off at a forty-five-degree angle when you're done."

She turned to Jeanine. "How are you feeling, sweetheart? I brought you some ginger ale. Please try to get up before Reverend Juliani gets here."

Jeanine moaned again and dragged herself to an upright position.

I took a stack of programs and scanned the first page.

Celebration of the Marriage
of Jeanine Elizabeth Peters
to Richard Derek Justice

Processional: "Canon in D Major" Pachelbel
Organist: Linda Juliani

Bridesmaid:	Pari Noskin Taichert
Groomsman:	Edward Neil Justice
Maid of Honor:	Cassandra Winifred Burdett
Best Man:	Michael Lewis Callahan
Ruth's Song:	Steve and Abby Bruce, vocalists
Scriptures:	Old Testament: Ruth 1: 16–18 New Testament: I Corinthians 13: 1–10

Marriage homily
Blessing of the rings
Exchange of vows
Lighting of the marriage candle

Hymn 272:	"Blest Be the Tie That Binds"
Recessional:	"Wedding March" Felix Mendelssohn
Officiating Minister:	The Rev. Dwight Juliani
Wedding director:	Camellia Toussaint

Two things jumped out at me. First, the service would go on forever. At least it would feel that way, standing in front of a full house wearing high heels and a strapless gown, trying not to look at Mike. I could only pray the minister wasn't long-winded.

Second, my name was spelled wrong. From the heft of the paper, the raised lettering, and the thick, purple, grosgrain ribbon, I could tell this was a high-class, expensive print job. I weighed the pros and cons of mentioning the mistake. The cons were substantial: all three of the Peters women teetered on the edge of flipping out. I didn't want to provide the last straw. Besides, no one but me was likely to notice the error.

"I brought your gowns over from the house, girls," said Aunt Camellia. "I thought it would be a good idea to wear them during the rehearsal. The train is unusual — the weight of the fabric could throw you off balance. Better to trip now than fall flat on your face in front of the congregation."

This was not the image I wanted in mind as I started down the aisle.

"Hurry, please," Aunt Camellia added. "The reverend should be here any minute."

I followed Pari to the dressing room, grumbling under my breath.

"Jeanine's arranged for all of us to go riding after we finish up," said Pari, slipping her blouse over her head and shaking out her thick hair.

"Riding?" I said, turning away to undress.

"Horses, you know, *neigh*." Pari laughed. I swiveled back in time to see her settle her breasts into the bodice of her gown. It didn't matter that I'd be marching down the aisle last. All necks would be craning ahead to follow her progress.

"I don't do horses," I said. "They scare me — they're too damn big. You look in their eyes, there's nothing there."

"Well, I'm going," said Pari. "It'll distract Jeanine. She seems so nervous. I wonder if she's having second thoughts about marrying Rick."

"I can't imagine that," I said, though after the fight I'd overheard last night, I definitely could imagine it.

"Michael's coming, too," said Pari, gliding over to stand in front of me. "Mind zipping me up?"

If I'd had the guts, I would have pinched a wedge of that perfectly tanned skin in the teeth of her zipper.

When we emerged from the ladies' dressing room in our gowns, Mike, Laura, Edward, and Joe had arrived. What was Joe doing here?

Mike whistled. "Now there's a pair of beautiful babes."

"You look lovely, ladies," said Joe.

Laura snickered and pointed at my feet. "I especially like the sneakers. They pick up the aubergine color so nicely."

"I didn't know we were supposed —"

Mrs. Peters entered the narthex with a woman she introduced as the society editor of the *Pilot* newspaper.

"Please, no photographs today!" Jeanine begged.

"I just have a few questions for the wedding party." She looked around. "Cassandra?" I raised my hand. "You're the maid of honor? That's Cassandra Burdett, *B-U-R-D-E-T-T*?"

"There's an *e* on the end," said Laura.

Mrs. Peters snatched up one of the parchment programs and ran her finger down the list. A bubble of saliva gathered at the corner of her mouth. "That means the programs are all spelled wrong. Camellia? There's no way we have time to get them reprinted." Her voice sounded high, close to tears and hysteria.

Aunt Camellia picked the top sheet off the stack and studied it. "I think we can hand write an "e" in on each one. No one will even notice. I'm pretty good with calligraphy. I'm so sorry, Cassie."

"Really, it will be fine. It's fine with me," I said, looping my arm around Jeanine's waist. "As long as the bride's name is right — it's her big day."

"And the best man is Michael Callahan," said the reporter. "You two are also engaged, correct?" She nodded at Mike, and then me. "Have you set a date?"

"Not yet," I said quickly.

What a total idiot. Why hadn't I said "just friends"? The other answer popped out unplanned. Mike looked at me, confused. His pupils began to dilate, the way they always did when he got surprised and then got mad. Laura's eyes had gone wide with amusement. Joe stared at his feet.

The reporter moved on to confirm the spelling of Pari Noskin Taichert. The moment where I could have laughed and gracefully corrected her melted away. Pari had launched into a mini-treatise on her heritage as reflected in her names when the minister arrived. The society page lady thanked us, promised exhaustive coverage, and retreated down the aisle.

"Good morning to all of you," said the Reverend Juliani in a hearty, ministerial voice. He was going to need all the tricks he had stashed in his robe to jolly this group up. "We'll do our best to get the kinks in the service worked out here this morning. But please remember, your guests are not coming to the wedding to be entertained. It's not 'a really big show.' They come to witness and celebrate your sacred union, sworn here before your loved ones and God, and to wish you Godspeed on the journey of your marriage."

Aunt Camellia introduced the wedding party to the minister. "And this is Dr. Lancaster. He's doing double duty, first standing in for Jeanine's father and then for Rick. Rick's team is still playing in the tournament."

She did not try to explain Mr. Peters' absence.

The organist, a petite woman with a cap of gray hair, launched into a vigorous rendition of the processional. Her knees pumped furiously beneath the keyboard. Aunt Camellia arranged Mike and Edward at the front of the church, then hurried back down the red carpet of the center aisle to the narthex where the rest of us waited.

"Remember girls," said Aunt Camellia, "as you recess from the front of the church, Pari will take Edward's arm. Cassie will do the same with Michael. On the way down the aisle, Pari will be first, then Cassie." She passed out bouquets of ribbons gathered from the wedding and shower gifts. "Walk a little more slowly than your normal gait and smile, girls, smile." She demonstrated a wide grin and gave Pari a small shove. "Smile," she hissed.

When my turn came, I clumped down the

aisle as gracefully as the voluminous gown and my sneakers allowed. Aunt Camellia was right — the train felt heavy and awkward. And my rubber soles had an unpleasant tendency to catch on the carpet. I pulled my lips back into a grimace and swung past the altar to take my place opposite Mike. He was not smiling.

The organist switched to "Here Comes the Bride." Joe goose-stepped down the aisle with Jeanine on his elbow. He looked adorable, his hair standing straight up, glasses askew, and a goofy smile on his face. He loved this romance stuff. I wondered again what had gone wrong with him and Rebecca Butterman.

The minister stepped in front of them, holding a worn Bible. He opened it to a page marked with a woven bookmark and cleared his throat. "We are gathered to celebrate the marriage of Richard Derek Justice and Jeanine Elizabeth Peters. Marriage is a journey. You have already taken many steps along the way, but today we witness the formal vows you will pledge to each other." He looked up from his notes and smiled. "Who gives this woman in holy matrimony?"

Jeanine burst into tears and ran off in the direction of the ladies' lounge, leaving Joe standing alone with the clergyman.

"That would be me," said Joe, raising one finger. "At least for today." He smiled and shrugged.

The minister removed his reading glasses and peered at Aunt Camellia and Mrs. Peters. "Do you expect Dan to be here on Sunday? I can certainly adjust the wording to accommodate a change in circumstances."

"He'll be here," said Mrs. Peters. She disappeared after her daughter.

"And the bridegroom? He's expected as well?"

Aunt Camellia sighed. "Far as we've heard."

"Why don't we run through the recessional once and then call it a wrap," the minister suggested. The organist began to play, and we shuffled back down the aisle.

"Off to the races, then," said Pari as we clustered at the church entrance. "You're coming riding with us, right Mike?"

Mike nodded and cocked his head at me. I shook mine.

"No. I'm going to give Aunt Camellia a hand with all those *e*'s."

"I can help with that," said Joe.

"Me, too," said Laura. "Horses and me don't mix. You guys go ahead and take care of Jeanine. We'll pack up the gowns."

We undressed, zipped the gowns into vinyl bags, and carried them out to Aunt Camellia's Toyota. Then I remembered I'd left my backpack in the lounge. "I'll meet you over at the Peterses'," I said to Laura and Joe. I wanted to avoid the delicate subject of my non-engagement to Mike for as long as possible.

On the way back into the church house, I heard raised voices in the chapel. I ducked into the hallway and stopped by the door. The minister was meeting with Kendra Newton and another woman.

"Tanya asked me to come along for moral support." Kendra's voice rang out into the empty sanctuary. The second woman honked into a wrinkled Kleenex.

"Fine," said the minister. "I think everything is in place for this afternoon. It will be a fitting tribute to a well-lived but too-short life."

I was relieved he didn't segue into how God must have wanted this fellow as an angel or some such clerical nonsense. By now, I'd figured out he was addressing Junior Mammele's widow. And I felt a little guilty about eavesdropping on the recently bereaved.

"The points she would most like you to make are his love for family, love for the arts, and love for community," said Kendra. Tanya Mammele snuffled softly.

"Yes, I had planned to talk about you and your boys, as well as the sculpture project and his service on the village council," said the minister. "Anything else?"

"His top ten crime targets," said Kendra. "He was so proud of identifying those law-breakers and having them prosecuted. In fact, Tanya and I were thinking about announcing rewards for information leading to the arrest of the criminals on the list who haven't yet been apprehended."

"Perhaps the funeral would not be the best time to get into that," the minister suggested, more diplomatically than I would have.

I vaguely remembered seeing a top-ten list on the bulletin board in the Pinehurst police station, posted next to the FBI's most wanted. Apparently, Junior Mammele had considered himself a vigilante for Pinehurst justice.

"We'll write up a piece for the *Pilot*, then," said Kendra.

"You should feel free to use the lounge before and after the service," said the reverend. "Do you know where it is? I'll show you the facilities."

I grabbed my backpack and slipped out the back door.

Chapter 20

Aunt Camellia answered the door and led me through Mrs. Peters' feminine living room to the dining room. A lace cloth had been rolled off the surface of the table and the stack of programs sat in the center. Two sets of china were displayed behind the doors of the cherry-wood hutch against the far wall: one rimmed with plaid and punctuated by crossed golf clubs, the other outlined by a simple gold band.

"I agreed to let Dan choose one set of china," said Mrs. Peters, coming to stand beside me. "I never promised to serve anything on it," she finished with a tight laugh.

Aunt Camellia distributed pens, drinks, and instructions, and we began to work on the program lettering.

"Have you heard anything more from the kidnappers?" Joe asked after several minutes of silence.

"Not a word," said Aunt Camellia, with a

sharp look of reprimand at Laura and me. Mrs. Peters slumped lower into her chair, the color draining from her face.

"We told Joe," Laura admitted. "He's a psychologist. We tell him everything."

Aunt Camellia looked furious. "Perhaps you don't understand just how serious this is."

"We do understand," I said quickly. "That's why we told him. He has a good head on his shoulders. And he can keep a secret," I added.

"I've bailed these two out of trouble more than once," said Joe. "I'm here as a kind of stopper." He laughed. "I make them quit when they're in over their heads. Which is almost always."

"We need to be able to confide in someone professional," Mrs. Peters said to her sister. "It's just too hard waiting alone." Aunt Camellia pursed her lips into a thin line. The thought crossed my mind that they would have done better to go with a private investigator than a golf psychologist.

"I hope you won't take offense," Laura said, "but we have a couple questions about Mr. Peters."

She summarized a watered-down version of the conversation we'd had in the bar with the Marines the night before, presenting it as though we had talked to the men several days earlier. Her description focused more on unsavory business partners that Mr. Peters might have inadvertently gotten tied up with, and skipped over his alleged tendency to recklessness and poor judgment.

"You specifically promised not to ask any more questions about Dan." Aunt Camellia was angry again.

"We didn't ask, these guys just started talking to us," I lied. "We didn't want to cut them off — that would have seemed even more suspicious."

"Let's say Mr. Peters realized he was in hot water. Isn't it possible that he might have decided to lay low for a couple of days?" Laura asked.

"To protect the family," I added, watching Mrs. Peters' lips pucker and her breathing quicken.

"I just don't know anything about it," she insisted. "And he wouldn't disappear during Jeanine's wedding. This is absolutely the biggest event in our lives. He would be here if he could." Tears seeped out of her eyes and started down both cheeks.

Aunt Camellia's eyes narrowed. "And what about the kidnapping note? You're not saying he wrote it himself? That would be terribly cruel." She rested her hand on her sister's.

Joe laid his Sharpie pen on the table. "We're just trying to explore all of the possibilities."

I wanted to ask about the lithium prescription, but I couldn't think of a graceful way to bring it up. So I went with clumsy and direct. "Another question. I noticed a prescription in the medicine cabinet yesterday when I was looking to borrow some aspirin. I wondered why Mr. Peters was taking lithium?"

Aunt Camellia glared. She'd discovered me in Mr. Peters' office. She knew damn well I'd been snooping, not searching for aspirin. "I can't believe this . . ."

"It's okay Camellia. There's no harm in telling them." Mrs. Peters heaved a heavy sigh. "For a while, the doctors thought he might have manic-depressive illness. He was so intense, and then he'd have these awful black moods."

"Is it still being prescribed?" Joe asked.

She shook her head. "He hated taking it. He said it made him feel dull and logy. He said the Marines would have canned him if they knew he had that weakness."

"May I take a look at the bottle?" he asked. "And while we're at it, I'd like to look

261

at his computer, too. Could you bring the note along?"

We trooped up the stairs and followed the women into the master suite. Aunt Camellia booted up the computer on Mr. Peters' desk, and Mrs. Peters disappeared into the mammoth limestone bathroom. She returned with the pill bottle and handed it to Joe.

He raised his head from studying it. "You held onto this a long time . . ."

"I kept hoping."

"And Dr. Harvey is . . ."

"A psychiatrist," said Mrs. Peters. "Dan only saw him the one time. He refused to go back. He said I'd have to learn to live with him the way he was. I think the doctor may have passed away now."

"Great," I said. "So we won't get anything helpful from him."

"Was there a particular trigger that caused Mr. Peters to go to the psychiatrist and try the drug?" Joe asked.

Mrs. Peters glanced at her sister, who seemed suddenly very involved in lining up the edge of the calendar with the beveled wood of the desk.

"Not exactly," said Mrs. Peters. "He just seemed out of control. He was hardly home. He drank too much and the credit card bills were enormous. Jeanine was just a baby. I was a wreck — just barely holding on myself."

"Sounds like a tough time," said Joe.

"Thank God for Miss Lucy. I don't know how I would have made it through without her."

Joe opened his mouth but before he could ask another question, Aunt Camellia said softly and slowly: "It was a hard time."

Joe scrolled through the calendar on Mr. Peters' desktop, but very few dates had been entered.

"He uses a PDA," said Mrs. Peters. "For business. I keep the family's obligations on my calendar — the old-fashioned way, stone and chisel." She chuckled.

"I need to get back over to the golf course," said Laura.

"I'm heading that way, too," said Joe. "I'm meeting a new client on the putting green in half an hour." He touched my cheek. "Cassie's playing so well now, I need to rustle up some new customers."

"I hope you don't mind seeing yourselves out," said Mrs. Peters. "I'm simply exhausted."

Aunt Camellia moved around the desk and took her arm. "We'll see you later at dinner."

I followed Joe and Laura back down the

stairs and into the kitchen to retrieve our belongings. Miss Lucy was rolling out pie dough on the counter.

"Miss Lucy," said Joe gently. "Did you hear anything unusual the other morning when the note came in the paper?"

He didn't give her the chance to deny she knew about it.

"I'm always up early," she admitted. "I always hear the paperboy. But I didn't hear nothin' unusual that day."

"Voices? A car? Anything different from other days?" Joe prodded.

Miss Lucy sat heavily on a stool beside the counter. "Maybe his muffler was startin' to go. It made like a coughing noise." She shrugged and nodded in my direction. "It sounded a little bit like yours."

"Mrs. Peters was telling us how much help you were when Jeanine was a baby and Mr. Peters was sick," said Joe. "Anything you can tell us about those times could be a big help."

She covered her ears with her hands, then covered her eyes, then pantomimed zipping shut her mouth.

Joe smiled, though I imagined he felt as frustrated as I did. "I appreciate your loyalty. You've been a part of the family a long time."

She smiled, one gold tooth flashing in the fluorescent light of the ceiling.

"Anything else unusual happen around here this week? Anything at all . . ."

The housekeeper stood up and began to tap the crust into a glass pie plate.

"Mr. Peters had a couple men out to the house before you all came to town. There was a lot of shouting," she said. "But they left all smiles." She shrugged again. "I got to get these pies in the oven."

We trailed down the hallway toward the front door. "About those men," Joe asked, "would you be able to describe them? Had you seen them before?"

"Never seen 'em before or since." She wiped one hand across her forehead, leaving a streak of flour. "White men, both of 'em. One kind of skinny, with a little mustache." She rubbed more flour on her upper lip and shut the door behind us.

We followed the driveway to the curb.

"Her description sounds a little like Salivetti," said Laura.

"What little she gave us," I said. "It could have been anyone. A thin man with a mustache? Really, that's half of Pinehurst."

"I'm beginning to think those three ladies have him stashed away somewhere," Laura said.

"For people who want their relative found, they sure aren't trying very hard to cooperate," I said.

Laura slid into the passenger seat of Joe's car and rolled down the window.

"Be sure you let us know when you and Mike set your wedding date," she said as they pulled away from the curb. I shook my fist at the retreating car.

I absolutely had to clear the air with Mike. Maybe it was even time to face my fears and get back on a horse. I pointed my car in the direction of the racetrack.

Chapter 21

My nose filled with the sour odor of horse manure and rotting hay. My heart beat faster. Short, shallow breathing forecasted the onset of an episode of anxious wheezing. I'd had two altercations with horses in the past. Both of them ended with me on my butt in the dirt, while the horses trotted off into the sunset unencumbered by their rider.

"Hello?" I called. My timid greeting echoed in the empty stable.

A woman stepped out of the farthest stall. "Can I help you?" She draped her canvas vest on the newel post of the stairs. She wore dusty jeans and a faded shirt embroidered with cowboy boots, and had her hair pulled back in a loose ponytail.

It took me a minute to recognize her. "You're Helen. Don't you work at the country club?"

"I wait tables for Forest Brook on special

occasions. Lucky for me, they needed lots of extra help for the Peters' wedding." She ran her hand across her hair, tucking the loose ends into the rubber band. "I mostly work here — I live upstairs." She pointed to a wooden stairway leading to the barn's loft.

How could she stand the smell?

"That was awful, what happened at the shower," she said. "It sure ruined a lovely party. Did they find out what happened to Mr. Mammele? How's Jeanine doing?"

"They still don't know who shot him, and Jeanine's still pretty shaken up. A terrible shame, all the way around. Poor Jeanine's been planning this wedding for a long time — years before she ever met Rick." I laughed. "The fairy tale princess bride. That's not for me."

"Really?" Helen said in a dreamy voice. "I want a big wedding, too. A white dress with a sweetheart neckline and lots of lace and a full train, and all the ushers in baby-blue tuxedos . . ." A wistful expression crossed her face. I wondered if she'd pasted in the face of the reluctant Pierre as her groom.

"Baby blue?" I asked. "That's an unusual twist."

Helen smiled. "It's my favorite color. But first I want my own riding academy — that's my real dream. One day a week I'll have a clinic for handicapped and orphaned children." She grimaced. "I have a lot of work to do, saving for that. The Peters are still having the wedding, right? I'd hate to lose the money."

"Oh, sure. I just came from the rehearsal. There's too much planning gone into it to give up now. I think Junior Mammele's family understands that. They'd never want Jeanine to postpone the wedding." So there'd been a sniper killing — never mind the abduction of the father of the bride; the show must go on.

Helen nodded. "The show goes on."

For a split second, I had the panicked feeling that she'd read my mind.

"Did you want to ride?" she asked. "The others got a head start. They've been gone maybe half an hour."

I hesitated. "I haven't had much success with horses."

"You can't let them know you're afraid," Helen said. "You have to act like you're in charge. You could try Mrs. T — she's very gentle. Even a beginner can handle her — she refuses to go any faster than a walk. If you like, I could just lead the two of you around the track a time or two, until you get the hang of it."

I nodded, still reluctant but not wanting

to play the sissy. Helen made it sound idiot-proof. She ducked into one of the stalls and retrieved a black nag with a white star covering the length of her snout. As she layered a blanket and the saddle on the horse's back, she chattered softly.

"This is Cassie. She doesn't have much experience with horses, so be gentle with her. Okay, Mrs. T?"

I stepped closer and, with Helen's encouragement, fitted one foot into the left stirrup. The wheezing started up again and I took my foot back out. I drew a deep, three-part yoga breath and scanned the barn: breathe in — horizontal, the boards of the horses' stalls; breathe out — vertical, the newel post and spindles of the staircase leading to the loft. Breathe in, the boards, breathe out, the post . . . I fitted my foot back into the stirrup. The horse snorted and bucked her head. I startled and stumbled backward, falling to the ground, my ankle still twisted in the leather strap. I groaned in pain and embarrassment.

"You scared her." Helen peered down at me with her hands on hips, then stroked my horse's flank. "Are you hurt? Remember what I said about acting like you're in charge?"

"Forget it," I said. "It's not for me. I'm no

actor. But thanks for trying." I untangled myself from the stirrup and stood up. Baxter's voice hammered in the back of my brain — something about learning which risks were worth embracing. Joe's voice whispered in the other ear — something about going easy on myself. I covered both ears and began to hum loudly. "Get out," I muttered. "Both of you."

Helen cast me a sidelong glance, probably thinking I'd lost my marbles.

In the distance, I heard the clip-clop of hooves. A horse and rider came into view — it was Mike, returning to the barn at a gallop. Canter, maybe, or trot. Whatever. The animal's muscles rippled as he ran, his chestnut hide shiny with sweat. And the muscles in Mike's arms rippled, too, and those in my stomach clenched in response. Would I ever again meet a man that confused me as much as this one? I hoped not.

He stopped just outside the barn, panting slightly in rhythm with the horse. "Did you change your mind? Are you coming out? I saw your car drive up, so I came back to get you."

"That's sweet. Thanks. I considered it. I tried, but horses just aren't me." I shrugged. "I appreciate your coming anyway."

He swung off in one graceful movement

and stroked the animal's dark mane. "How about we shoot some skeet instead? They have a nice range here — the only one in town." He called into the stable, and Helen reappeared from Mrs. T's stall. "Can you take care of Custer here and set us up to shoot some skeet?"

Helen took the reins of Mike's horse and started into the barn. "Give me a minute and I'll meet you over at the shed."

We seemed to be the only customers at the shooting range. Perfect conditions for clearing the air — no one to overhear and plenty to keep our eyes and hands busy while we talked. If I had the nerve to step up and take control. I hadn't done too well with the horse.

"I've never tried this," I said, leaning on the counter and tapping my fingers on the rough wood. Mike already knew that, but I felt compelled to start talking just to break the silence. "I hate hunting. I hate seeing animals hurt. If I had any real principles, I'd go cold-turkey vegetarian."

"It's not hunting," said Mike, instantly exasperated. "It's skeet shooting. There are no animals involved. You'll be shooting at pieces of clay. Do you have any moral issues about blowing up pieces of clay?"

I had a real knack for bringing out the

prickliness in him. And he in me. Over the past year, small flashes of comfort in our relationship had expanded into occasional stretches of easiness. But mostly it felt like we were making our way across a minefield. Or climbing a mountain that doesn't look that challenging, but the footholds keep crumbling beneath your feet, so you slide backward more than you ascend.

Once Helen arrived at the desk, Mike arranged for two guns, waved away my offer to pay half, and led me out to the trap shooting range.

"These are Winchester twelve gauge over-under shotguns," Mike explained, looking pleased to have an audience. "Rick uses a Browning Citori back in Texas."

Which meant zippo to me. He demonstrated the proper shooting stance, left foot pointed to the target, front leg bent at the knee, weight balanced evenly.

"The idea is to swing from the hips so you can follow the target. Don't roll your body."

"Aha," I said. "Like swaying in golf. Death to the novice. And the expert."

"The pigeons get shot out of those little sheds, called trap houses," he said. "Get in your stance, sight over the bead, then point your gun towards the spot where you want to break the target. Then swing back to the trap house and lead the target. Follow-through is crucial. Watch me first."

He loaded the gun, raised it to his shoulder, and pointed it skyward. The first clay disk hurtled out of the shed. His gun belched smoke and noise, the disk burst into pieces.

"Great shot!" I yelled. We both smiled — it sounded like one of our few good moments on the golf course.

"Just like golf," Mike said, "you're looking for a rhythm. Visualize, anticipate, then fire. The trajectory of the shot is going to vary according to which station the disk comes from. Here, you try it."

I hoisted the gun up, squeezed the trigger, and stumbled backward, stunned by the strength of its recoil.

Mike laughed. "I think that bird got away — you were only half a mile off. Here, try it again."

I shot a second time and missed by a large margin.

"You're not leading the target," he said. "You're stopping to shoot and the disk's already gone by."

I shot again, this time clipping the edge of my clay pigeon.

"Got it!" I felt a rush of excitement, not quite equal to hitting a pure seven-iron, but a thrill all the same. We shot for half an hour in silence, when Mike signaled we would take a break. He removed his ear protectors and flopped down on a bench in the shade of a large pine tree.

"You're doing good," he said. "With your eye-hand coordination, I knew you'd pick it up quickly."

I grinned.

"You looked sharp on the golf course, too, the last two days. All those years of feeding me tips seem to have rubbed off."

"Thanks," I said, shy with his praise. I leaned against the back of the bench, chewing on a stalk of dried grass, and watched two dark-colored birds squawk over some prize in the distance.

"So what's the story with Julie Nothstine?" I asked.

The lines around his mouth tightened.

"No story there. She's just a friend I had some drinks with." He shaped the brim of his Mets cap. "What do you know about her, anyway?"

I blurted it out. "She wanted my advice — should she ask you out or wait for you to call. I told her I'd be damned if I knew how to handle a relationship with you."

A series of expressions progressed across his face — embarrassment, sympathy, and finally, annoyance. In his mind, I'd spoiled a perfectly good afternoon.

"I've been thinking it's time for us to go our separate ways for a while." He stood up and brushed a piece of lint off his jeans. Then he looked down at me and cleared his throat. "I guess I was having some trouble saying it out loud because I didn't want to hurt your feelings. It's not that we couldn't have a nice enough life together. But . . ."

I squinted up at him. "Save yourself the song and dance, I'm right behind you."

"So what was that comment about how we haven't set a date for a wedding?"

I leaned back, feeling the crossbars of the bench press into my spine, my face burning. I couldn't stop a parade of images from running through my mind. How I'd started out as his caddie, and pictured wearing the white caddie coveralls of Augusta National — *Callahan* emblazoned across my back in green letters, a small map of the U.S. and the Masters' flag embroidered on the pocket, and a green cap to match the letters. Then I'd collected articles about fighting jet lag with melatonin and a wacky no-protein diet, all in the service of Mike's future performance at the British Open. But the caddie fantasy died early, and Laura went to

Scotland with him last summer, not me. Over the past year, the dreams had more to do with living together, sharing our lives, golfing and otherwise.

It wasn't going to happen. I wasn't buying his "for a while" comment — if we broke it off, this time it would be permanent. And for the best. So I had no idea where the wedding date comment came from. Some dark psychological recess that I didn't care to explore.

"I think it's time for a change," he said again. "We've got too much between us right now, it's not working with us. I know you see it, too."

I did see it, but that didn't mean it felt good. I shrugged. He plunged ahead.

"Here's my advice. You've got to make up your mind whether you want something, or someone, or not. If you do, just go for it. Look: I never really knew where I stood with you. It's like you're jealous of everyone — Julie Nothstine, even that silly Pari. But you still can't take a stand and say 'I'm Mike's girl.' I suspect it's the same when you play golf."

Oh, great, now my very, very recently exboyfriend was distributing therapeutic maxims and golf tips. I wished I could barf on command.

"And if you'd like some other advice . . ."

"I don't . . ."

Mike made a face and blazed forward. "I'm aware that Jeanine and her family are worried about her father. Just stay out of it, Cassie. You get mixed up in these things that are none of your business, and it doesn't help anyone. Besides that, it ruins your concentration."

"I don't recall having trouble concentrating the last few days. It wasn't me who scored eight over par. Besides, how would you know what's going to help Jeanine?" I was shouting now. "For all you know, her father could be in serious danger. You've got your head so far up your ass you can't find your way to the next tee without a baby-sitter."

I turned and marched to the parking area, barging past Helen in front of the barn. She called out a tentative good-bye.

On the way back to town, I dialed Laura. Her phone was turned off. Okay, so it was a serious faux pas to have a cell phone ring on the golf course during a tournament — but her best friend needed her. Now. So I tried Charlie. He'd be likely to dish out the right mixture of sympathy and "good riddance to the bastard." The tears welled up as soon as he answered. I took a breath.

"Hello?"

"It's me. Just wanted to let you know that Mike Callahan is history."

"Good show," he said. I sniffled into the phone. "Oh, Christ," he said, "don't tell me you're feeling sad about the son of a bitch."

"A little."

"You know what I do when I'm feeling down?"

"You're not going to start singing about raindrops on roses and whiskers on kittens, are you?"

"Swimming," he said. "It works like a charm. No one asks you why you're crying, you hash out a lot of stuff thrashing around in the water, and you get your exercise to boot."

"But then I have to go to the rehearsal dinner and act like nothing's wrong," I whined.

"Just show up, shut up, look gorgeous, and skip out early. Look, things were never going to work out with you and Mike. It's like asking Mom and Maureen to get along."

"I don't see the connection."

"Competition. With you and Mike, it's golf. With the ladies, it's Dad and the family. Maureen can't let go of her fear that he might have loved Mom, or us, more. She hates that he loved someone else first. Mom can't forgive him for moving on and loving someone else."

I'd had wisps of these thoughts pass through my consciousness before, but Charlie fitted them all together this time. And he would know — he was the only one in the world who'd been through exactly what I had. Well, not exactly. He'd bailed out to go to college, leaving me with Mom at her worst. I didn't know when I'd forgive him for that.

"I have to run to a meeting. I'll check in with you tonight, okay? Love you."

The phone clicked off. Alone again. Naturally.

Chapter 22

Cars jammed the parking area next to the brick church on the village green and spilled down the surrounding streets: Junior Mammele's funeral. The crush of vehicles included a phalanx of cop cars. Uniformed officers flanked the tall white columns of the entrance. Maybe I could help Jeanine by attending the service — listening and watching to see if any snippets of information fell into place. This had been useful in the past. On the other hand, the Pinehurst police looked like they had it covered.

Besides, if there were ever the right mood for a funeral, I was not in it today. Charlie's suggestion sounded best — swim forty laps, make a token appearance at the rehearsal dinner, and get to bed early. As maid of honor, there was no way I could skip the dinner, even though the idea of more time anywhere in the vicinity of Mike Callahan made my skin crawl. I remembered with a sickening lurch that we had planned to give a tandem toast — a light-hearted roast comparing the development of their relationship to ours. *Just say no,* Cassie, I told myself. The wedding tomorrow promised to be even worse — an emotional fun house, especially if Mr. Peters didn't show. Monday morning couldn't get here soon enough. I drove down Dogwood Road in the direction of the spa.

A pleasant but aloof woman checked me in at the desk, handed me a robe, slippers, and towel, and returned to studying *Allure* magazine. I squeezed into my suit, showered quickly, and click-clacked out through the relaxation chambers to the indoor pool. New-age Muzak featuring crashing waves and tinkling bells followed me. All three lap lanes were empty and the water sparkled, clean and blue. I dropped my terry robe on a wicker lounge chair, slid into the pool, and settled my goggles in place. Just then, Violet, my masseuse from the previous day, walked by with her hand placed protectively on the back of her outgoing customer.

"Oh, Miss Burdette. Nice to see you again. Don't forget to spend some time in the hot tub — it will do wonders for those stress knots."

I waved and pushed off into a brisk crawl.

Once I'd remembered the trick of the flip turn and worked into a stroke-stroke-stroke-breathe rhythm, my mind started to wander. The talk with Mike had been a bust. I'd gone in planning to take charge, announce that it was time to move on, and shake hands, still friends. *Bravery. Honesty. Dignity.* That could have been my motto. Instead, Mike took the lead and I crumbled. So embarrassing to have left the stable shouting like a banshee.

Besides all that, I did not expect to feel this sad.

I swam faster, pushing my thoughts toward the missing Dan Peters. Had he really been kidnapped or was he hiding out? And what was his family holding back? Southern families do have a tendency to reticence, declining to air familial grievances publicly. And we're proud of it. Leave that ugliness to the Yankees.

But this felt like a deeper secret.

I made a smooth flip turn at the end of the pool and pushed off into the breaststroke. Would Mr. Peters really have killed Junior Mammele at the shower? He just didn't come across as the kind of man who would murder someone and spoil his only daughter's wedding. If he had, would he be stupid enough to leave the smoking gun in his home office? It seemed unlikely, even for a man with poorly controlled manic tendencies. If he hadn't killed Junior Mammele, then who had? And why? Was the timing random? Like Mr. Peters, Mr. Mammele seemed to have acquired his share of enemies during the process of securing safety and justice for Pinehurst.

Then I mulled over Joe's question to Mrs. Peters: what was the trigger for her husband's visit to the psychiatrist? All shrinks want to know what exact moment brings their customers crawling on their knees for outside psychological intervention. I spotted one common theme in our investigations and conversations so far. Mr. Peters loved women, to put a fine Southern face on it. He appeared to be a philanderer, in blunt Yankee terms. Had Mrs. Peters caught him *in flagrante delecto?*

Lingering beyond this buzz of ideas was the worry that I had been drugged in the bar. We'd made no progress on that front the night before.

Once I'd logged forty laps and two extra for good measure, I climbed out of the water and wrapped myself in the plush robe. I felt pleasantly tired, but a little chilled. A dip in the hot tub would feel just right.

The spa Muzak still hummed in the background, but there were no other customers in the relaxation room. Ignoring the warning on the wall about not indulging alone, I stripped off my suit a la Pari and eased into the steaming tub. I practiced clearing my mind of clutter by counting the vertical green stripes of the wallpaper and cataloging the pattern of green and gold tiles. Ten minutes later, I emerged lobster red and just beginning to relax. I decided to squeeze in a quick visit to the steam room before facing down Jeanine's rehearsal dinner. At least I'd heard the food was outstanding at the Carolina Inn. Maybe they'd serve ribs. Probably not — Jeanine's prospective mother-in-law was more likely to choose something elegant to suit the occasion. Chicken breast dogpaddling in some odd fruit sauce, or flabby, pink poached salmon — even worse. *Ugh.*

I left my robe on a hook outside the door and spread a towel on the top shelf. Then I lay down on my stomach and felt the thick cloud of steam waft over me. I shifted gears and ran through my performance over the two days of the Pine Straw Challenge. Once the chaff of my partners' collapse and the intrigue of multiple family members caddying was swept aside, my golf game looked solid. I'd been a little disappointed about the hooked driver on the fifth hole. And on fifteen, I certainly should have stuck my sand wedge nearer to the pin. If you're seventy yards out and don't end up putting for bird, you need to —

The door to the steam room swung open, allowing in a rush of cool air. I pulled a section of terrycloth across my buttocks and kept my face to the wall, hoping to discourage conversation. Footsteps padded across the small space in my direction and suddenly a towel was over my head and hands fastened around my throat. I thrashed and tried to scream, my own towel falling away in the struggle. I fought harder, coughing and tearing at the choking fingers and the material covering my eyes. I couldn't breathe.

I reached around to try to scratch at the attacker's face and felt my finger sink into his eye.

"Ahhh!" His grip loosened, and with a burst of energy I flipped the body off me and onto the step below. The man's head hit with a horrible clunk. I broke completely free and dashed for the door. Once outside, I grabbed my robe and jammed my spa sandal into the handle of the steam room door. Then I ran out of the room, across the deck of the pool, and down the hallway until, chest heaving, I slammed into Violet.

"Miss Burdette! What's wrong?"

Tears poured from both eyes and my neck and throat burned. I'd bruised my left elbow and both knees in the struggle. Violet led me to a chair just down the hall. She blotted my face gently, and asked again: "What's wrong?"

Then Pari, hair wrapped in a towel turban, appeared from the direction of the pool. "Cassie, what's the matter? What the hell happened?" She put her arm around my shoulders and squeezed.

"Someone attacked me in the damn steam room, that's what happened." I pulled my wet hair back from my face and shook off Pari's embrace. "So much for your advice on relaxing," I said to Violet.

"Attacked you? Who would attack you? Why?" asked Pari.

"I didn't ask for his résumé," I snapped.

"Gosh, we'd better talk to my supervisor," said Violet, her eyes wide through her thick glasses.

She placed a sheltering hand on my back and steered me down the hallway past the treatment rooms and into an office. A large arrangement of yellow roses reflected the honey tones of the wooden desk. A brass nameplate identified the supervisor as Miss

Joan Cox. She stood to greet us with a pleasant but strained smile on her face. The white coat worn over her tailored gray dress leant her an air of efficiency and medical expertise that she probably hadn't earned. She had on low black heels and too much eye makeup: the same woman who'd informed Jeanine yesterday that we were short two facials.

"Miss Cox, there's been an incident. One of our patrons was assaulted in the steam room." Violet rubbed my back gently, pushing me closer to the desk. Miss Cox offered seats to me and Pari and asked Violet to shut the door. She perched on the corner of the desk, her thin, penciled eyebrows arched in dismay. At her urging, I described everything I could remember about my fifteen minutes in the steam room.

Miss Cox approached me.

"May I?" She folded down the collar of my robe to inspect my neck. "Oh, my goodness, I believe you can actually make out fingerprints."

"It just looks like red blotches to me," said Pari.

"Would it help if I rubbed your shoulders?" Violet asked.

"It would help if I could get dressed and go home," I said.

Miss Cox tapped a pencil on her red lips and reached for the phone. "We'll have to call the police and the paramedics."

I shook my head. "That's not necessary — I'll be fine."

She picked up the phone and began to dial. "Oh, but it is. We can't have our patrons harassed. Besides, the perpetrator could still be on the premises."

I shivered. She was right — the cops needed to know. And the spa wasn't about to allow some madman to disturb their carefully cultivated environment of pampered tranquility and relaxation. So I negotiated my way out of the only thing left — a medical examination.

While we waited for the police to arrive. Violet escorted me to the locker room where I put on my jeans and long-sleeved T-shirt with "Life Is Good" embroidered on the pocket. It didn't seem all that great just now. My neck was raw, and my hair a wet and tangled mess. I reeked of chlorine and my jeans smelled like horse manure. And I was scared, too. But just changing out of that damn spa robe and into my own clothes made me feel less vulnerable.

"Should I call Mike for you?" asked Pari, when I emerged from the locker room.

"No!"

Was she joking? The solicitousness sounded real.

I tried to smile. "Thanks, anyway."

Officer Cutler, the female cop who'd pulled me over on the way home from the Tarheel Bar and Grill, answered the supervisor's call. Dressed in full uniform, she looked awkward and out of place in the muted womb of the spa. She did a quick search of the premises and then listened to my report along with interpretations from Pari and Violet, and concerned murmurs from Miss Cox.

The cop shoved a small notepad into her breast pocket. "Let's see the steam room again," she said to Miss Cox.

Cutler followed the supervisor to the space containing the hot tub, the sauna, and the steam room. "You'll need to close this area off so the team can come in and dust for prints," she said.

"Fine," said Miss Cox, "We'll just close the spa early today. But no crime scene tape until we get everyone out. Please!"

Donning a pair of latex gloves, Cutler entered the small space and waved me in. Through chattering teeth, I pointed out the shelf where I'd been lying and showed her the towels heaped on the floor. She gathered them into a plastic garbage bag. After examining the sandal that I had jammed in the door handle, she dropped it into a bag decorated with the Pinehurst Spa logo.

The niggling thought surfaced that it was odd for Pari to have shown up so quickly after the attack. Her story: she'd been so impressed by my praise of Violet, that she'd scheduled a massage to follow her horseback ride. Had she had the time to try to strangle me first? I glanced quickly at her hands. Had she tried to choke me? I took another quick look at her hands, attempting to compare them to the feeling of the ones that had circled my neck. They seemed a normal size, not particularly large or small. And both of her eyes were intact. But who else knew I was here? I palpated the bruises on my throat.

The Peters women simply had to tell the police about the ransom note. This had gone too far.

"I'd like you to come down to the station to give a formal statement," said Officer Cutler. "I need to bring my boss up to speed."

I didn't want to go back to the police station. On the other hand, time with cops would reduce my sentence at dinner. "I'll follow you there."

Chapter 23

I parked along the curb in front of the police station and followed Officer Cutler into the reception area. The gum machine was now plastered with a hand-lettered "out of order" sign.

"Take a seat," she said. "I'll be right back with Detective Warren."

I paced the length of the waiting area and checked out the bulletin board again. No new FBI suspects had been posted. But this time I studied Junior Mammele's top ten crime targets. The "De-greening" of Midland Road headed the list, followed by a rash of burglaries in gated communities. The desecration of the Sculpture Mile took third place, and congestion of the Moore County jail system was fourth. Two of these subjects tied Mammele straight to Dan Peters. Mr. Peters' planned commercial development was currently the biggest threat to the natural appearance of Midland Road, and Mammele had been a fierce opponent. Peters certainly had a stake in catching the thieves plaguing the golf course communities — that had been part of the argument I stumbled on my first night in Pinehurst. And Kendra Newton had told me enough about Mr. Peters' objections to the sculptures that I could imagine him behind the airplane prank. *Ha.* If he had really killed Mammele, maybe he'd be contributing to jail congestion, too.

Several of Mammele's pet peeves, including the capture of the ringleader of an embezzlement scheme at a local country club, had been successfully accomplished. These coups were marked with large red checks. Articles detailing his role in these successes as well as the unresolved burning issues (in Council Chair Mammele's eyes) were pinned to the bulletin board beneath the list. I was scanning an article about the preservation of open farmland space when Officer Cutler reappeared and ushered me into the conference room where Jeanine had been questioned several days earlier.

"This is Detective Warren."

I nodded at the tall, thin man with a receding hairline and a neat mustache, who I recognized from the tailgate shower disaster. I spilled out my description of the

attack in the steam room. Both police officers took notes.

"Thank you, Miss Burdette." Moving
from left to right, Warren roughed up the
hairs of his mustache and then patted them
down flat. "Who was in the spa when you
arrived?"

"There was the woman at the desk, of
course, who checked me in and gave me the
robe and all that." The police nodded like
bobble-head dolls. "Then I saw the masseuse coming through with a customer
when I was starting my swim." More nods. I
pictured the empty pool. "It was pretty
quiet, I remember thinking that. There's a
gym where they do golf fitness evaluations
on the other side of the pool from the ladies'
locker room. I think there were some folks
in there using the exercise equipment, but I
couldn't swear to it. Other than that, no
one."

"No one in the hot tub? No one in the
sauna?"

I shook my head. "It was dead quiet."

"Why were you the target of this attack?"

How the hell would I know? And what I
did know, I wasn't free to say. "I've been
wondering that myself," I said, trying to
stay calm. "I'm afraid I don't have an
answer."

"You visited with us the other night, did you not?"

I nodded, though I wouldn't have called it a "visit."

"Don't you find that a bit peculiar, two police incidents in the span of a four-day stay in Pinehurst?"

I shrugged, my shoulders sagging. I felt tense and exhausted, all at the same time. The two incidents weren't peculiar, they were frightening. The missing link was Jeanine's father. How could I enlist the cops' protection and support without mentioning Mr. Peters' kidnapping? On the other hand, it was not my decision to spill that news. His abductors had been very clear about the consequences of contacting the authorities. I couldn't live with that responsibility.

"You probably heard that my breathalyzer reading was under the legal limit for drunk driving, right?"

Detective Warren raised one hand. So?

"I believe someone spiked my drink the other night. If that's so, that makes two attacks in three days. Someone's after me, Detective. But I don't know why."

I spent another forty-five minutes in the conference room, spelling out all the details of my visit to Pinehurst — the wedding activities, the golf tournament, and back around to walk the same tired details of my problem at the spa. Everything but Mr. Peters' kidnapping.

Suddenly I flashed on my first night in Pinehurst, when I'd overheard the argument between Peters and Mammele. Maybe I could point them in the direction of finding Mr. Peters without specifically mentioning the ransom demand.

"One more thing," I said slowly, "it may be related, or maybe it's not. But as I arrived at Forest Brook on Tuesday, Mr. Peters and Mr. Mammele were fighting about the Midland Road development. Any way the hit-and-run incident could be tied into all of this?" Even as I said it, I didn't see how it could be related to my attacker in the spa. Officer Cutler cracked a wad of gum and rolled back on her chair legs until she rested against the wall. Detective Warren made a short note and frowned at his paper.

"The thing is, we've arrested someone in that hit-and-run. A thug from Aberdeen. Far as we can tell, there's no connection at all with these other incidents."

"Just thought you should know."

He nodded, but with a puzzled look on his face. "That's all for now. We'll be in touch. Be careful out there."

I stopped back by the Magnolia Inn and changed into rehearsal dinner attire — a cream-colored silk shirt, boxy brown velvet pants, and my grandmother's pearls. I buttoned the shirt to the collar, disguising most of the red marks, hoping to avoid a public scene about the sauna incident. Then I combed through my tangles with a tablespoon of styling gel and scrunched the curls around my face. It was the best I could do under the current rough circumstances.

A teenage boy in a green jacket accepted my car at the entrance of the Carolina Inn and directed me to the ballroom. Maureen waylaid me at the door, Zachary and David on her heels. She was zipped tight into a sleeveless silk maroon jumpsuit that set her sculpted arms off perfectly. The diamonds at her neck and earlobes twinkled when she moved. My mother would have flipped out.

"Pari said you were attacked in the spa today!" said Maureen, thrusting a glass of champagne at me. "Are you all right? What happened?" She had abandoned this morning's rudeness in the exciting wake of another police incident.

"Cassie, you're late, we're about to begin with the formal toasts," said Aunt Camellia, pushing in from the other side. She dropped her voice low. "We're going to try to cut the evening short. Jeanine's a wreck."

I squeezed Maureen's wrist and followed Aunt Camellia to the head table. Thanks be to some kind soul who had seated me on Jeanine's right and Mike on Rick's left — an almost-comfortable two-person cushion for recent exes. The Carolina Inn, in conjunction with the Justice family, had eschewed golf-theme table settings. With hundreds of tiny white café lights, garlands of holly, and pinecones strung through the room and down the center of the tables, it looked like an enchanted forest. The only other touch of green was in the salads, which had already been served: baby spinach leaves, real bacon bits, chunks of tomato, and creamy blue cheese dressing.

Jeanine did look bad — a porcelain doll with a frozen smile. I kissed her cheek. "Buck up," I said. "We'll get through all this." I leaned over to tap Rick's arm. "How was your round?"

"Real good —"

Mr. Justice stumbled to his feet and held up a mug of beer. "We are so pleased to have the opportunity to share this evening with our nearest and dearest friends, and to reciprocate the grand hospitality that has been so generously offered by the Peters family." He went on to praise Jeanine and her family and wish the bride- and groom-to-be well in their married life. The crowd applauded noisily.

Aunt Camellia tapped on her wine glass with her fork and nodded at me and Mike.

I stood, knocking the chair to the floor in my hurry. Laura and Joe smirked and waved from a table across the room. I ignored them. I would never, ever, accept a position as maid of honor in another wedding. Well, maybe if it was Laura. Or maybe not even then. I'd have lots of time to recover and think it over: she'd have to find a boyfriend first — as far as I knew, there wasn't even a Y chromosome on the horizon. Besides, she'd go for an extravaganza like this when Bobby Jones came back from the dead to win the U.S. Open. The Women's Open.

"I'm Cassie Burdette. I introduced Rick and Jeanine not too long ago, though it turns out their two families have connections that go back years. Ain't it a small world?" The guests chuckled politely. I didn't care — I wasn't on the stand-up circuit, just get through the damn speech and sit back down.

"Anyway, I don't believe in fairy tales. But I knew Rick had a thing for smart, gorgeous blondes, and I knew Jeanine was partial to sweet, accomplished golfers. And once they came together, it turned out to be a perfect match — not a rocky moment between them, as far as I can tell." A lie, but I wasn't working for the *National Enquirer*, either.

Several of Rick's buddies called out rude suggestions about what might have really gone on behind the scenes. I raised my voice and plowed on.

"I'm thrilled to have been able to grease the skids." I glanced over in Mike's direction. "On behalf of Michael and myself, we send you off with all our love. And I wish that you prove me wrong about fairy tales and live happily ever after. To the princess and her prince . . ." I raised my glass, righted my chair, and sat down to a smattering of "here-heres" and applause. I hadn't given Mike any chance to butt in. Jeanine smiled gratefully, but I noticed that she had yet to make eye contact with Rick.

There were other toasts — Aunt Camellia with a reminiscence about Jeanine in purple ruffles on the playground and how all the little boys flocked around her . . . Mr. Justice — again — visibly drunk now, emphasizing how thrilled they were to have the Justice family join with the Peters . . . and

Rick, looking tired and drawn, toasting his bride-to-be and thanking his future in-laws for hosting the multi-day event at their home. His distinct emphasis on "multi-day" brought on a rash of warnings to Jeanine about his apparent lack of stamina. In truth, the whole affair had gone on way too long. And they weren't even married yet.

After dinner — at least the salmon had a crispy teriyaki glaze — my father and stepfamily crowded around me. The boys looked both bored and worried.

"What's this about someone trying to choke you in the spa?" demanded my father. Maureen pressed in next to him, her breathing bordering on hyperventilation.

"I'm okay, now," I said. "And the police have dusted for prints and so on. They'll take care of it."

"But Pari said it was awful — she said you could actually see fingerprints on your neck!" Maureen exclaimed.

"Why don't you come and stay in our suite tonight," my father suggested. "One of the boys can sleep on the floor. In fact they can both sleep out in the living area, and you can have their bedroom to yourself. We'd love to have you."

Zachary grinned. "Yeah, we can play a

family game of Boggle! Come on, Cassie, we'll teach you."

"I'm the champion so far," David announced, then wrinkled his forehead. "Maybe we should give her some points so she has a chance to catch up."

Maureen scowled, but even she didn't have the balls to uninvite me when genuine physical safety was the chief concern. I took her off the hook.

"I'll be fine. My hotel is right in the middle of town. My pad's on the main hallway. I'll be perfectly safe. Thanks so much for asking." I patted both boys on the back. "I'd love to play another time. I'm whipped tonight, guys."

I hit the sheets hard in my rented room, craving dreamless sleep. Sooner the morning came, sooner the wedding would be over, and I could blow town. If I stuck to O'Doul's and sparkling water, I could leave immediately following the reception. Just as I was drifting off, my cell phone chirped.

A couple of breathy sobs, and then Jeanine: "Cassie, can you come over right away? And bring Joe. We've received another note."

Chapter 24

I threw on sweats and sneakers and vaulted down the stairs to meet Joe. Pacing back and forth outside to the pounding music from the jukebox in the Magnolia bar, I wished I'd worn a jacket. It had to be hovering near freezing. Joe's forest-green Honda careened to a stop, and I collapsed into the passenger seat and slammed the door. On the short drive to the Peterses', I filled him in on the details of the spa incident, the police station visit, and Jeanine's frantic message.

"I don't like the way this is headed," said Joe sternly. "You should have told the cops everything."

"Do you think I like the way it's going?" I snapped. "Check this out, Mr. Pompous-Know-It-All: how would I feel if these lunatics killed Jeanine's dad because I spilled the beans?"

"Sorry for the tone. You scare me." He

flashed his lights and waved at the guard in the Forest Brook gatehouse. The gate swung slowly open. I snuck a glance at Joe while we waited — he looked more rugged than usual, wearing a plaid flannel shirt and blue jeans, with a worried frown and the shadow of a beard on his face. I tried to picture him growing that out. He'd look good in a full beard.

"We'll see what's happened at Jeanine's, and then we can decide whether to call the police," he said.

I'd already made that decision. But I held myself back from snarling at Joe again. Tense with anxiety, fear, and too many nearby blood relatives and wedding preparations, I would have been testy with Mother Teresa.

The figures of Jeanine and her mother and aunt were silhouetted through the pleated shades of the living room windows when we pulled into the drive. Jeanine opened the door. She looked like she was fighting to hold herself together, but her cheeks were marked with trails of tears. Joe gathered her into a comforting hug.

"We're here now," he said, moving her to arm's length and wiping a wet spot off one cheek with his finger. "We'll figure it all out."

Aunt Camellia appeared in the hallway. "Come upstairs. You'll need to see this for yourselves."

We followed the women up the main staircase and into Mr. Peters' study.

"It's on the computer," said Jeanine. "Aunt Camellia ran a copy off, but the picture's clearer online."

We clustered around the laptop. Mr. Peters' haggard face filled the screen. His eyes looked bloodshot and his color poor. A wide scrape ran the length of his left cheek, snaking through a stubble of whiskers and meeting his unwashed hair at the temple.

Jeanine manipulated the mouse and rolled the screen up so we could read the attached e-mail.

"Bring the money in a brown paper sack and leave it under the statue of the squatting woman at two a.m. One person alone. No cops, no private investigators, no FBI, or you will never see Dan Peters again. Return home and we will release our prisoner."

"Is that definitely him?" Joe asked.

We all nodded.

"He doesn't look too bad," said Joe, his voice artificially cheery. "A little tired maybe, but not like he's been tortured or anything."

"How did you find this?" I asked.

305

"When we got home from the party I checked the phone messages," said Mrs. Peters, who was beginning to look tortured herself. "The first one instructed me to read my e-mail, so we came right up."

"Was it a man or woman on the answering machine?" I asked, flashing on the attack in the spa.

"A man, definitely. A deep voice, right Camellia?" Mrs. Peters turned to her sister.

"That's right. By the way, Cassie," said Aunt Camellia, with a pale smile, "your toast was lovely." She smiled again. "We do have to work hard to find the bright spots in all this."

"Thanks. So what's next?"

"That's why I called you and Joe," said Jeanine. She straightened her shoulders and thrust out her chin. "I think we have to do exactly what they say, but my mother thinks we should call the police."

Finally, a sensible decision.

"Excellent move," said Joe.

"I don't know what to do," Jeanine's mother sniffled. "I just couldn't bear it if Jeanine went and something happened to her, too."

"But what about Daddy?"

The three women circled the question of whether to call the cops for the next five minutes, landing back on the same square: the risk was too high.

Joe sighed heavily. "I'll take the money over."

He was the only guy here — I'm sure he felt obligated to offer. Though the determined set of his jaw made me believe part of him really wanted to go. I felt sharp prickles of both worry and irritation.

"But you're not supposed to be involved," Aunt Camellia pointed out. "They told us not to discuss this with anyone." Her eyes squinted nearly closed. "Have either of you been talking to people about this? I just wondered if that's why Cassie ran into trouble today at the spa."

I was indignant. "We haven't said a word." I thought for a minute. "Well, only to Edward. Laura let it slip, and we swore him to secrecy."

"You told Edward?" asked Aunt Camellia. "But we —"

"Thanks for the offer, Joe," said Mrs. Peters, with a sharp glance at her sister. "I'm afraid if a man showed up with the money, it would scare these terrible people off, and we'd lose our only chance."

"Why don't I just go then?" I asked. "If someone's already pissed off at me, it shouldn't make things worse."

"That's ridiculous. It's my father, I'm going, that's final."

Mrs. Peters and Aunt Camellia tried arguing her out of it, but Jeanine wouldn't budge. She didn't often take a firm stand — for or against any issue. This could be just the beginning for Rick.

"Where exactly is the squatting woman?" Joe asked.

Aunt Camellia described the sculpture's position on the edge of the village green. "It's sheltered by a stand of pines, so it would be easy enough for the kidnappers to park on one of the nearby residential streets without attracting attention, or even at the Magnolia. Then they could wait in the shadows for the money."

"Is there a place we could hide and keep an eye on Jeanine?" I said.

By 11:15, after reviewing all the possibilities, we settled on a plan. Joe and I would go early, park behind the church — neighbors sometimes used the lot for overflow at night — and slip across the street to hunker in the shelter of the heavy bushes near the Sandhills Women's Exchange, a historic building on the green. We should have plenty of time to get set up before the kidnappers arrived. And we'd be in shouting distance if Jeanine needed help, but not close enough to scare off the kidnappers and queer the drop. Aunt Camellia would wait at home with Mrs. Peters in case Mr. Peters showed up. And they'd be poised to call the cops if two a.m. came and some part of our arrangement went sour.

Joe and I drove back into town in silence. The euphoria generated by brainstorming for a plan was fading quickly. In spite of the bulky, black coat I'd borrowed for warmth and camouflage, I was cold, tired, and more than a little scared. Joe, now dressed in one of Mr. Peters' navy turtlenecks and a down fishing vest, coasted into the back parking lot of the brick church house and turned off his lights.

"This is one damn dumb idea," he said.

Headlights tunneled through the darkness, signaling the approach of another vehicle. My skull knocked against Joe's elbow as we slid down in our seats.

"Ouch!" he said.

"Shh . . ." I laughed softly. "Ready?"

We cracked the doors open, squeezed out, and pressed them closed behind us. Then we crept past the church, hugging the shadows. Joe peered around the corner to check for other cars, and then motioned me forward. We dashed across the road and into the bushes. I wedged myself between a large holly bush and the weathered siding of the building, a position that allowed me a clear view of the statue. The squatting woman's pale marble limbs glowed in the quarter moon. The sharp leaves of the holly dug into my cheek and neck. I felt my skin for evidence of blood, wishing I'd chosen a magnolia. Joe crouched next to me — I could hear the soft whistling of his exhale. Was he nervous, too?

At a quarter before two, Mrs. Peters' silver Audi stole along the road in the direction of the statue — Jeanine.

"She's here," I whispered. "Damn, I wish we'd called the cops."

Then I felt cold metal pressing against my neck.

"Hands up, back out of the bush, now!" commanded a loud voice.

We scrambled out of the underbrush and turned with our hands raised to face Officer Cutler. Her partner, the cop I'd met on the Peterses' front stoop and in the police department basement, had his gun trained on Joe's chest. A confused look crossed Cutler's face.

"Miss Burdette? What the hell are you doing here?"

I felt a surge of panic. How could I explain this quickly without implicating

Jeanine? And how to get her and her black-and-white cop car out of the middle of the road? If the kidnappers saw her, saw it, our plan was screwed. Mr. Peters' life was at stake. More important was Jeanine.

"Put your hands against the car and spread your legs. Moving slowly," said Officer Cutler, "no funny business."

We shuffled to the cop car and planted ourselves, as instructed, in the position I'd seen in a hundred bad TV crime shows. Cutler patted me down from head to toe, while her partner examined Joe.

"I'm freezing my ass off out here," she said. "Let's talk this over in the cruiser."

The police opened the back door and ushered Joe and me inside. They slid into the front seat and turned to face us through the protective grate. Officer Brush spoke first.

"Now what in the hell were you two doing in the bushes?"

I glanced at Joe. My heart was hammering and I'd broken into a soaking sweat. Joe gave a slight nod. With a trembling voice, I explained how we believed Mr. Peters had been kidnapped, and that Jeanine was in the process of delivering a million bucks, and that we were her backup.

"You should write fiction," Cutler said,

"you have quite an imagination, doesn't she, Officer?"

I started to cry, and Joe fumbled for my hand. "It's the truth," Joe said.

"I just hope to God Jeanine got out of here before you guys drove up," I said.

Officer Cutler snorted. "I hate it when civilians play cops and robbers. Everyone gets hurt." She put the key in the ignition, fired up the cruiser, and headed down the street toward the statue. "Let's have a look."

Officer Brush called the dispatcher to report a possible kidnapping and request backup. "You cowboys stay here," he said, as the cruiser pulled to a stop. "In fact, I'm going to lock you in." The two officers stepped out with flashlights and guns in hand.

"Jesus, what a mess," said Joe.

I pulled my hand out of his grip and wiped my eyes. "We had to tell them, right?"

"Either that or go to jail. That wasn't going to help Jeanine."

The flashlight beams played over the tall trunks of the pine trees and reflected off the angles and curves of the marble sculpture. Jeanine's car was gone.

"There's no paper bag anywhere," said Officer Cutler, settling back into the driver's seat with a thump.

"Jeanine must have dropped it off while you were busy searching us," I said, angry and very worried. "I hope she's not in trouble now."

"Let's take a ride out to Forest Brook." Cutler ignored my accusation and started up the car. "Call Detective Warren and have him meet us at the Peterses' home," she said to her partner.

Chapter 25

The backseat of the cruiser smelled faintly of urine. My fingers brushed something sticky on the vinyl upholstery. Gross. I shifted toward the middle. My cell phone vibrated as we lurched onto Route 5.

I pulled it out of my back pocket. "Hello?"

"Where are you?" Laura demanded. "I decided I should sleep on your floor tonight, but I stopped by your room and you were MIA."

I cleared my throat and lowered my voice. "We're on our way to Jeanine's. It's a long story, but there's been a ransom demand and Jeanine was dropping money off —"

"Hang up the phone," snapped Officer Cutler.

"Who's that?" Laura asked.

"We're with the cops. I'll call you later." I pressed end and made a face at the back of Cutler's head, taking a chance she wouldn't be looking in the rearview mirror. And not really caring if she was. Joe took my hand, squeezed gently, and let it go.

The cruiser stopped at the Forest Brook gate only long enough to be identified, then accelerated through the streets of the development to Payne Stewart Way. There was no silver Audi in the driveway.

"She probably pulled into the garage," said Joe, reading my mind and squeezing my hand again. The cops unlocked our rear doors and waited for us to emerge. With the officers' hands poised by their weapons, we trooped up the front stairs and banged the lion's head against the door.

"Oh, my good lord," gasped Mrs. Peters when she saw us. "What's happened?"

"Don't panic, ma'am," said Officer Cutler. "We found these two in the bushes near the village green. We need to come in and speak with you for a few moments." There was no question of waiting for an invitation.

We followed her back into the living room, the delicate flowered furniture and knickknack displays now overwhelmed by sweating bodies.

"Detective Warren is on the way. While we wait, suppose you take us to the beginning and tell us everything." Officer Cutler looked sternly at Jeanine's trembling mother, and then stared at her aunt. "Your friends claim that your husband was kidnapped earlier in the week and that you received a ransom note."

The women exchanged worried looks. Aunt Camellia began to describe Mr. Peters' disappearance, followed by the receipt of the note in the newspaper, and finally, tonight's e-mail. A sharp knock from the front hallway startled all of us.

"That'll be Warren," said Officer Brush, heading for the entryway.

But it was Laura. She burst past the policeman and into the living room. "What the hell is going on here?"

"Who is this?" barked Cutler in return.

While Joe made the introductions and tried to calm everyone down, I watched Mrs. Peters' eyes gradually widen with a look of terror.

"Where's Jeanine?" she whispered from across the room. And then a little louder, "Where is Jeanine?"

"We were assuming she'd arrived back home and parked in the garage," said Joe. "She isn't here?"

Mrs. Peters shook her head. "No . . ." she said, her voice hoarse with fear.

"When we didn't see the car, we

thought . . ." I turned to Officer Cutler. "We were supposed to be backing her up."

"Let's be certain she isn't here," said Joe in his most soothing shrink tone.

He sent Laura to check for the Audi in the garage. She returned quickly, shaking her head.

"Try her cell phone," Joe suggested. I dialed the number and got instructions to leave a voicemail message. I told her to call ASAP — that everyone was very worried.

"Okay, then," said Aunt Camellia. "Let's think through all the logical possibilities. She and Rick had a spat at the end of the rehearsal dinner. Do you suppose she could have gone back over to the Carolina to make up with him?"

"That's ridiculous," said Mrs. Peters, "she would have come back here directly to let me know she was safe. Those terrible men have her, I just know it." She dissolved into a weeping lump on the sofa.

I sat down next to her, Joe taking her other side.

"Aunt Camellia, could you kindly call Rick and double-check whether she's with him?" he asked. "Rick's her fiancé," he explained to the police. "It does seem unlikely under the circumstances, but we should cover all our bases."

"Just ask the question," said Cutler. "Do not discuss the details with him."

Aunt Camellia reached for my phone and dialed up Rick. "Sorry to wake you, dear. Is Jeanine over there by any chance?" She shook her head as Rick talked. "No, don't worry, dear. She must have gone out with Cassie. They said something about karaoke." She handed me the phone and sagged into the rocking chair. "He doesn't know where she is. When precisely did you lose sight of her?" From the look in her gray eyes, I could imagine a lawsuit under construction featuring the negligence of the Pinehurst Police Department. Mrs. Peters just cried.

Joe told them how we had stationed ourselves in the bushes alongside the Women's Exchange. Just as Jeanine's vehicle rolled down Cherokee Road, but before we could witness the drop, we were accosted by the cops.

"She must have left the money while we were being searched," I said in a snotty voice.

"We were doing our job," said Officer Brush. "The circumstances were suspicious, and the search was necessary. For all we knew, you could have been carrying —"

Cutler silenced him with a scathing look.

"By the time we'd been frisked and seated in the cruiser," Joe continued, "her car was gone. We assumed, we hoped, that Jeanine had dropped off the package and returned home."

Cutler asked for a complete description of the car and its occupant. "Call in an APB," she said to her partner, thrusting her notepad at his stomach. "And find out where the hell Warren is."

Within minutes, the detective arrived. We began our explanations again, starting at the very beginning and, with his prompting, moving through the week in minute detail.

According to Jeanine's mother, Mr. Peters had last been seen shaving early on the morning of Jeanine's steeplechase shower. Mrs. Peters explained that he had been called away on business.

"Except," said Laura, "we have a video-tape of the steeplechase shower. Cassie and I think we saw your husband on the tape."

"But that's not possible —," said Mrs. Peters.

"Continue please," said Detective Warren, waving Mrs. Peters to silence.

So I reviewed the facts: Junior Mammele had been shot at the party. Later that evening, I had been stopped for suspicion of DUI and retained at the police station. On

Friday, I had chatted with Kendra Newton about Mr. Peters' conflicted relationships with people in the town. We'd all had dinner at the Forest Brook clubhouse and returned to the Tarheel Bar and Grill with Edward to look for suspects who might have drugged my drink. We found no suspects, but talked with two Marines who described Mr. Peters as a man willing to take dangerous risks for large payoffs. They admitted to a meeting with Mr. Peters on Tuesday night. Earlier today, during Mammele's funeral, I was attacked and nearly strangled in the spa. After the rehearsal dinner this evening, Mrs. Peters found the e-mail with Mr. Peters' photo, demanding a ransom swap at two a.m. The cops grabbed us on the town green and Jeanine disappeared.

"I think that about sums up the bare bones of it," I said. "I'm sure you have questions."

Detective Warren ran his hand over his bald spot. "Where is the first note?"

Aunt Camellia moved across the room and slid open a narrow drawer in the coffee table. She pulled out a Ziploc bag containing the typed message. The two officers crowded in to peer over Detective Warren's shoulder.

"Have any of you touched this?" he asked.

"Camellia and I handled it before we realized what it was. Then we put it in the plastic baggie." Mrs. Peters looked almost as ghostly white as had the marble squatting woman in the moonlight.

"Put a call in to Major Crimes," Detective Warren told Officer Cutler, then to Mrs. Peters: "When did you think something had happened to your husband, that he wasn't actually away on business?"

"Saturday morning, when we got the note in the newspaper," said Mrs. Peters, nodding. "We were terribly concerned on Saturday. But the note said not to contact anyone in authority." She hiccupped and blew her nose. "When he left the house on Wednesday morning, he said he had to take care of some business."

"Jeanine was worried as soon as her father didn't show up for the shower. That was Wednesday afternoon," I said, frowning.

"I told her he had to be out of town," said Mrs. Peters. Tears filled her eyes again.

I shrugged an apology. I did feel sorry for her, but I couldn't help wondering if whatever she'd been holding back had put Jeanine — and maybe Mr. Peters, too — in danger. "You told her two different things, Atlanta and Washington, D.C. And Jeanine didn't believe either of them."

Detective Warren interrupted. "Did she discuss her concerns with anyone?"

"Yes." I nodded across the table. "She asked me if I'd help her look into her father's absence — maid of honor and all that."

"And your name again . . ."

"Cassie Burdette. Cassandra." Was his job so demanding that he'd forgotten the interview we had earlier in the day? Or was he just dense? Or playing with me?

"She's the one who spent half the night in the drunk tank on Wednesday," said Officer Cutler, striding back into the room. I could have thought of many other descriptors I'd have preferred as an introduction. "And then she got herself attacked in the steam room at the spa earlier this afternoon. You interviewed her, sir."

"I know that, Cutler." Detective Warren stared at me and scratched a patch of whiskers on his chin. "Where did this conversation with Miss Peters occur? Could anyone have overheard?"

"It happened at the shower. After Junior Mammele was shot. She was worried her father's disappearance was related to that. There were a couple hundred women there. I imagine one or more could have overheard."

"So she thought her father shot Junior Mammele," Officer Cutler crowed.

"No. She was only worried that other people would think it was true. And she just didn't know where he could be."

Mrs. Peters began to sob.

"I'm going to get you a tranquilizer," said Aunt Camellia. She stood and squeezed her sister's shoulder.

"We're not through questioning her," said Detective Warren.

"You won't get anything out of her if she's hysterical," said Aunt Camellia firmly, and left the room.

Laura sprang out of her rocking chair. "I just remembered. I have the video out in the car that Rick made at the party. Want to take a look?"

"Can't hurt," said Detective Warren.

Laura came back with the small camera and hooked it up to the large-screen TV in Mr. Peters' pool room. Aunt Camellia returned with a pale orange pill and a glass of water and watched protectively as her sister popped the medicine and swallowed. The television came to life.

"Rick may make a fine son-in-law," I said, "but his photography makes me dizzy." Only Laura chuckled.

The video started at the entrance to the

ballroom and spun around the room. Rick had paused for a cameo of Pari in her mermaid costume.

"Pari's the other bridesmaid," I told the cops. "She's the one who found me right after the incident in the sauna." I paused. How to say this without sounding too dramatic? "It might be worth your while having a chat with her later." I raised my eyebrows for emphasis.

"Is that Mrs. Newton?" asked Officer Cutler.

"Yes, and I'm there next to her," said Laura. "The whole thing was ridiculous. We were supposed to be representing the riding world in Pinehurst. Can you imagine someone pegging me for a jockey?" She laughed. "I'm at least fifty pounds over regulation."

"Was Kendra Newton having an affair with Mr. Mammele?" I asked suddenly.

"Of course not!" said Mrs. Peters, now slumped against the back of the couch. "They were very good friends."

The video lurched forward again, then stopped on Jeanine, dressed in the Bo-Peep bride's gown. Jeanine accepted a glass of champagne from Helen, the Forest Brook waitress, and raised it in a toast.

"Here's to you, sweetie." She took a large

swig, giggled, and raised the glass to the camera. "To finally landing the man of my dreams." The champagne sloshed out of the crystal flute across her hand and dribbled down toward her elbow.

"Are you already tipsy, honey?" Rick's voice asked from behind the camera. "You better pace yourself."

"Let me help you with that, Miss Peters." The waitress set down her tray and patted Jeanine's arm dry with a white linen towel.

The video continued, capturing snatches of a luau and several other booths I hadn't noticed at the time.

"Where were you?" Detective Warren asked me.

"Dragging her feet," said Laura. "She didn't care for her costume, either. Look! There's the guy we thought was Mr. Peters." She pointed at a burly man at the back of the crowd, wearing a houndstooth-checked hat.

"I don't think that's Dan," said Aunt Camellia, "though I could see how you might make that mistake."

"Then who is it?" Laura asked, glaring.

Aunt Camellia looked away and shrugged.

"This is when Rick turned the camera over to me," Laura said. "But then all hell broke loose with Mr. Mammele, and I never used it."

"It's not much help," I said. "Rick never got a picture of me talking to Jeanine, so we don't have any idea who might have been eavesdropping."

Detective Warren patted his mustache. "Let's take a look at this e-mail."

We followed Aunt Camellia and Mrs. Peters back up the stairs. Mrs. Peters clutched the metal railing all the way and reached for her sister's arm as we turned into the study.

Mr. Peters' haggard face still glowed on the computer screen. The detective manipulated the mouse until the words came into view. "Whose address was it sent to?"

"It's the one I use mostly," said Mrs. Peters. Her words sounded slightly slurred. "For family business."

The message hadn't changed. "Bring the money in a brown paper sack and leave it under the statue of the squatting woman at two a.m. One person alone. No cops, no private investigators, no FBI, or you will never see Dan Peters again. Return home and we will release our prisoner."

"You see why we didn't call you?" said Aunt Camellia. "We were afraid to jeopardize Dan's life."

"And now you see what happened because you didn't call," said Officer Cutler. "We know how to handle these things."

Detective Warren silenced her with a sharp look and continued to study the screen. He clicked on "reply" and an empty return message popped up addressed to smithjones@hotmail.com. "Call the office and ask Wilma to trace this e-mail address," he told Cutler. "Probably an alias, but we'll try."

Warren's phone rang. "Yep?" He listened intently to the tinny voice on the line. "On our way," he said. "Send back-up and tell them to wait until we get there." He closed the phone and faced Mrs. Peters. "They've located a silver Audi that appears to be yours. We'll let you know as soon as we find something out."

The three police officers clattered down the stairs and out the front door.

"I'm going to be sick," said Mrs. Peters. She ran for the master bath.

Chapter 26

"Damn, I hope she's okay."

I paced across the study to the window and watched the cops drive away. The printout Jeanine had mentioned earlier in the evening was lying on the floor next to the wastebasket. I leaned over and picked it up. Something seemed familiar. I squinted at a blurry line in the background of the photograph.

"Oh, my God," I said. "I think I know where they're holding him. This is the newel post for the stairway that leads to the loft in the barn."

Joe took the page, and I pointed out the thin rounds of decorative wood that appeared to emerge from Mr. Peters' left ear. "I started to have an anxiety attack about getting on a horse and I used those spindles to focus myself and calm down."

"What barn?" asked Joe.

"The stables. Where we went riding this afternoon."

"The Pinehurst Race Track," said Aunt Camellia.

"Can you call the police and tell them?" I asked her. "I'm going over to check this out."

"Hold on," Joe said, "How can you be so sure?"

"I'm sure." I started toward the door.

He strode across the room and gripped my arm. "Let the cops handle it."

"I'm going." I shook him off.

"I'll drive then," said Joe. "Laura, do you mind staying here?"

She did mind. Disappointment and worry blazed across her face.

"Someone needs to stay at home base," said Joe, tipping his head toward the two women. She nodded.

I clutched the armrest as we swerved out of Forest Brook, Joe's tires squealing a warning. "I'm beginning to think Helen must know something about all this," I said. "She doesn't just work at the stable, she lives there, too."

"Who's Helen?" asked Joe.

"The waitress. You saw her on the video. She was helping Jeanine with the champagne? She's the one who kept plying you with wine the other night. She has blonde hair with dark roots and a dimple in her chin." I thought for a minute. "She asked questions about Jeanine and the wedding yesterday when I was at the race-track. I didn't think much of it — it seemed like normal politeness at the time."

"You think she's involved with the kidnapping?"

I shrugged.

Joe drove too fast through the side streets to Route 5. My phone rang.

"The Audi's been abandoned," said Detective Warren without identifying himself. "Mrs. Peters told us you identified the background in the photograph. We're headed to the racetrack. You stay out of this."

"Too late," I said, "we're just about there."

"Park along the road at the entrance and remain in your vehicle. That's an order."

I repeated the instructions to Joe, who turned off his headlights and coasted to a stop just outside the grounds of the track.

Minutes later, Detective Warren pulled in behind us. Officer Cutler's Crown Victoria screeched around the corner, nearly rear-ending his cruiser.

"Jesus Christ, Cutler's a maniac," muttered Detective Warren as he approached the passenger side of Joe's car. He pulled a gun out from a holster under his blazer and fiddled with the bullets. "What's the layout inside the barn?" he asked me.

"Stalls are lining the left side, maybe ten of them. Maybe eight. There's a little office on the right side in front, and behind that are the stairs. The saddles and other stuff are stored along that wall."

"So the steps start at the rear and lead up toward the front of the building."

I nodded, following his pointing finger. Several hundred yards in the distance, a dim light shone through the window in the loft.

"You two are to wait here. Do not get out of your vehicle. Do not enter the barn. Stay in your vehicle. Is that clear?"

I glanced at Joe.

"Believe me, we're staying put," he said. He tapped the steering wheel and then reached over to snap my fastened seat belt for emphasis.

Cutler and Brush got out of their car, hunkered low, and darted forward to join Detective Warren.

"Damn, I hope Jeanine's okay," I whispered. "I can't believe we let her go alone."

"She'll be okay," said Joe. "These guys know what they're doing."

I snorted and turned back to watch them zigzag through the shadows to the barn.

Small-time cops in a small-time resort town? They might know what to do with a perpetrator who'd snuck onto Pinehurst No. 2 without paying greens fees, but I very much doubted they'd handled hostages before.

"I smell smoke," said Joe, sniffing the air.

A chorus of frantic neighing began to issue from the barn. And then I saw jagged fingers of orange light.

"It's on fire!" Joe yelled.

I fumbled my cell phone out of my back pocket and punched in 911.

At that moment, the driver's side door was flung open by a bulky figure in dark clothing. His features had been flattened by a nylon stocking. Something in his hand glinted dully: a gun — pointed at Joe. I yelped.

"Give me the phone," he hissed. I handed it over, and he hurled it into the bushes alongside the road. The back door opened and a second, smaller masked figure slid into the rear seat of the car.

"Get in back," the man told Joe. "Don't try any idiot moves." He tossed his gun to the person behind me. Joe scrambled over the headrest from the front to the backseat.

The horses' neighing had escalated into terrified screams. "Are Jeanine and her father in there?" I asked. "We can't just leave them — they'll die!"

"Shut up, both of you." The man's voice was harsh and fierce. "Not one word." And then over his shoulder to Joe: "Not one move or the girl dies."

He pressed the child-lock button on the driver's-side door, reached for the keys that Joe had left dangling in the ignition, and fired up the Honda. We lurched out of the driveway and back onto the main drag, heading away from town. As we passed under a streetlight, even with his face mashed flat by the hosiery, I recognized our driver as Pierre from the Forest Brook gatehouse.

Joe cleared his throat. "Excuse me . . ." His voice trailed off.

Pierre, who looked dirty and very tired, glanced into the rearview mirror and scowled.

"Excuse me," said Joe again, this time addressing the woman next to him, "Helen, is it? If you'll just let us out, you're welcome to the car." Helen pulled the stocking off her head, shook out her hair, and glared.

Pierre grunted. "Shut up, Doctor. You and the girl aren't going anywhere until I say so. And that won't be anytime soon."

We rode quietly for what felt like hours.

In my mind, I tried out avenues of conversation and negotiation. None of them resonated with probable success. And I didn't want to piss him off worse.

"Is Jeanine all right?" I finally asked in a timid voice.

Pierre let go of the steering wheel and slapped the side of my head with the back of his hand, hard. Tears sprouted from my eyes.

Joe leaned forward and grabbed Pierre's headrest. "Don't you dare touch her again."

Helen spanked her gun against Joe's temple. The gun fired. The rear windshield shattered into a spider's web of broken glass.

I pressed my neck against the seat, both ears ringing painfully from the loud blast and my heart banging with fear. I felt back with my right hand and reached my fingers along the door. Joe touched them quickly. At least I knew he was alive. His cell phone buzzed.

"Don't answer it," Pierre barked. "Turn the goddamn thing off now."

There was silence again from the back, except for the wind whistling through the broken window. Now what? I peeked at Pierre. He was gulping in air and sweating heavily. Terrifying to be at his mercy.

"Maybe we should let them out," Helen whispered.

"For what? So they can run to cops and tell them who we are? Why not just drive to the station and turn ourselves in." His voice was cold and angry.

He had no intention of letting us live. I stared out the window. We whipped past a stand of pines and then the murky black of an open field.

As we rounded a sharp curve, I reached over and jerked the steering wheel hard. The car flew off the pavement, veered down a bank, jumped a ditch, and flipped over. We rolled — one, two, three times. Then we crashed into a lone pine and jerked to a stop. I hung from my seat belt upside down, stunned. The dome light flickered on. Unsecured by a seat belt, Pierre had been flung partway through the windshield. Blood trickled down his neck, which was canted at an awkward angle.

"Joe?" I heard my voice, small and terrified. "Joe, are you okay?"

No answer. Then Helen whimpered. "What did you do that for? Are you crazy? You could have killed all of us."

"Are *you* crazy?" I snapped back. "Is Joe all right?"

"It looks like he hit his head. He's

breathing and not bleeding too bad."

She reached over to the driver's side and flipped the lock off. The sheet metal groaned as she pushed open the door and wriggled out into the night. I heard her footsteps, then a small scream as she saw Pierre. She came around to my side of the car and stared in at me, the gun hanging loosely from one hand.

"Shit. What the hell do I do now?" She sounded desperate enough to be either dangerous or easily led. I had to bank on the latter.

"For God's sake, I'm choking to death here. Help me out," I said. "Then we'll get the guys out and call an ambulance. I'm pretty sure Joe still has his phone." I believed her friend to be past helping, but I wouldn't tell her that.

"Oh, my God, what if he's dead? What the hell am I going to do then? This is so bad . . ." She trailed off into quiet sobs.

"Helen," I said, reaching out the window to touch her hand. "Please let me out. We'll figure this out together. Whatever the trouble is, it's only going to get worse if we let someone die here."

She walked to the rear of the car and returned with a roll of duct tape. Good old Joe — he carried a trunk-load of supplies so he could be prepared for anything, anytime. Helen taped my hands together in front of me at the wrists and then wrestled open the clasp of my seat belt. I crashed down onto the roof of the car, and moaned. My neck and head and knees ached.

"Just get out," she said.

I crawled out of the car, stumbled to my feet, and peered in the back window. Joe hung upside down by his seatbelt, his face beet red. He appeared to be breathing.

"We're out of here."

"I'm not leaving Joe."

She jabbed me in the ribs with the butt of her gun. "Move, now."

We set off at a fast clip through the woods.

"Please," I begged, panting. "My knee is killing me. Can we rest for just a minute?"

She pointed to a half-rotted stump. I sat, stretching my wrists against the duct tape.

"Where are we going? What are your plans?" I asked once I'd caught my breath.

"I'm going to get my car and get the hell out of here."

No mention of her plan for *me*. How could I reach her? "Helen. Listen. There's a big, big difference between being an accessory to kidnapping versus murder. You can't let Joe die. Pierre set this up, didn't he? You don't seem like the kind of girl to push things this far."

"You have no idea what kind of girl I am." Her words were cold, angry, but the hurt and disappointment floated underneath.

"Tell me about it. I know how it feels to be pushed up against a wall. Maybe we can figure a way out together."

Her eyes shone with tears. "You can't possibly understand."

"Try me." I wedged a lifetime's worth of empathy into those two words.

"Did you know Jeanine was my sister?"

Then, through her sobs, the story began to pour out. Mr. Peters had met her mother at a military retirement party at a bar in Jacksonville, not long after Jeanine's birth.

"You know the military," Helen said bitterly. "Work hard, play hard. My mother was part of the fun. And so I was conceived. But when she contacted him to let him know, he denied responsibility. Mother said he was afraid that neither his career nor his marriage could take the stress of the truth. So he turned the whole mess over to his wife's sister."

"Aunt Camellia knew about this?" I was dumbfounded.

Helen nodded. "There was no proof. Mother didn't have a legal leg to stand on. She kept a Polaroid — the only 'family'

338

photo in my album — my father's arm draped around my mother's shoulders in that tacky bar." She wiped her eyes. "Camellia arranged to send a lump of cash to help with child support. But she said he'd never claim me as his own."

I heard a slight crack in a stand of holly nearby. Had someone come to rescue me? Silence. Just an animal moving through the night. I had to keep her talking.

"Why would you kidnap your own father?"

Helen sighed and slumped next to me on the tree stump. "Mother died five months ago. Pancreatic cancer," she said. "She went fast. She told me everything at the end because I begged her."

"You didn't know Mr. Peters was your father growing up?"

"No. She wouldn't talk about it. And my stepfather wouldn't have allowed any mention of him, either." She frowned. "The truth doesn't set you free, it ties you in knots."

I tried to adopt a sympathetic look. "What happened after your mother died?"

"I convinced myself that if I tracked him down, he'd be happy to see me. I told myself that he'd been thinking of me all these years."

"Your name is Lorimer, right? How did you ever find him?"

"Through the photograph and the bar — I talked to the man who retired that night. He's an old man now, but he recognized *my father.*" She spat the last two words out.

As she talked, I studied her face. She had Mr. Peters' chin dimple and Jeanine's blue eyes. But instead of Mrs. Peters' delicate features, the fine lines around her mouth and eyes bore witness to a hardscrabble life.

"I came to Pinehurst and found work a couple of months ago, waiting for just the right moment. I finally got the courage to approach him outside the gatehouse one evening. I wasn't asking for much. Just to have him accept me. And maybe a little money to make up for the years I had so little. I thought he'd stake me to my dream." The frown lines bit deeper into her face. "I saw how much money they were throwing around for Jeanine's wedding. Surely he would see the unfairness."

"What did he say?"

"He said he was broke. He told me to go away," she wailed. "He had Pierre throw me out of Forest Brook." Her head dropped to her lap.

The gun hung loosely from her hand. I yanked my hands apart, tearing them loose from the duct tape, and twisted the gun away from her. Leaping to my feet, I trained the barrel at her forehead. After an afternoon at the skeet range and the wild car ride, I was pumped with confidence and adrenalin.

"I'm sorry for you," I said. "But we're going back to help the men and call the police. Now move."

I prayed that I wasn't hallucinating the faint sound of a siren in the distance.

Chapter 27

Officer Cutler and Laura waited at the hospital until I'd been cleared in the ER.

"I'm just banged up," I told them. "Nothing rest and ice won't cure. I'll meet you outside." I jutted my chin out. "I'm going to check on Joe."

I found him on a gurney behind a beige curtain. One lone rooster tail of curly hair poked through the bandages that swathed his head. An IV apparatus hung from the ceiling, clear liquid dripping through a tube and feeding into a needle taped to his left arm. His eyes were closed. Under the faded blue johnny, his chest rose and fell with his soft breathing. I reached out to touch his hand. His eyelids fluttered, and then closed again.

A nurse bustled into the cubicle carrying a clipboard and another bag of fluid. "Are you a family member?" she asked. "If not, I'll have to ask you to leave. Visiting hours are ten to eight. Only immediate relatives allowed overnight."

"How is he?"

"You'll have to talk to his doctor in the morning. Unless you're Mrs. Lancaster?"

I shook my head. She patted my back as I shuffled toward the door.

"You look like you should get some rest yourself, honey."

Laura circled her arm around my shoulders when I emerged. We moved outside and through the parking lot toward Cutler's cruiser, the policewoman hovering close behind. "How is he?" Laura asked, opening the back door for me.

I shrugged. "Sleeping. The staff wouldn't tell me anything because I'm not family," I paraphrased. "His wife" sounded too strange, too scary, and made me want to cry. "How about Jeanine?"

"Good. I mean good, considering what she's been through. She and her mom are both home, pumped up with enough tranquilizers to lay out a couple of those show horses. Mr. Peters was dehydrated, so they're keeping him a few days to push fluids and for observation before they turn him over to you know who." She glared at the back of Cutler's head. "Are you sure you're up for the police station? You've been through hell and back, too."

Cutler's shoulders tightened. The interview at the station had been more of a command performance than an invitation.

"I can manage."

Laura handed me a fragrant white bag. "I did bring reinforcements."

I slid into the backseat of the cruiser and opened her gift. The barbeque take-out from John's was exactly the way I liked it: a soft, white roll piled with shredded pork and chopped slaw, and slathered with hot sauce. Sweet tea, though the ice had already melted, on the side.

"Geez, don't spill that crap on my upholstery," said Officer Cutler.

"You've got to be kidding. At this point, a little hot sauce could only help the situation back here."

Detective Warren, Officer Brush, and Aunt Camellia waited in the conference room at the station with a man I didn't know. Aunt Camellia looked worse than even Joe — dark bags of flesh under her eyes, drooping shoulders, and a general air of defeat. I couldn't wait to get her side of this story.

"I'd like to record our discussion. Any objections?" Warren glanced around the table and indicated that Officer Brush should start the small tape recorder that sat in the middle of the conference table.

"This is November sixth, 2005, Pinehurst, North Carolina. Present are . . ." He listed off our names and the names of the police officers present. "And Police Chief Mason Meredith."

He nodded at the chief, who had not spoken since we entered the room.

"Let's take it from the top, then, Detective Warren. I'm especially interested in how, during the twelve hours I was away in Raleigh and you were in charge, two hostages were taken, resulting in one serious civilian injury and a fatal car crash."

The detective swallowed and patted his mustache. "Following a tip, we approached the Pinehurst Race Track. Miss Burdette and her companion, Dr. Lancaster, had arrived ahead of us and were told to remain in their vehicle. A fire broke out in the barn, with arson strongly suspected. While Officers Cutler and Brush and myself worked to free the victims —"

"And put out the fire," inserted Cutler. "The fire department was slow in responding."

"The alleged perpetrator fled the scene with his accomplice, Miss Helen Lorimer, and commandeered Dr. Lancaster's vehicle," continued Warren. "Miss Burdette and Dr. Lancaster were passengers in the vehicle at the time of the theft. I had instructed them not to exit the car under any circumstances."

The detective swallowed again. "The two passengers were not suspects. And the barn was on fire, sir. I acted quickly in the attempt to save lives."

Chief Meredith frowned. "Could someone kindly enlighten me as to what went on with this kidnapping, about which, I must point out, I had heard nothing previous to this evening . . ." He glanced at his watch. "Morning." He crossed his arms over his chest and waited.

"We only just became aware of it ourselves," said Officer Cutler. "We —"

An angry look from Detective Warren silenced her.

"As the officer said," he continued, "the Peters family contacted us earlier yesterday evening to alert us that they had received a ransom note. Two notes actually, one delivered by hand and a second by e-mail. They did not approach us until they received the e-mail."

"They warned us that Dan would be killed if we talked to the police," Aunt Camellia added in a quavering voice.

"Prior to our contact with the family," said the detective, "Officers Cutler and Brush found Miss Burdette and Dr. Lancaster lurking in the bushes by the Women's Exchange. Only then were we informed of the alleged kidnapping." He cleared his throat. "While the officers were taking their statement, Miss Peters disappeared. We determined that she might have been abducted as well and taken to the racetrack."

He didn't bother to credit me for identifying the barn.

"Once we arrived at the track, we saw the building on fire and the safety of possible hostages became our primary and urgent concern."

The chief's eyes shifted and bore down on me. "Suppose you fill us in on what happened while Detective Warren was gallantly rescuing hostages."

"Pierre — that's one of the Forest Brook gatekeepers — got into the driver's seat with a gun. He slapped me when I tried to talk to him about Jeanine. Then Helen slammed Joe's head with her gun and it went off." I fingered the bruise on my left temple that had swollen to the size of a quail egg. "I was terrified. I just couldn't imagine how we'd get out of it alive. We had nothing to bargain with. So when Pierre took a curve at high speed, I grabbed the wheel and yanked. I didn't mean to kill him. I just hoped somehow we could get away from him. I couldn't see any other way." Tears gathered at the corners of my eyes, and my nose started to run. I wiped it with the back of my hand. "I didn't mean to kill the guy. I was straight scared."

"Who is this man, and why did he kidnap Dan Peters?" asked Laura, sliding her chair closer to mine. "We'd like some answers."

"His name is Pierre Foutin," answered the chief. "We believe he's behind the rash of systematic thefts in the gated communities around Pinehurst."

"Then he was on Junior Mammele's top ten hit list!" I said.

The police chief nodded. "He was also Helen Lorimer's boyfriend. Miss Toussaint, perhaps you would care to enlighten us further on this angle of the case."

Aunt Camellia looked drained of the spunky confidence she'd shown all week. She sighed heavily. "I believe Helen is Dan Peters' illegitimate daughter."

"The hell you say?" Laura's mouth gaped open. "She's Jeanine's half-sister?"

Aunt Camellia nodded. "Just eleven months younger."

"You knew this all along, and you never said anything? We came damn close to dying because you didn't speak up!" I was furious.

"Just wait a minute," she said, holding her hand up. "I knew Dan had been accused of fathering a child out of wedlock. I made a large cash settlement to the girl's mother almost twenty-five years ago, just the way they had agreed. I had no way of knowing this child had become a criminal. I certainly didn't suspect or recognize Helen. I'd never seen her."

Detective Warren turned to me. "What did she confess to you?"

"She moved up here from Florida a couple of months ago hoping to reconcile with Mr. Peters," I said. "She approached him outside Forest Brook, and he turned her down flat. Said he'd have nothing to do with her and would deny any connection if she pursued him further. Pierre overheard them arguing and broke things up. After Mr. Peters drove off, he persuaded Helen to tell him her story." My voice was soft. "Once she moved here and got wind of the extravagant wedding plans, she saw Jeanine's life as Camelot. Their father adored her. She had a stable, loving mother. Helen was an orphan."

"Pierre smelled an opportunity?" asked Laura.

I nodded. "He convinced her that her father was bullshitting about being broke — the money was there, and the family would come through with it if they thought he was in danger. And Mr. Peters would never say anything after he was released — the news would torpedo both his professional and personal lives."

"Good lord," Aunt Camellia moaned.

"Helen claims the plan was to hold Mr. Peters briefly, get him to turn over the money she felt she was due — and some extra for Pierre — and then leave town. She wasn't thinking felony kidnapping."

"Who killed Junior Mammele?" Laura asked.

"Helen said Pierre had planned to grab Mr. Peters as he left the shower," I said, "but he saw another opportunity — a chance to pick off Junior Mammele and leave the smoking gun pointing at Peters. That's when she knew for sure she had gotten in way over her head. That must have been the argument that I witnessed in the bar."

"Why shoot Mammele?" Laura asked.

"He had leads that could have exposed Pierre's involvement in the robberies," said Detective Warren.

"What about the hit-and-run death on Mr. Peters' property?" I asked. "Was it connected to all this?"

"We'll interview the man we have in custody again," said Detective Warren. He shrugged. "With Mammele dead, it may be hard to find the truth."

Or maybe they preferred not to find it, I thought.

"We'll have your statements prepared by midmorning," said the chief to Aunt Camellia and me. "Please stop by tomorrow to sign them."

Aunt Camellia hurried out of the police station ahead of me and Laura. I caught up and grabbed her wrist. "Can I have a word?"

"I'm all talked out," she said.

"You knew he had an illegitimate daughter, and you said nothing about her? Didn't you think it might have some bearing on the kidnapping?"

"No. You can't possibly understand the man. He lives on the edge of one disaster or another all the time. I truly believed he was hiding out until some problem he'd manufactured with his business blew by. Amanda chooses not to know what's going on with him. Jeanine, the same. They made their peace with this arrangement years ago."

I dropped her hand. "If you'd had even an inkling that this woman had kidnapped him and put his life in danger, I can't imagine what would have kept you from speaking up."

She stared at me, her eyes pooling with tears. She tightened the sweater draped over her shoulders and walked off toward her car.

Chapter 28

Joe was sitting up in bed spooning in applesauce and Cream of Wheat when Laura and I stopped by the hospital the next morning. He looked ashen, and his scalp was half-shaved and still flecked with blood; but most of the bandages had been removed, diminishing the mummy effect.

"The doctor tells me I had a concussion," he said. He gestured at his tray. "But the dieticians seem to think something's wrong with my teeth."

Laura began to fill him in on the discussion at the police station the night before. I stayed quiet, watching him eat, almost weak with relief just seeing him alive and relatively well.

He whistled through parched lips when she finished. "Did Mrs. Peters know about Helen?"

"Aunt Camellia said she didn't and wouldn't want to. She's always known he was out of control in lots of ways, especially after Jeanine's birth."

"Why would she stay with a man like that?" Laura asked.

Made sense for Laura to be puzzled — she wouldn't take anything off of any man, for love or money. I admired that.

"He probably allayed her fears by going for psychiatric help," said Joe. "Then once he had the medication, he convinced her he didn't really need it. Who knows what the trade-offs were for her? Obviously, it cost too much for her to see the truth and take the consequences."

"It fits with what Mr. Justice was telling me about bridge bids — some relationships only work if one person takes the lead."

"What about the attacks on you?" Joe asked. "What did the cops say about that?"

"The episode in the bar was courtesy of Helen," I said, wincing. "We saw on the party video that Helen was hovering around Jeanine. We just didn't understand what that meant. She was afraid I'd mess up their plan or piss off Pierre. She heard me agree to help Jeanine find her dad, so she followed me to the bar and dropped a roofie in my beer." I laughed. "I was the only one drinking Budweiser. She hoped a little trouble with the cops would scare me off."

"What about the spa?"

I blushed and looked out the window. "Helen overheard me telling Mike that I thought Mr. Peters was in danger and I wasn't going to back off. This time she told Pierre."

"When did this happen?" Joe pushed his tray away and trained his gaze on me.

"At the stable on Saturday. We had a little argument. I guess I was yelling." Joe's eyebrows rose. "Pierre intended to kill me before I got any closer to the answers." I shivered. "Lucky for me, my finger found his eye socket or my last breath would have been pine-scented steam in the sauna."

A redheaded nurse bustled into the room and headed for Joe. "Time for your bath," she said cheerfully.

Jesus, were they taught to make it sound like nurse and patient would both enjoy what was coming? I glared at her and kissed Joe on the forehead. "I'll call you later, okay?"

I paused at the door. "Geez, I'm really sorry about your car."

"A car can be replaced." He laughed and blew a kiss to me and Laura. "But next time, I'll drive."

Out in the hallway, I reached for a squirt of antiseptic hand lotion from the dispenser on the wall. "What the hell did ever happen with him and Rebecca Butterman?"

Laura winked. "Sure you want to know?"

I punched her in the arm. "Out with it."

"Butterman told him there wasn't any point in going out with a guy who was obviously interested in someone else."

She socked me back and stepped into the waiting elevator. I stood staring at her until the doors started to close, bolting in just before they did. Laura grinned like a monkey all the way down.

I drove to the Peterses' home after leaving the hospital. A security guard who I didn't recognize waved me in when I held up the guest pass. Jeanine would have had a perfect day for her wedding. Sunny, sixty-five degrees, not a breath of wind. My father's Winnebago and Rick's silver Porsche were parked at the curb in front of the house.

Miss Lucy answered the door. "Miss Jeanine's upstairs. I can't get her to come out of her room. No one in this family wants to come out of their rooms," she grumbled and limped back down the hall to the kitchen. "Your folks are in the living room. Mr. Rick's shooting pool. Jeanine refuses to talk to that boy. She's gonna break his heart."

My father, stepmother, and two brothers surrounded me as soon as I stepped into the parlor. "We were waiting to say good-bye to you before we took off." Dad reached out and brushed a strand of hair off my forehead. "That's some shiner you're working on."

"How fast were you going when the car went off the road?" Zachary asked. "Man, I wish I'd been there."

"I would have jumped all over that guy," David said. "I would have grabbed the barrel of his gun and threw him over my shoulder and out the window, maybe cracked his head right open." He twisted his brother's arm behind his back and wrestled him to the ground.

"Boys! Cut it out!" said Maureen, rescuing one of Mrs. Peters' china figurines from near-catastrophe. "I can't believe you solved another crime," she said to me, her voice loaded with admiration (maybe ten percent) and envy (the other ninety).

"I didn't really solve anything," I said. "Though I did point the cops in the right direction by recognizing the staircase in the photo. As for the car wreck, I just couldn't think how else we'd survive."

Maureen clapped her hands together. "Let's get this show on the road. Do come out and visit us in Santa Monica. I'll take you to one of my new classes."

"And we'll go to the beach club," said Zachary. "We can rent roller blades; it'll be awesome."

"Be safe," said my father. "And hit 'em straight. I'll call you soon. I love you."

I knew he was hoping for an echo from me. We exchanged hugs. "Me, too," I mumbled, finally.

When the door clicked shut behind them, I headed over to the poolroom. Rick was slumped on the leather couch, a pool cue dangling from his left hand.

"Aren't you supposed to be playing golf?"

"I withdrew when I heard what happened last night. And now Jeanine's called the wedding off, and she won't speak to me."

"I guess she's shaken up pretty badly about the news. The half-sister and all that."

He jumped up off the couch and grabbed my shoulders. "Cassie, please, can't you talk to her? I know it's been a terrible week, and I haven't been there for her the way I should have been. But if I lose that girl," he finished in a strangled voice, his eyes beginning to glisten, "it would be worse than choking down the stretch at the Open."

"I'm sure *that* will make her feel better," I

said. "Which Open, U.S. or British?"

"Please, take this to her." He pressed a fat envelope into my hands. "Tell her I'm wild about her and I'm so, so sorry. Tell her I only want to take her in my arms and —"

"Stop! You'll have to tell her the X-rated stuff yourself. I'll see what I can do."

I traced the curve of the decorative railing up the stairs with my palm and turned down the hall toward the front of the house. The door to Jeanine's parents' suite was closed tight, as was the guest room, and Jeanine's.

I rapped on her door. "Jeanine, it's me, Cassie."

Jeanine cracked the door open, then launched herself across the bed and buried her face in a pink flowered comforter. Her wedding gown hung from a padded hanger on the closet door — yards and yards of antique lace and French silk dotted with seed pearls. Jeanine looked up as I straightened the train.

"At least you can wear your dress again," she said, her voice bitter. "I'm taking mine to the consignment shop tomorrow."

I bit back my first thought. Like which stop on the LPGA tour called for a strapless purple gown with an awkwardly weighted train?

"I can't believe this is happening. I've

planned this wedding forever. And dreamed about it since I was five years old. And now my own father ruined it."

"I bet Rick's disappointed, too," I offered.

She lifted her head to glare at me. "Believe me, that guy is thrilled he doesn't have to make the trip down the aisle later today."

I extracted the envelope from my back pocket.

"He asked me to give this to you. You should at least read it over. Give the guy a chance." I dropped the letter beside her.

Jeanine rolled off the bed and walked to her dressing table. She came back with a silver knife and slit the envelope open. Then she scanned the papers and handed them to me.

Four, round-trip, first-class tickets to Maui. "I don't get it. He wants you to go on vacation to Hawaii with another couple?"

"Gosh, you can be thick sometimes, Cassie." She flapped a handwritten letter in my direction. "He wants us to elope to Maui. He even lined up a chapel on the beach."

"Sorry." I thought for a minute. "Actually, that sounds perfect. No family, no newspaper stories about your father's business dealings or the other stuff . . ." I didn't dare bring up Helen's name. At some point, Jeanine would have to sort through her feelings about the sudden acquisition of a half-sister who'd kidnapped their father, but I wasn't going to play her shrink now.

"And the flowers could be amazing," I added, sure this would get her attention. I didn't mention that the golf courses on Maui are supposed to be out of this world — that wouldn't be a selling point for Jeanine.

"I don't think I even want to get married anymore," Jeanine wailed. "How can I trust Rick after all that's happened?"

"That's not fair. What did he do wrong?"

Jeanine started to cry again. "I feel like I went through all this by myself."

"He had no clue what was going on with you. You didn't tell him your father was missing. You told him to focus on the golf tournament and he did. If you're going to be married to a golfer, that's part of the package."

She shot me a furious look. "I know you heard us fighting in the parking lot."

"Okay, maybe he had a little case of cold feet, too, but other than that, he's solid," I said. "A rock. An immovable object."

I laughed at my own golf jargon joke, but Jeanine kept crying. "Look at my parents. Who could get married after the mess they made? And why would he even want to marry me now? He thought he was getting one girl with a normal family, and now he's engaged to someone entirely different."

"You're the same girl he fell in love with." I perched on the bed and patted her leg. "Rick won't let you down. You'll have rough spots. Everyone does. But you'll talk them over, and you'll get through them — even the worst of times."

What the hell did I know about talking things over and making it through? And her parents had unveiled a spectacular marital disaster. But somehow I knew my platitude applied here. Jeanine and Rick's union had as good a shot as any to be among the sixty percent of first marriages that aren't doomed to fail.

"Besides," I added, "you're thinking your father is one-hundred-percent bad guy and that's just not true. He loves you and he loves your mother and you know that, even if he did some bad stuff, too."

She was bawling now. I squeezed her hard, trying not to let my own tears show. I could have been talking about my father — just transpose the words and leave out the part about loving my mother, and it all fit perfectly. My father had made mistakes — big ones. But he had loved me, too. And I did not need to define myself for the rest of my life by the failed relationships in his past.

"Will you come along?"

"Come where?"

"Maui, silly. Maid of honor, right?"

"No way. Not the way things went with Mike this week. You better ask Pari." My lip curled. "She certainly seems fond of him."

"Mike wouldn't come anyway. He's going off to the Leadbetter Academy to rework his swing."

"He'd be better off reworking the wiring in his brain."

Jeanine laughed. "We may have to wait a week or so, but Rick says here," she waved the letter again, "he wants to ask Joe to be the new best man."

The blush spread down my neck and up to the roots of my hair. "Now that's an interesting proposition."

I jogged downstairs and sent Rick up to Jeanine's room. Time to get on the road myself. Time to get back to the range at Palm Lakes and hit a couple hundred balls and sink some putts. Down the hallway, I spotted Miss Lucy working in the kitchen.

"Just came to say good-bye," I said, resting my elbows on the counter beside her mixing bowl. "One thing I still don't understand about all this." I swiped a finger of chocolate chip cookie dough. "Why wouldn't Aunt Camellia mention Helen as a possible key to Mr. Peters' kidnapping? She risked his life not coming clean."

She swatted my hand away from the bowl and gazed out the window. "Could be you don't understand what it would feel like to lose your whole family, all at once."

"You mean Jeanine and Mrs. Peters?"

"And Mr. Peters, too." The bill of her Citifinancial cap bobbed. As she turned away, I could read the sadness in her eyes.

Chapter 29

I kicked off my flip-flops and curled into my regular chair. "You would have had a field day last week," I told Baxter. "You wouldn't have even known where to start."

He tented his fingers and widened his eyes. Shrink-speak for "tell me more."

So I summarized the week's action, emphasizing the moments where I'd made the most sensible decisions. Even mental health professionals get discouraged if you stumble into the same damn mistakes over and over. Breaking up with Mike was on the highlight tape, as well as a few reasonable interactions with my father and stepmother. And I gave him Charlie's analysis of how competition made the relationship with Mike and me impossible, and bode poorly for Mom and Maureen, as well.

By the time I'd finished the week's roundup, half an hour had elapsed and Baxter was looking glazed. He shook his head slightly and asked me to repeat the reasoning behind not calling the cops in to help with the kidnapping.

"It's still a little confusing," I said. "Jeanine's mother and aunt were so definite, and then Jeanine started to beat the same drum — she believed her father would be killed if they didn't follow the instructions to the letter."

"What happened to Jeanine that night?"

"Pierre was waiting in the woods behind the statue so he could grab her and the ransom money. He tied her up in the barn loft with her father and left them both to burn alive. When he saw Joe and me waiting in the car, he must have thought 'hostages.' He was in up to his neck at that point."

We had a moment of silence. I was pretty sure Baxter was hoping I'd gotten the message — again — about leaving police work to the police.

"So you believe the two women were protecting Mr. Peters' secret," Baxter said.

I hemmed and hawed and then offered up the only conclusion that had seemed remotely possible after three hours of solitary rumination on my ride home: Aunt Camellia had had an affair with her own sister's husband. I couldn't be sure when — probably before Jeanine was born and before Helen's mother became a factor. Like the other women in his life, she had gotten caught up in the magnetic field of Dan Peters. If she told her sister about Helen, she was afraid her own involvement with Dan would come out, too.

"I have this image of him as a vat of acid," I said. "No matter what got dropped in, it disappeared without leaving a bubble."

"But in the end, secrets are poison," said Dr. Baxter, rubbing his eyes. "And they grow bigger in the dark." He glanced at the clock on the end table next to my chair. "Our time is up for today."

I paused on the way out, my hand twisting the doorknob open. "Did I mention my father offered to stake me on the tour next season? I might take him up on it. And remind me to tell you about Joe."

I left him gasping like a goldfish in a dirty bowl.

Glossary

Approach shot: a golf shot used to reach the green, generally demanding accuracy, rather than distance

Back nine: second half of the eighteen-hole golf course; usually holes ten through eighteen

Birdie: a score of one stroke fewer than par for the hole

Bogey: a score of one stroke over par for the hole; double bogey is two over par; triple bogey is three over

Bump-and-run: chip shot for which the aim is to get the ball running quickly along the ground toward the green

Bunker: a depression containing sand; colloquially called a sand trap or trap

Caddie: person designated or hired to carry the golfer's bag and advise him/her on golf course strategy, also called a looper

Card: status that allows the golfer to compete on the PGA or LPGA Tour

Chip: a short, lofted golf shot used to reach the green from a relatively close position

Chunk: to strike the ground inadvertently before hitting the ball; similar to chili-dipping, dubbing, and hitting it fat

Collar: the fringe of grass surrounding the perimeter of the green

Cup: the plastic cylinder lining the inside of the hole; the hole itself

Cut: the point halfway through a tournament at which the number of competitors is reduced based on their cumulative scores

Dewsweeper: an early morning golfer

Divot: a gouge in the turf resulting from a golf shot; also, the chunk of turf that was gouged out

Draw: a golf shot that starts out straight and turns slightly left as it lands (for a right-hander); a draw generally provides more distance than a straight shot or a slice

Drive: the shot used to begin the hole from the tee box, often using the longest club, the driver

Eagle: a score of two strokes under par for the hole

Exempt status: allows a golfer to play in official LPGA tournaments without qualifying in Monday rounds. Exemptions are based on past performance in Q-school, previous tournaments, or position on the money list

Fade: shot that turns slightly from left to right at the end of its trajectory (right-handers)

Fairway: the expanse of short grass between each hole's tee and putting green, excluding the rough and hazards

Fat: a shot struck behind the ball that results in a short, high trajectory

Flag: the pennant attached to a pole used to mark the location of the cup on the green; also known as the pin

Front nine: the first nine holes of a golf course

Futures Tour: a less prestigious and lucrative tour that grooms golfers for the LPGA Tour

Gallery: a group of fans gathered to watch golfers play

Green: the part of the golf course where the grass is cut shortest; most often a putter is used here to advance the ball to the hole

Green in regulation: reaching the green using the number of strokes considered par for the hole; one is regulation for a par three, two for a par four, three for a par five

Greenie: prize for hitting the ball closest to the pin in one shot on a par-three hole

Hacker: an amateur player, generally one who lacks proficiency; also called a duffer

Handicap: a measure of playing ability used

in tournaments to allow golfers of varying skill levels to compete with each other; lower handicap, better golfer

Hazard: an obstacle that can hinder the progress of the ball toward the green; includes bodies of water, bunkers, marshy areas, etc.

Hook: a shot that starts out straight, then curves strongly to the left (right-handers)

Irons: golf clubs used to hit shorter shots than woods; golfers generally carry long and short irons, one (longest) through nine (shortest)

Lag putt: a long putt hit with the intention of leaving the ball a short (tap-in) distance from the hole

Leaderboard: display board on which top players in a tournament are listed

Lie: the position of the ball on the course; killer lie — extremely challenging position, fried egg lie — all but the top of the ball buried in a sand trap, plugged lie — ball sunk into the surface it lands on

Looper: caddie

Money list: cumulative record of which golfers have earned money in the official tournaments and how much

Out of bounds: a ball hit outside of the legal boundary of the golf course, which results in a stroke and distance penalty for the golfer; also called OB

Pairings sheet: sheet listing which golfers will be paired together for the round

Par: the number of strokes set as the standard for a hole, or for an entire course

Pin: the flagstick

Pin high: ball has come to rest on the green level with the flagstick

Pitch: a short, lofted shot most often taken with a wedge

Pre-shot routine: a set of thoughts and actions put into practice before each shot

Proxy: closest to the pin on a par-five hole in regulation (3 shots)

Pull hook: a shot that turns abruptly left (for right-handers)

Putt: a stroke on the green intended to advance the ball toward the hole

Qualifying school (Q-school): a series of rounds of golf played in the fall that produces a small number of top players who will be eligible to play on the LPGA Tour that year

Rainmaker: an unusually high shot

Range: a practice area

Rough: the area of the golf course along the sides of the fairway that is not closely mown; also, the grass in the rough.

Round: eighteen holes of golf

Sandy: a par made after at least one of the

shots has been hit out of a bunker

Scramble: team format in which each player hits her shot from the team's best ball after every stroke until the ball is holed out

Shank: a faulty golf shot hit off the shank or hosel of the club that generally travels sharply right

Short game: golf shots used when the golfer is within 100 yards or so of the green, including pitches, chips, bump-and-run shots, and putts

Skull: a short swing that hits the top half of the ball and results in a line-drive trajectory

Slice: a golf shot that starts out straight and curves to the right (for right-handers)

Solheim Cup: competition pitting the best twelve U.S. golfers against an international team; occurs every two years. Equivalent to the Ryder Cup for men

Swing thought: a simple thought used before hitting a shot intended to distract the golfer from mental chatter

Tee: the area of the golf hole designated as the starting point, delineated by tee markers, behind which the golfer must set up

Tour card: *see* Card

Top: to hit only the top portion of the golf ball, generally resulting in a ground ball

Trap: colloquial term for bunker; *see* Bunker

Two-putt: taking two shots to get the ball in the cup after hitting the green; a hole's par assumes two putts as the norm

Wedge: a short iron used to approach the green

Wingding: an informal tournament with players assigned to teams according to skill

Woods: golf clubs with long shafts and rounded heads used for longer distance than irons. The longest-shafted club with the largest head used on the tee is called the driver

Yips: a condition involving nervous hand movements that result in missed putts

Yardage book: a booklet put together by golfers, caddies, or golf course management describing topography and distances on the course

About the Author

Roberta Isleib is a clinical psychologist and avid golfer who lives with her family in Connecticut. Visit her website at www.robertaisleib.com or e-mail her at roberta@robertaisleib.com.

We hope you have enjoyed this Large Print book. Other Thorndike, Wheeler or Chivers Press Large Print books are available at your library or directly from the publishers.

For more information about current and upcoming titles, please call or write, without obligation, to:

Publisher
Thorndike Press
295 Kennedy Memorial Drive
Waterville, ME 04901
Tel. (800) 223-1244

Or visit our Web site at:
www.gale.com/thorndike
www.gale.com/wheeler

OR

Chivers Large Print
published by BBC Audiobooks Ltd
St James House, The Square
Lower Bristol Road
Bath BA2 3SB
England
Tel. +44(0) 800 136919
email: bbcaudiobooks@bbc.co.uk
www.bbcaudiobooks.co.uk

All our Large Print titles are designed for easy reading, and all our books are made to last.